THE MAN

illustrated

Keith Hulse

ISBN 978-0-9553971-4-1
ISBN-13: 9781234567890
ISBN-10: 1477123456
ISBN9798433176546 PAPERBACK

Cover design by: Art Painter
Library of Congress Control Number: 2018675309
Printed in the United States of America

Dedicated to the idea,
Rulers are meant to serve the people,
not the people serve the ruler.
What is the ruler for then?

Then a brown rat ran over her hand and left pee dribbles. Like rats do, so why they soiled food, the blighters.

But it was a sign from a God: rats do not wear space helmets.

The rat was her yellow canary in a yellow submarine.

Then amidst the quiet the reliable hum of the nuclear turbines in the engine room heard, and now Nesta sat until her aches ceased, and then she got scared for she was all alone, except for orange oil gauge lights and yellow temperature flanges.

Where were the others? On the fluorescent bright yellow lifeboat, had they pulled the BLUE lever?

CONTENTS

FOREWORD

The storyteller was an archaeologist, soldier, jack of all trades, now Veteran Scottish War Blinded and artist. (Saatchi-art.com) He gets visits from spirit people, he is not a medium, just ghostly folk like him.   His house is full of cats.   He gets words tumbling into his left temple and come out his right temple as a story.   This one is called The Man, a science fiction adventure.

INTRODUCTION

The subject matter is imagination.   To look at space and wonder, "Am I alone?"   No, The Man, a ruler of planets is out there, trying to serve the people, warring with despots believing they must be served.   Lo, the introduction takes us to Church reformers Knox and Calvin, discussing early Christian ideas on reincarnation.   For The Man existed before and fought for humanity.   He also meets Nesta, prearranged before birth to be his woman.   The Church Council of 451 A.D. accepted reincarnation as a Christian dogma.   But a hundred years pass and The Empress Theodora of The Eastern Roman Empire, who got her man, Emperor Justinian banning ideas on reincarnation amongst early Christians. [553 A.D.]   The early Christians believed in a loving God that gave you another chance, hence The Man is born again to serve.

PREFACE

This tale is to bring joy to science fiction readers and introduce the subject to new readers.   Read this discovery, a star older than the universe that is of billion years, 13.787±0.020 old.

The star Methuselah is 14.5 billion years old.

Huh? Older than our universe?

Let us read science fiction.

PROLOGUE

Now A Man Zadok had a house as he liked privacy and did not like to just lay down where he was when night came, like so many others. There was no need for houses, no one had any nervous systems so, did not feel the wind or soft rain. In fact, just outside A Man Zadok's house with no roof, a lion was sleeping on the most vivid of light greens coloured soft grass, grass that felt like satin and snuggled into the lion a young boy using the lion as a pillow and company, for the night. Never mind, no one had any stomachs and that included the lion, so the boy was perfectly safe.

THE MAN

BY
Keith Hulse
79586 words 412 pages

Keith Hulse
Aberdeen
lugbooks@gmail.com
lugbooks.co.uk

[CHAPTER 1] — ABOUT US

A lion does not eat the man, and he does not kill the lion.

There was no need for a roof or even a house with a roof for when it rained the water was so fine it was like dust.

No one wanted a roof, so they could gaze up at the night sky and tune into the oneness of creation.

"Twinkle, little star how bright you are?"

Now A Man **Zadok** had a house as he liked privacy and did not like to just lay down where he was when night came like so many others. There was no need for houses, no one had any nervous systems, so did not feel the wind or soft rain. In fact, just outside A Man Zadok's house with no roof, a lion was sleeping on the most vivid light greens colored soft grass, grass that felt like satin and snuggled into the lion a young boy using the lion as a pillow and company, for the night.

Never mind, no one hand any stomachs and that included the lion, so the boy was perfectly safe.

Now A Man Zadok was expecting company, special people, friends were coming over to plan their futures. Using his mind, A Man Zadok thought up a table with white tablecloth; silver cutlery appeared and water fresher and clearer than, Earth mineral spring water.

"Hallo **Tintagel**, always Tintagel, eh?" A Man Zadok and hugged his friend who had arrived.

"Hello handsome," **Natasha**; she was more beautiful than A Man Zadok remembered from behind Tintagel.

"Remember me," *a boy* asked entering the house that did not have a door, there was no need, thieves lived elsewhere.

"Will you ever grow into a man, or perhaps a girl, always the undecided youth," A Man Zadok.

Then "Hello," she was a beautiful woman called **Vega**, and hugged A Man Zadok to the jealousy of Natasha.

"I am sorry; my feelings for A Man are

always the same."

"And mine for you my sweet," A Man Zadok.

Now they sat down and each from his mind produced succulent food they remembered of their favorite physical dishes.

And they feasted and had no stomachs or nervous system, but the food was at the correct temperature and did not burn or scald their flesh and ate till full.

And their flesh was of the finest light particles one could see.

"I will return first," A Man Zadok, "I must be a legend so

Natasha will know who I am before she meets me?"

"I always know who you are dearest as my soul belongs to you." Natasha.

"What will you call yourself this time round?" Tintagel, "Nesta perhaps?"

"I like that, Nesta; I will be called Nesta, what about you A Man Zadok, something big and tough sounding?" Natasha.

"The Man," Tintagel suggested.

"To The Man and Nesta, times immortal lovers," all.

"Will you be my mother again and you, my papa?" The boy asked, looking at the other beautiful woman, Vegas.

"Is it alright Natasha?" The woman asked.

"I suppose so Vega," Natasha a little sulky.

"Natasha no wonder we must play this same game repeatedly till you realize jealousy is only a feeling, I, like you are making my own responsible decisions, my own progress and we are here tonight to plan our next school when we return," A Man Zadok chided his wife as she was always his wife when they materialized in the flesh.

"One day I won't agree and be the boy's wife, he is always after me," Natasha.

"Speaking of souls always after you, the evil ones must agree to act in the physical world also," Tintagel, "I understand missionaries have approached them and offered them again the chance to progress out of their grey dimensions into our worlds, soon we will be told if they are coming."

"Posidoctopus gives me the creeps," Natasha shivered.

"He must come, none of us here can function as evil ones, we have progressed beyond that stage of our developments," A Man Zadok.

Now when all had fallen asleep Natasha came to A Man Zadok in a room where there was no roof.

"Hug me dearest," Natasha asked coming to him.

And he did and their bodies dissolved into each other, and they became one light, and it was like stars coming out of their union and then they parted. It was a union of love for they had joined and is popular in the other light realms.

Now why they loved Tintagel and Vega came together.

"Why don't you choose me to marry, you wait for no soul mate?" Vega.

"I chose you now and tomorrow I might choose another, and I do wait for one, she is late, she has agreed to be a female cyborg for my pleasure on the physical dimension, she is called *Wendy*," Tintagel and waited for Vega to make her move.

"Well, she is late, so I chose to have union with you Tintagel, come to me," Vega and the pair met, glowed, and became one light as A Man Zadok and Natasha had, for such unions valued for closeness and love.

And layers of light below them in a world of darkness and grey light the evil ones had agreed to meet A Man Zadok and the others in the physical dimension Earth. They were looking forward to physical pleasure in the extremes that stopped them evolving into bright orbs of light in their worlds of light.

*

And John Calvin seen speaking to Mr. Knox about predestination on a higher level where the brown dust of a road was as fine as powdered milk, and the flowers were of colors never seen on Earth and the colors sang notes also never heard of.

"When I asked people to believe it was them that go to heaven as predestined to do so," John Calvin muttered "and the rest to hell."

"Yes, now we have the likes of Posidoctopus escaping when he should suffer for his wrongs till the end of time, what is our God thinking off," Knox replied shaking his head and because of this was stuck in his level of light. Posidoctopus was a brother and one's child; of light like him and so entitled to progression and just maybe might overtake Knox?

"I hear A Man Zadok is planning to return, has carved himself an empire to rule and given himself alternate roads to follow when he makes a CHOICE," John Calvin.

"It goes against everything we have taught about predestination," Knox complained: the idea of choice, of more than one path to follow. One good, one bad and one ugly!

And a passing man was hurrying to catch a ship anchored in the sky above; it had sails and was full of people, and the next this man was aboard her and the ship then sped towards A Man Zadok's house. He had just come from the Library of Memories where he had been looking up what is written about Earth, and her colonies in space. He was *Thesaurus* and had decided when he returned with A Man Zadok he would be *Tintagel the Clone* and he was late for the dinner party.

He was glad he was getting another chance to make things right on the physical dimension, everything he was going to do was being planned right now at A   Man Zadok's house by elders come down from higher light levels; glad he would have alternative roads to walk after he decided whether right or wrong and knew each road would bring other choices and people, he would have agreed to meet at the dinner party.

"Yes, it was all predestined but not the way Calvin and Knox said the rest of society was damned to hell, if so, why bother to go back to school and learn things the right way?" *Tintagel the Clone* thought and liked his new name, it had a ring to it.

"Hello again," Tintagel the Clone said sitting down next to a handsome girl.

"We are both late, I don't know why we just don't think ourselves to the dinner party," the girl replied smiling.

"Because going by ship is much more fun, and do you know what you are to be called this time?" Tintagel the Clone asked.

"Wendy, and I am going to be your cyborg lover."

"Fine by me," and his left hand dissolved into her right hand and they both tingled with pleasure, later when alone they did and become one light and sparkle and shine and glow love.

[CHAPTER 2] — WHO

The Man used prism light as a shield for use in battle.

An orb of light, headed towards Planet Old Earth so fast it was incredulous, it did it by passing through doors that led from one dimension of light to the next and suddenly, the orb was hovering in a darkened bedroom; a human man and woman were hoping for a child below it.

"I hope you want a son like me," A Man Zadok mused inside the orb of light. "Better hurry," Natasha prompted behind him.

"Nesta, better get used to it the human way," and he quickly joined with Nesta's orb of light for one last union before?

"Look, fireflies, how beautiful, I have never seen them before," the human woman in the bed seeing the sparkling lights from the union of A Man Zadok and Nesta; the last time as orbs of light till Nests went back to the school A Man Zadok had entered, Earth, and she would know him here as The Man, and he would be hers again, in the physical.

A man needing daily shaves.

And the Earth woman's companion strained his head back and saw little orbs of colored light in the bedroom.

"The Man," Nesta whispered to A Man Zadok's mind for she was in love with him and could not wait till they met again, "I will always be close to you till I am born."

"It is time, love you to the end and beginning of time, till the end and beginning again," The Man and his orb of light was vibrating faster than the ions about him went through the Earth woman's belly to her womb, where an egg had just met a sperm.

"Miss you," Nesta mourned.

*

"Born Cluny James Smith, Glasgow, Dept. of Europe, United Earth, Old Earth, A.D. 50123. Immigrated to Dept. of United States, United Earth, Old Earth A.D. 50143.
First genetic transplants A.D.
50144. Second genetic transplants A.D. 50145.

Joined Space Foreign Legion
A.D. 50146. Promoted colonel
in the field 50148.

Declared Protector of Space Field Army on the field 50149.

Such was the meteoric rise to power of one man of common origin, Cluny James Smith. For war gives the poor the chance to prove their worth and end up KINGS.

Who?

The Man."

Taken from the surfaced Chronicles of Tintagel Tasciovanus the Wise Spy.' Works written by the original human grown from the fetus of a human mother and not the clone or robot, during the years A.D. 50147>50220.

And on New Jupiter where the clouds come in shades of the gaseous atmosphere, white, yellow, green, and red and change their color pitch as the sun sets and rises and whose six rings leave six illuminated bands on the planet at night and whose cities are domed, like other planets and contain an Earth atmosphere with white Columbus clouds, a nuclear firing ball as a mini sun, fertile soil, and Earth germs; and the largest dome is Jupitermegapolis, here is Castle Jupiter, a great Gothic folly on a manmade mountain of dirt, concrete and steel frames, and home to Aelfric Europe:

"We have fed him Simon, a whole vial of Uranus Black Plague and he still lives," Posidonus a small over fed man with a dyed green Mohican hair cut in an oversized blue silken track suit complained. So, smooth the smock his belly button showed as his large round stomach pushed it forward, and his true brown chest hairs showed, for Posidonus was full of FEAR for if discovered as a spy, he knew what would befall him.

The Man.

Yes, The Man would have injected him with a dose of the substance in the vial but in a public execution square with a cloth sign hanging from his neck on his naked body to add humiliation.

"SPY."

The sign would read.

And Posidonus knew he would take days to die under the two hot suns of New Saturn 12, home planet of The Man and the Dictatorship.

And Posidonus, dehydrated as the red ravens there urinated in his empty eye sockets after they gladly fed on them, then moved to feed on his slit abdomen.

And he knew the red ravens were not afraid of man and are three times the size of those back on Old Earth.

And Posidonus did put all his trust in his long Black haired friend Aelfric that this would never happen to him? He knew Aelfric was the only man alive capable of removing The Man from society, and then things would return to the old imperial system, where those with wealth

like himself

need not worry and stay awake nights fearing The Man's police knocking at the door.

So, Aelfric Europe looked at his little Fourth Secretary with disgust and was not surprised The Man had survived sixteen previous assassination attempts.

Aelfric had the ugly Posidonus to work with.

"Why does the man deliberately make himself out to be ugly/" Aelfric often thought.

Anyway: Aelfric did not see Posidonus as a friend but as a tool to an end.

To bring back liberty, freedom of speech, free living to the rich.

Posidonus, not beautified like most men, by genetic implants, paid by the wealthy who wanted youthful virility publicized and forced   billions of their servants, slaves, serfs, and contracted laborers, so masters would not have to look upon ugly faces, such as Posidonus.

Posidonus could afford to be ugly. Women and boys, he

could buy, friends he did not want for they always asked for loans. So, he enjoyed his large lips, that said something against society.

Posidonus with his green Mohican put FEAR into his victim's by simply being outrageous.

Why Aelfric wished Posidonus was visibly pleasing to look at for he had to look at him often. He must demand Posidonus get genetic implants or else did terminate the relationship.

Now Aelfric waved his ruby encrusted brown gloved right hand and the lone human red head dancer fell flat on her stomach. All knew Aelfric bored easily and became dangerous.

ALL?

SILENCE of the grave.

For the chamber suit had stopped playing Nutcracker.

"I am afraid," Posidonus as saliva dribbled from his bright red lips. Posidonus liked to keep in fashion, he liked the brightest of reds and it was fashionable in high society for men to wear cosmetics and fine linens for their silken smoothness.

Aelfric wondered why he kept such a Fourth Secretary in employment.

But Posidonus saw the curled lips of Aelfric's and responded, "The Man cannot silence everyone and alienate himself totally from the upper classes you know? Why my family members have loaned him fortunes to stay in power.

PAUSE.

Besides, I get my job done." Posidonus meaning he was a double agent and fed Tintagel lies.

And Aelfric thought, "Loans that will take The Man a

century to pay back without interest and you will still not be advanced beyond the kitchens. The Man simply does not want your types influencing government, and you do not have The Man's intelligence to see it, so fools go ahead and loan your money to your enemy."

Why Aelfric left it at that, the Fourth Secretary ran the domestic side of his household, and all knew The Man's tastes thanks to Posidonus, and all knew the tastes of Posidonus were different from The Man for he was not into the bizarre.

But Posidonus had a gift with kitchens and ran them well so Aelfric could ask for a sudden banquet for visiting aliens and get it.

The real reason he kept Posidonus was, keep your enemies near you.

And Posidonus saw Aelfric's yellow mascara eyes narrow and so became nervous and fidgeted.

Aelfric like anyone else disliked traitors; they might betray you any day.

And it was Aelfric who had spoiled the soft Posidonus to get him to spy on The Man, turning him into a double agent.

And Aelfric grabbed Posidonus by the cheeks and kissed those big red lips. THEN LAUGHED.

The dancer gave a timid
glance. A moth landed
on a harp string,

not a musician moved,
Aelfric was a dangerous
bored man who had ex-
perienced ALL life.

And the moth flew on and landed on the dancer's right nipple. It was the bright yellow feathers that passed as clothes on the girl's bosom, rump and other parts that attracted the insect.

The moth had eggs to lay.

Two minutes later the dancer tried to blow the insect unsuccessfully away.

SHE HAD MOVED.

Guess who noticed.

Aelfric.

And drummed his fingers on his chair resembling a throne.

"Come here," he ordered, and the dancer gingerly crawled over to him.

"Kiss my feet," he commanded, and his silken red slippers removed, and the act done.

Aelfric craned his neck to see if she had removed any rings from his toes.

He was extremely wealthy and she extremely poor.

"MY feet," he is using them pushed the girl backwards.

Besides him Posidonus no longer afraid, for his friend Aelfric was no longer angry at him.

The dancer saw in Aelfric's eyes hate for all life and hate directed at her. "I am contracted to you for one month master," she said in New English which was a mixture of English, Chinese, Russian and Spanish with a smattering of other tongues?

In the last three weeks she had seen horrors in this house and servants with missing limbs sent to Posidonus for correction.

SHE WAS INDEED
AFRAID.

"I am aware of Madam
Butterfly Chou's con-
tract of employment,"
Aelfric. SILENCE.

"You are mine to bid as I desire for that time; everything I bid, I own you lock stock and barrel girl. Mine,"
Aelfric was losing it.

He could find nothing more about LIFE to interest
him apart from trying to rid society of The Man.

The girl was as if she had become a white grub,
a thing to loath and hurt. "Take her away," he
shouted.

Posidonus brightened and squirmed excitedly as guards
resembling newts on hind legs covered in ceramic plated
armor approached the girl dancer. Aliens with no sympathy for the human dancer, Aelfric fed them well.

In her eyes was terror directed at Posidonus, of all
men to be handed over too.

ALL WORKING GIRLS AVOIDED HIM.

They knew the truth about him.

HE WAS WORSE THAN JACK THE RIPPER.

Scores said he was, a reassembled Jack when cloned. So,
great was her fear that she screamed hysterically.

Aelfric understood and smiled; she was entertaining after
all.

Beside him Posidonus's mind was playing doctors, but the
trouble was, he was not a qualified surgeon?

Never had been.

There was a handful of truth in the whispers of girl employees, 'Jack the Ripper reassembled.'

Posidonus just always wanted to be a doctor.

And his money made it real without the
years of study involved, and exams.

Money bought Posidonus everything he desired so he
could not care if he had big red lips with a green Mohican
hair cut; greed ruled.

Money counted when needed; greed ruled.

And money did not care what you looked like; greed ruled.

"Thank you, Aelfric," Posidonus said rubbing his
hands with a low bow and Aelfric was pleased Posidonus knew his groveling place.

Now Aelfric was alone, it was time to think, so he turned
up the rose-tinted light on the chandeliers above.

His left sparkling jeweled index
finger twitched. Quickly the chamber suit played Swan Lake.

And Aelfric thought of the seventieth way to assassinate
The Man rather than what Madam Butterfly Chou's contract said he could and not do with the dancer.

Compensation would demand and paid;
greed ruled.

The dancer was just that, a dancer, a no
one.

       In six yellow feathers.

       But Aelfric was wrong, there was one who
       knew LIFE was not boring and he was

The Man: and greed did not rule him but liberty.

*

And The Man was young, and his once handsome face
scarred for a sword cut from his left temple to his right
upper lip.

And his left eye was not an eye but a camera lens.

And his left eye stabbed out by an assassin's dagger; Aelfric's first
assassination attempt.

And unflinching The Man had strangled the assassin as his grey remaining eye focused, such the metal of The Man.

The assassin would not talk anyway; war had hardened The Man and made him a killing machine when required, with the mind and reactions of a beast, sorry, human.

And his left hand was gone, blown away in battle and replaced by an eleven fingered electronic hand.

An extra finger allowed one to do wonders.

And his legs were bionic for a tank had crushed the originals.

And from his back sprouted silver wings and bulging bird wing muscles interlaced
with nuclear mini power plants; thanks to the first genetic implant surgery.

For he was **The Man.**

And his body was not his own but machine shop cogs, hydraulic works,
and regrown shell splintered organs.

He was a soldiers' general and loved by his men for he fought up front with them to the dismay of his staff officers.

And the above was thanks to the second genetic implant. Now he was mostly bionic and no longer human, *well!* Except his soul and spirit were human and of a divine spirit origin. Often, he remembered a name, A Man Zadok and wondered who he was?

And his brown hair was long, and a gold head band kept it out of his eyes.

And his remaining grey eye was cold and hard.

But it would twinkle kindness to a child and mischief to a woman.

And his teeth white, strong, and not the originals but grown from implanted

Genes.

And apart from these wounds, once called handsome, still was for his face showed the original gentleness he had been born with.

He had no flab and exercised daily for his new body parts demanded it or MALFUNTION would occur.

And he was a renowned space warrior who would give a screeching war yelp before going into battle and his enemy would become afraid and ask, "What do we fight? A demon or a man?"

"No, The Man," he would laugh back,

For he was **The Man**, Cluny James Smith.

Dictator.

He who had risen through the imperial war machine in wars against aliens, pirates and rebellious planets and had seized New Saturn 12 as his own declaring himself DIC-TATOR, and enemy of the imperial system. "LET ALL LIFE THAT HATES CORRUPTION COMETH TO ME AND DRINK FROM THE PURE WATERS OF THOUGHT THAT IS NEW SATURN 12."

So, he started his wars of conquest at the expense of the Emperor Augustus who could not forgive this commoner stealing the empire from under his nose.

"1,000,000,000 gold imperial dollars for the dictator's head," was Augustus's

reward and answer to The Man.

And The Man lived in Saturnmegapolis that still fabled city of light, masses of shiny stainless-steel skyscrapers that reflect the original two sun's rays and threw them down upon the teeming streets below. Where the sky is orange three miles up and blue below for massive apparatus pump out Earth's copied air.

And Planet New Saturn 12 is The Man's and has 2 types of huge plastic domes, one to contain polluted war and not the living, and one for his cities. As he said, "Take your recycled air away; give me just air to breath."

For it was his intention to clean all New Saturn 12's air but knew he needed the domes for they were radioactive proof.

And as for Posidonus?

"I have not condemned yet for he will lead me to his paymaster," The Man.

[CHAPTER 3] — THE FAILED ATTEMPT

Color: New Saturn 12, mercury storms, green clouds, black sky with red, yellow clouds and light green lighting streaks.

Tintagel the spy dressed as a tramp.

The Man was not happy, he who held absolute power over half the known human universes. His food taster Simon the large bald Frenchman with him since the beginning.

Once a sergeant in the Space Legion and a complete swine to the men until a grenade had blown the back of his skull away. Not to worry, the bone people

had regrown it and missing grey matter from *implanted genes;* he had been lucky; The Man had crawled under barbed wire and dragged him back to their lines.

And The Man won another medal,
And became more of a hero than he was.

And remembered Simon's cruelty and Simon had driven a tank over his legs so The Man said, "He did me a favor, now I can run the mile in ten seconds," for he was referring to his bionic legs and so rewarded Simon with the job of food taster when he knew machines could do it.

Such a promotion went down well with the troops!

For the dictator could do as he pleased for, he was The Man and that night Simon had eaten roast duck, sweet and sour fish, special fried rice along with the vial of plague belonging to another Aelfric Europe assassination attempt.

But The Man had not feasted that night for he had been indisposed with a beautiful woman. And if Aelfric had poisoned the woman, he might have succeeded for the vices of The Man were:

War, woman, food, exercise and drink and the spoils of war; And food was not the top priority at times.

And now Simon lay dying.

Such was the Dictator's justice for the absolute cruel and insight gained into one of space's greatest human dictators.

"How could poison get through the kitchen food scanner?" The Man asked furious.

"A traitor?" He whom he
asked replied. "I want IT
found,

NOW," and he whom he addressed went with the dictator's feared palace police in a swirl of black fluffy robes with a large black hat resembling a chef's hat to question the human, alien, and machine kitchen staff.

And his name was Tintagel Tasciovanus the Wise, he

whose chronicles have been raided for the information needed on The Man to write the truth about The Man, we the Historians of New Saturn 12 in the year 70,000 A. D for the two dictators, human female and Rhegid.

Now Tintagel was amazed dinner was from the second kitchen and   could find no trace of who gave the order. (Posidonus possibility.)

And the staff of the second kitchen was not trustworthy as they were new. AND POSIDONUS THE SPY HAD MADE SURE THE MACHINE THAT TOOK THE ORDER WAS NOW SCRAP. Posidonus could keep smiling, killing a machine was as enjoyable as dissecting a human dancer. How the machine had squealed in a tin voice for mercy as Posidonus had poured acid into its memory circuits. Then to be on the safe side, had used a screwdriver and dropped the remains down a rubbish chute that fed the incinerators below the palace for waste disposal.

The rats here were not fat.

And the vermin Posidonus were safe.

So, the new kitchen staff rounded up and the huge second kitchen palace doors sealed. Tintagel knew the innocent would suffer as the guilty would have escaped by now, *yes,* he saw the **fear** in their fresh faces for the second kitchen was a training area.

> Saw them looking at the red-hot
> plates on the ovens. The brown
> wooden chopping blocks.
> The big silver sharp cleavers.
> The big bronze pots of boiling water.

All because they had a dictator as a ruler and not a prime minister, what difference, both yield power?

And Tintagel's job would be easier for already FEAR

had their tongues at wagging point.

"Who is missing?" Tintagel asked.

CRUNCH   he slams a meat cleaver into a block slicing a big orange carrot in half.

The effect was good.

The orange carrot halves went flying,

This   way
and   that.

So, Tintagel gave a twisted little smile which he thought deserved a professional actor's praise. How he loved his little theatrics; hated violence, respected all life, and only killed when he was in battle with The Man. Sometimes he wanted to replace his job with a nice Deep Space Thought Monastic Cell, but knew he was vital to the peaceful existence of billions of life forms.

FOR WITHOUT HIM THE EMPEROR WOULD RECLAIM THEM BACK INTO THE EMPIRE.

And now those addressed babbled together and Tintagel watched his droid yellow microcomputer floating balls, with blinking LED lights as their microchip brains separated voices and filed them away in their note pads. He felt sorry for the two scribes holding the reins to the computers who feared they would error, and they would have the unenviable job of decoding the mess of data to separate the voices picked up here.

Then the newest dish washer shouted louder than the rest and advanced throwing her towel at Tintagel, "I isn't getting chopped up like that carrot for something I didn't do."

The room went into a shocked silence.

As everyone looked at the wet towel draped over the open orange sandals of Tintagel.

"Unseal the doors," Tintagel commanded and left taking the young girl with him, behind he could hear sighs of relief. The staff was no longer under investigation "for the moment," Tintagel added.

He was the primary spy of The Man and knew a plant when he smelt one. This SHE did not want questioning, she knew something, and she had drawn attention to herself; besides his aurora life indicator showed she had two life forces inside her. A good spy always carried an indicator in his pocket for extending his *own* life.

He also noted this SHE had wit and spark and burning intelligence behind her green eyes. A great pity she was working against them as his gut told him.

Tintagel had lots of ego; he would not admit the aurora machine had helped him detect her; he liked to see himself as a modern-day Sherlock Holmes.

SHE WAS JUST THE SORT HE WANTED WORKING FOR HIM AND THE MAN.

She would hang Posidonus and Aelfric Europe, therefore he would start tampering with her brain, it was his job to do that, he was The Man's primary spy.

Which gave him licenses?

And the Dictator would be pleased no one was racked and Tintagel was glad too for he did not like hurting folk, and The Man had issued secret instructions to him, NO PHYSICAL TORTURING SUSPECTS, use drugs instead.

So, it was right to let the suspects think they were going to the hot coals, it made tongues wag before you knew it.

As he The Man said, "The fighting is mainly over, we have got to win the hearts and minds, let's do it Tintagel."

So, Tintagel the Wise stayed in his job and only dreamed of that Deep Space Monastic Thought Cell.

The Man was The Man and there was no other like him. And Tintagel wondered how The Man became who he was and that was a mystery too.

ALL SPACE FEARED HIM.

Feared what?

An image of a ferocious beast and behind that image Tintagel knew was a softie. Given time everyone who worked for The Man would

come to know that truth making it that much easier for an assassin to kill. And Tintagel knew that, and the huge size of The Man's palace had prompted The Man to open wings, to house orphans and homeless types; any of whom might be a disguised assassin.

"A palace, this is a hostel for street urchins," Tintagel had shouted once.

So, Tintagel wondered what The Man would do without him and the generals who backed his humanitarian ways.

If The Man had been a cruel dictator would Tintagel or the generals love him?

"No," Tintagel's thought allowed, and the girl looked at him.

She was trying to read his mind, good, so had given away she had a mind reading implant under her scalp.

Indeed, a plant this pretty SHE.

At least The Man had learned one important lesson,

KEEP YOUR ARMIES WELL PAID, FED, AND TRAINED.

And The Man saw to it that Simon lived, for he was a collector and valued the advice of this former sergeant now a food taster, for this man was full of kitchen gossip.

And where did kitchen gossip come from, from the streets of course!

And The Man knew Tintagel Tasciovanus was wrong, for The Man was his own man and had everything under control.

He knew his generals, handpicked all. He also knew how to divide and rule amongst them so that they looked to him for reward, protection and punishment and each general knew that if he declared himself ruler of their galaxy the other generals under The Man would come for him or her.

Tintagel Tasciovanus worried too much about the state of the Dictatorship and that is why The Man kept him for he was The Man's conscious.

"Come this way my dear," Tintagel told the young girl whom he liked the look of. Of course, he did, he was walking behind her, and the movement of her hips drew his eyes to them. Tintagel you see was a male and we all know what they cannot help themselves looking at?

"Little girl how old are you?" Tintagel asked and at once he had given his thoughts away for, she stopped and faced him, and her eyes said it all, "Dirty old man."

Tintagel was at a loss; he had caught off guard. This girl could better him if he were not careful.

"So much unbroken spirit," he changes the subject.

"So, you are going to break it by handing me over to jailers or do it personally?" She challenged.

Whatever Tintagel had been thinking about personally behind her he was not any the more the more!

"Are you a badly treated slave too hate so much? And if you are who is your owner" He asked knowing millions of

The Man's subjects flouted his antislavery laws.

She did not reply, "Yes and he is Posidonus."

"I know The Man's laws, they are supposed to be for the oppressed," she more softly for his laws were on her heart.

The Man who passed good laws without a meeting house to ratify them. Who cares if the laws were good?

YOU SEE HE WASN'T REALLY
ALL THAT BAD.

He did care about his citizens, who were
not born to serve him,

He was to serve them.

But because he was a dictator and his palace so big and impressive, they automatically got the wrong impression about The Man.

"Only those who break his laws meet The Man," Tintagel warned. "So, what I have met worse?" She snapped back.

But he saw *fear* in her eyes at that prospect and allowed Tintagel to walk in front this time and walked silently behind now realizing the predicament she was in.

Tintagel rummaged in his pockets for a sweet.

And for an instant Tintagel knew fear for even if palace police lined the walls, why only two months past a man had tried to stick a dagger into Tintagel's waist.

Tintagel had been badly shaken but his master The Man did not think less of him, Tintagel was a spy, not a soldier or ACTION MAN.

And the police had used their lasers, cauterizing the assassin into blocks of tissue and Tintagel had been sick on the spot, never used to the sight of battlefield gore, especially stuff that had stuck to him.

The memory made him feel faint.

And the aurora machine in his pocket had failed him; it had not detected a corrupted color field made that way with evil thoughts. And the assassin had been in a cleaner's cupboard rummaging about tins of polish till Tintagel had passed and then sprung his suicide mission.

"Machines can fail," he muttered, and the girl looked at him questioningly. "They don't fail, or we would never have conquered space," she said behind him. *'By the gods the girl knew nothing about social boundaries, she was fresh and innocent or only plain awkward,'* Tintagel thought and answered, "It is the human spirit that conquered spirit not machines."

Suddenly a door slid open.

The girl stopped until she saw it was an elevator.

UP, UP, UP, UP, they quickly sped in an anti-gravity lift that was so fast the young girl struggled to keep her light summer flower printed kilt down.

Tintagel was a male; males notice these sorts of things *out of the corner of their eyes when they are trying not to notice!*

And he made no effort to keep his black robe down so his ankles showed and his white Bobbin ankle socks, then his knees, then his boxers, it was one of the indignities of an advanced civilization and either accepted this, or walked UP, UP, UP, UP, thousands of stairs.

HE SIGHED; his eyes had noticed what lovely legs she had.

He was a man and out of the corner of his eye he had of

course unintentionally seen these details.

He was also a primary spy and it had not gone unnoticed she disliked lifts.

Was she from an agrarian community where lifts were few?

But she cast venomous eyes at him, and Tintagel made it obvious he was reading the level indicator lights flashing as they zoomed past floors; *men are good at that too! He was a man and out of the corner of his eye he had of course unintentionally seen her look.*

Then the lift stopped, and the doors opened, and greeted by two-woman guards in silver body armor waiting to escort them to a luxurious wall papered room

in imperial Russian design. It was obvious the young girl was shocked, never seen the likes of this opulence, pomp, splendor, and tidiness.

"It is all lies then; The Man doesn't live in Spartan living quarters?" She triumphantly restoring her faith in what she believed about The Man.

"These are your rooms, The Man's guests are always given such rooms," and he saw her triumph vanish replaced by suspicion.

"I get a private loo, no two ways mirrors?" The girl and," Hey soft loo paper, perfumed soaps, so what happens when I have a bath, get electrocuted?"

"I am not Posidonus," he said it deliberately and watched for reaction.

She flushed, not trained as well as he would have trained her.

"First we debug you," and he waved to a purple machine

that had floated in uninvited with trailing octopus black tentacles.

She did not have a chance; the two guards knew their job and the tentacles had suckers on them.

"Born 50204.

Parents unknown.

Sold to Dictatorship 50221 A.D.

Granted freedom and citizenship rights same day. Known anti-social person.

Recommend mental reprogramming to readjust back to society," the machine bleeped.

Not a mention about Posidonus or Aelfric, the gods had forgotten Tintagel this day.

If reprogramming rejected offer settler ship on a pioneer world or sold back to previous owners," the machine bleeped.

Tintagel liked the last bit; **he had personally added that bit.**

The girl heard it too and did not like it, her past masters were not kind, and slowly he was breaking down her defenses.

"Ouch give me back my hair?" The girl annoyed as suckers floated away from her. Tintagel left her to soak in the bath and think.

Outside he sucked on a sweetie, his tenth Victory V today.

He wished the machines could see things the way The Man did, that slavery was bad. But the Master machines in the Senate House of Machines were proud they were

machines and not humans, slaves to logic and an antisocial life form should be in slavery till it mourned for the rights it had taken for granted and abused.

"Machines," he mused and sucked harder enjoying the burning sensation in his mouth from the sweet.

It gave him a warm glow in his mouth.

"Machines gave loyalty to The Man, but The Man wanted the flesh and blood of citizens loyal to him, to win their hearts and Tintagel could not understand why the likes of Posidonus existed? They ran about shouting 'FREEDOM OF SPEECH' and ??pp wanted liberty to do whatever they liked; what a shame the dictator put limits on their liberties for the good of all," and only the spying machine devices in the walls heard Tintagel muse.

The Man was not the Emperor Augustus who seeing how beautiful one of his woman courtiers was, had her eggs removed and now he had over a hundred thousand duplicates of her; *all loyal of course with slightly different characters?*

Yes, baby farms existed on all sides; they bred desperately needed troops for the wars. Robots were fallible on the battlefield, like a war elephant once hurt could go berserk and cause havoc.

And it was common knowledge the Emperor Augustus had instructed his First Minister, Po Wei to experiment further, to breed super soldiers and to use the duplicate courtiers as gifts to his loyal troops and generals.

Augustus being a man had bored with so many beautiful looks alike.

And such a baby farm program disturbed The Man and Tintagel for they did not sleep well at night.

THEY MUST DEFEAT THE EMPEROR NOW BEFORE HE BECAME TOO

POWERFUL and absolute.

And Tintagel prided himself at being an honest man, but he knew he was good at his job and lies came cheap.

It didn't cost the taxpayer anything for Tintagel to open his mouth carelessly in a crowded place, "The Emperor Augustus is playing with people's genes and turning the undesirables of society into mindless slaves, human robots.

Po Wei has factories altering this human tissue market.

Only The Man can stop Augustus and his madness," and all knew Tintagel was right, at least The Man's laws were good even if freedom of liberties and speech were curtailed.

"Posidonus could complain all he wanted that it was his civil right to open a shop to sell narcotics at the end of a tree lined road, but The Man would argue back it was his right to stop him," Tintagel would say, and it was true too.

Of course, The Man had his robots too; the 10th New Saturn Infantry regiment was all robotic and good fighters, cyber machines with living tissue on their inner robotic frames.

Why there was robotic woman, whores and friends, doctors, and judges; even robots who owned human slaves, even owned intergalactic trading companies and one was Aelfric who was not the original Aelfric Europe but a clone who had murdered his parents to gain control of the family trading empire and of course the real Aelfric.

Only murdered in turn by the robot Aelfric Europe who knew a good thing when he saw one.

FOR HE WANTED TO BE ABSOLUTE LIKE THE ORIGINAL.

And shared common characteristics!

Which explains his apathy towards human/aliens and why he did not flinch when he gave the original his master a bath in nitric acid to dissolve all the evidence the man existed.

There would be no clone appearing to accuse him of murder and steal him of his wealth.

The Emperor Augustus Sutherland knew how to deal with *malfunctioning robots*, he crucified them under the elements to erode slowly, and slow was the word, and plastics took thousands of years to decompose.

Yes, Aelfric had seen them on the Appian Ways into the capital Saturnmegapolis, moaning as a limb dropped off, rusted away, and seen rare metal scavengers take away a head to dismantle to sell the rare elements.

To end up in the circuitry of a, a, a, a, toilet flush.

AELFIC EUROPE
HATED HUMANS

HE WANTED ABSOLUTE
POWER LIKE HIS
MURDERED MASTER
BUT FOR ROBOTS

NOT HUMANS

"So?" The girl in question asked.

The two women guards smiled
at each other and laughed. "This
is your room," one repeated.
"And what do I have to do to keep it?"

"Anything you like dearest," the other guard and both

guards laughed and blushed. That last bit worried the girl, she was not born yesterday you know.

"We were like you once, antisocial until we met The Man," they told her simultaneously.

"Pros,' are we?" The girl insulted them, but the two guards took it in their stride, yes, they had been just like her once.

"Welcome to the family," one of the guards as the girl sat on the king-sized bed. It was so corrupting for it was so big and inviting her to sprawl and GET CORRUPTED and stretch and yawn and be LAZY.

Further down the hall Tintagel switched off his receiver, a scarab beetle that pinned his black fluffy robes together on his chest; would record all heard and send it to his computer in his room where later he could listen.

He loved his toy spying bugs that infested this palace; he was after all, good at his job.

"Welcome to the family," he repeated and made his way to Rest and Recreation and sucked on another Victory V.

Watching the girl's rump had made him think about a robot called Wendy.

She was not antisocial.

She was the replica of Ms. Pluto 38765 A.D. and loved him.

Beautiful people reincarnated as he called it, reassembled was the word?

And as two weeks passed the girl learned that part of the family did not mean entertaining The Man in that giant bed, although she was sure the two guards entertained with the police and whoever took their fancy in the adjoining rooms.

The girl could not understand such behavior because FUN had never come into such acts for her, *for she had been a slave with no rights.*

Her life she had spent on imperial planets where The Man's good laws did not exist. Only the avarice of the greedy; power was the norm, you got power then lorded.

Power to buy someone and then
abuse them.

Power to kill someone who you
took a dislike too.

Power to covert another's property either land or body.

Imperial society had its arenas for the disposal of undesirables, those who no one wanted to buy as a slave, and so did the mines.

Imperial society did not have the mental attitude of The Man who saw knowledge as being close to the animated spirit that he called God.

So treated all men and woman as he treated himself for, he believed treat one another as you do yourself.

And The Man did not treat himself well, for he did live in Spartan conditions for he was a soldier.

But he always had an insane desire to put his hand on sick stray dogs, and rid them of their mange. And The Man was not against genetic science for he knew old age was a disease and there was sickness amongst the human, alien poor and The Man was absolute!

And he knew his destiny had chosen for him before he was born, a handful of people just know and go and accomplish what others dream to do.

And he had opened doors and the secret he knew was not to languish in luxury and become soft that in any door that led away from light. And the light often went out in his heart and then The Man knew he had erred.

"You lie in the bed you make," he often said meaning *you did not have to be the person you were meant to be,* or a man would remain an addict to a certain way of life and never bother changing.

And looked out across dark space from a cock pit window and felt he was not alone.

Because he was THE MAN.

And destiny had chosen him because he was born to be a soldier and at the same time his spirit was full of love and compassion for the least too the greatest to the holiest to the most sinful for all possessed by a divine spark that animated all.

*

And The Man approached Simon his food taster.

"From now on be my ambassador to the Emperor Augustus." And Simon was pleased having suffered much from the plague Posidonus had fed him.

And both knew Simon had longed to visit Old Earth where he had been born and would not come back.

"You will give Augustus a gift of rare Orwellian Ostriches, but the troop of dancers come home," The Man told him but not that he had transferred $100,000 gold dollars into Simon's account. Simon had paid his debt to society for bullying recruits in the Space Legion and it was his severance pay from his *good soft job as food taster.* And when Simon discovered this any bitterness in his heart towards The Man melted. He would not be coming back; he would buy a pub come restaurant and thrill the customers with his tales of adventure riding into battle with The Man.

"And to think I might have crushed more than his legs with

that tank?" Simon mused in private thoughts glad he had not.

But when Simon reached Old Earth, it was Po Wei who gave him audience and opened the green envelop The Man had asked him to give Augustus.

'An invitation to a
roast duck dinner
Accompanied by
sweet and sour fish.

And special fried rice.'

And behind Simon the troop of dancers
and ostriches waited patiently.

Now Po Wei sat on his red dragon throne in his finest muslins as he deciphered what The Man had intended in the invitation.

Then Po Wei smiled, it was of course a peace offering, a way to get talks started between the two powers. But Po Wei wanted none of it, war he profited from, he was

 the real power not Augustus who would especially like to see the dancers. And Po Wei believed The Man in war, defeated by a brilliant general, himself. And then there would be no Augustus or The Man, *only of course* Po Wei.

And sent to The Man the frozen boiled head of Simon with a green cooking apple stuck in the mouth with this message stuck on the forehead:

'Undercooked.'

And the dancers sent to Augustus
who did not return them to The Man
and

the ostriches went to the emperor's private menagerie.

And The Man rent his purple robes of state when he saw the head of Simon and heard the dancer's fate.

And The Man swore he did avenge all and try to bring the dancers home to their loved ones.

SUCH THEN THE MAN

who was a mighty man?

Who knew he was here to serve the people,

not the people put here to serve him.

SUCH THEN THE STATE OF THE
GALAXIES OUTSIDE THE
DICTATORSHIP.

"And the scales of justice titled against the evil doers."

From Tintagel Tasciovanus his Chronicles.

And Po Wei continued his imperial duties unperturbed, cutting colored ribbons to open new munitions factories in front of flashing press cameras; and yes, he owned those factories and the wars against The Man had made him an extraordinarily rich and powerful being.

*

And The Man hated pomp and sometimes wished he were not The Dictator. "Space I need but three hundred rooms?" He often shouted while Tintagel sucked his Victory V's.

"These sweets I suck clear my mind and remind me of the power of spring," Tintagel.

And this day of spring 50220 The Man was alone in his private rooms and that was all it was, an old military keep that existed in the middle courtyard of his palace and The Man refused to have it demolished.

And since the roof of the mess hall had long collapsed, he could often lie flat and stare up at the dome surrounding Saturnmegapolis and see space beyond and know he belonged to?

And thought, these days of Posidonus needed hanged,

without or without a trial; Posidonus needed terminated, from his present existence.

"What goes round comes round," he mused but if he clung to that alone he would not give judgement upon evil Posidonus. "As long as I want your paymaster to hang with you, I let you live a little longer Posidonus, do you hear me?" And Tintagel heard instead for there was a motionless black **ant** resting on the table leg that The

Man lay upon; and the ant heard all.

"Well said," a voice behind The Man who sprang cat like to his feet as his hands and arms blocked the air.

But Tintagel had expected such moves so had stayed safely out of reach.

"Posidonus?" The Man asked of him.

"There are rumors in the streets there is one law for Posidonus and another for the street," Tintagel.

Now The Man was not a weak ruler who allowed the press to sway his judgements, but he did listen to his people, "Then let us hang Posidonus now."

"A dangerous act master as then they will shout you are Augustus," Tintagel replied meaning no trial allowed.

"Is there nothing I do that satisfies the street?" The Man raged.

"Patience master, I have a new recruit, Nesta, a wonderfully intelligent girl I believe Posidonus planted in the second kitchen, she I believe poisoned Simon and she will be a double agent and trap Posidonus and his paymaster very soon," Tintagel offering good news. He offered a Victory V and The Man surprised him taking one.

> The Man finally gave a smile and laughed, "She must be pretty Tintagel?"
>
> "I will first instruct her in manners before I present her too you master."

"That rustic?"

"Quite master."

And The Man hated Tintagel calling him master for it reminded The Man *his friend was but a slave.* But that was how Tintagel wanted it to confuse their enemies,

for hundreds sought him out offering him freedom as a reward to betray The Man.

And both knew The Man's proclamation offering slaves freedom in his domains believed because slaves trust slaves, and the most trusted adviser of The Man was a slave, not a free man who was bribable.

So, slaves left the empire of Augustus and came to the lands of The Man bringing their skills in lace making and olive oil pressing, and the economy strengthened. And Po Wei foamed for he was a free man and no slave trusted him!

"Such the mentality of salves master that only we slaves understand," Tintagel tried to explain.

And Tintagel the slave had sold himself into slavery to pay for his fourth microchip implant to make his brain faster than a computer; nothing was free in life apart from love and death.

Character update Tintagel

To my students, please leave this update after page 37 and on no account remove and paste elsewhere................ Tintagel Clone 44... 70000A.D.

The Man's friend and adviser born New Mars, parents' stable Red Martian marrow farmers' intent on making Tintagel a farmer. But Tintagel had plans for from his planet he could see the Milky Way, all its colors, its brightness, **its pulling,** like a boy on Old Earth brought up by the sea, watching the crashing white waves, knowing that over the horizon are worlds beckoning a visit.

"The grass is greener here boy."

So, the young Tintagel studied hard in secret while laboring for his parents to make the biggest juiciest marrows out. "They would have me travel space slicing marrows in a liner's kitchens when I would be on the bridge steering," Tintagel would joke to the marrows growing in lines in his parent's fields until at last they out of love, seeing him gazing sickly at the stars helped him to study.

"Come home lad, come home," they pleaded seeing his itchy feet would take him far from them.

"Who will put flowers on our graves?" They asked themselves.

And so, it was then that Tintagel obtained a ticket in ship's computer navigation and left New Mars on the ship S.S. Liberty as a second officer.

"I will return, I promise," Tintagel had bidden them farewell, but his parents had been young once and knew space was so large it could fit in a pint bottle of   sea water.

And Tintagel wanted away from the rule of the emperor for he wanted liberty so paid for the first free genetic implants to increase his memory, for he wanted never to forget what he saw and learnt on his travels.

And soon began to realize there was no freedom for his kind for the emperor owned all space he travelled in.

But there were the legends of the sea, of free worlds deep in uncharted space of free men and women building new planets with liberty on their minds

Unfortunately, their star co-ordinates hidden, less the empire swallows them up.

Then fortune smiled, Tintagel met The Man, a young private in the Space Legion who gazed at the stars on deck as Tintagel did.

"I will take space from under the emperor's feet till he has no planet to call his foot stole," Tintagel remembered The Man boasting and was not ego but truth.

And Tintagel saw this young soldier believed in himself and saw he was special so kept an eye on him and sure enough The Man rapidly rose through the ranks.

"But always doubt assailed me; did fate and the gods exist to have chosen him?" Tintagel asked often.

Then one year Tintagel heard a man called Cluny James Smith had declared himself Dictator of New Saturn 12 in A.D. 50149.

"Immediately I went there, a most perilous journey for war existed between The Man, and the new Emperor Augustus William Sutherland.

And cost me every dollar to get into New Saturn 12 on a gun runner with passengers wanting off the planet.

War was coming.

And saw immediately the troops of The Man were without fear, they had a brilliant general leading them to war unlike the corrupt Grand Marshalls of the Empire facing them.

And The Man welcomed me to sit always beside him for I had memorized all space I had seen hadn't I and he remembered me?

And there were rumors of a messiah that the imperialist tried hard to suppress for it aided The Man, so I went about creating myths for a man who was about to conquer space must come out of myth, must not he?

And the first war against Augustus ended in victory and The Man wined and dined as women threw themselves at him seeking advancement in the new order, for none had seen the likes of The Man since Alexander and Julius Caesar.

Except Tintagel went off with his books and star gazing for he had heard the astronomers of old had been able to see the future in the stars? *And I took my share of the admirers: I am a man?* Then I met Wendy the robot cyborg and never sought a relationship with another of my species.

She was a man's dream, a friend and more, and so drifted off to my pursuit of studying life forms and became a spy from it.

And often wondered if I am a failure because I devote myself to The Man when I have a life to lead? What am I afraid of, of a son leaving the roost and promising to return and he never does?

The heart break I caused my parents for how often they gazed into the sky hoping my return. *And all that came was the troops of Augustus to execute them because they were my parents.*

Had that affected me so much? Is that why I remained with a cyborg?

And one day the scientists would ensure Wendy and her kind could carry a womb and would the child have a soul? It is only a womb, the growing tissue that lives in there must have a soul, for it is living.

And would I fall to temptation and select the coloring, the eyes, hair, and such? Or would I stand back and allow chance to choose? Or is it chosen already, and I am just a foolish actor playing my part.

My children where the citizens of The Man, those who lived and died every day in the dictatorship, billions.

CHAPTER 4

Who is Aelfric Europe?

This is he.

Original born 50150 Old Saturn, Dept. Milky Way, scion of the wealthiest human family Old Earth. Father, Henry Cedric De Wattigern, trader and Milky Way Senator.

Father disappeared as well as clones 50123 A.D. Old Saturn. Mother and two

brothers and one sister perished in ferry shuttle explosion between Old Saturn and Old Jupiter 50123 A.D.

Suspected bomb.... police reports.

Sole inheritor Aelfric Europe the youngest child.

"Yes, blame cuddles the cat."

100,000,000, gold dollar transfer noted from De Wattigern family bank accounts to imperial treasury accounts same time as ferry disaster.

Pilot error......new police report that appeared soon after.

Free papers called it a *'bribe to clear a conscious.'*

And Aelfric had known real power all his life and now he was absolute and the bored click of a finger could send a hired entertainer to the acid baths.

He was not a genuinely nice man.

Another bored click and an alien scribe notified the master computer to withdraw clone deposits of one entertainer from all listed clone banks.

And the clone banks would expect and receive a small gift.

And Aelfric safely entertained in the knowledge he had really killed, exterminated, made extinct a living being.

That was fun   *he was not a nice man.*

FOR THIS WAS THE CORRUPT

FUTURE WHERE CONVICTION

WAS IN ONESELF

WHERE A STRONG MIND WAS

NEEDED TO SURVIVE. BODY
BEAUTIFUL WAS THE NORM.
HEALTH AND YOUTH WAS AVAILABLE TO ALL,

OF COURSE, AT A PRICE.

There was nothing wrong in that.

It was the top that was wrong,
the law makers, For they were
corrupt and immoral, rotten.

The rulers were out for themselves and the enslavement
of all. Power was the turn on, the abusing of the weak
their joy and the security of their wealth their aim.

AND THE TOP WAS ABSOLUTE EVIL CORRUPTION.
THE EMPEROR AUGUSTUS WILLIAM SUTHER-
LAND

Who sat on a gold throne encrusted with diamonds?

As street beggars outside in the streets starved.

They were addicts, the evicted and the runaways; the
criminal element who deserved what they got and that was
begging. And when beggars appear on the streets something has seriously gone wrong with society.

And since Augustus spent his time at the arena, in bed
with courtesans, gaming, hunting, eating, and drinking
and pretending to rule by crucifying a tax evader or allowing his hounds to scent out an escaped slave, their
evening meal; it was Secretary Po Wei who ruled the empire.

"And Augustus would tether barbarian and rebel kings
behind his golden chariot as he made his way back to his
white crystal palace for, he knew the power of display. It

was pomp; it sent a message to the cowering citizens that it might be their slave remains roped up instead of the barbarians and the hounds bayed in anticipation."

Tintagel, Chronicles, vol: 11: pp 4908.

And Aelfric made sure there was no evidence but there was still The Man too worry about.

"I condemn the guilty," The Man's words and Aelfric fretted over them as did

billions of the ABSOLUTE RICH.

For Aelfric Europe lived on the disputed planet of New Jupiter that now was part of The Man's Dictatorship. Next year if the emperor's admirals won a battle, New Jupiter would once again become an imperial planet.

IT WAS A HARRING TIME FOR AELFRIC.

It meant one could not relax under imperial law and not have to worry about 'what to do with trash?'

'TRASH' was rich slang for disposable slave flesh.

Why last year The Man had re invaded and his wise man Tintagel had plugged into the Deaths and Register master computer, found evidence of mass murders, and sent those responsible, a hundred wealthy traders back to New Saturn 12 as workers in a sweat shop that removed toxic metals from machines.

It was The Man's justice and made The Man popular with the mob that Aelfric feared.

So, Aelfric worried for under imperial law it was legal to state on the death certificate a slave whipped to death for insolence, and Aelfric had bribed dozens to remove his entries; just in case Tintagel should find them.

He did not want to contract cancerous sores from those metals like the hundred had.

"I condemn the guilty to death," Aelfric mimicked and added, "I condemn you to

death as you are The Beast to Rich.

I WILL KILL YOU DICTATOR," therefore 'Aelfric Europe De Wattigern' was not   absolute, and he was aware of this FACT and hated The Man for it. For he was answerable and accountable for murder under The Man's strict regime of law, and even under imperial laws if a bribe was not forthcoming.

That is all Aelfric wanted to be   ABSOLUTE.

Without FEAR of the law for he would be the law.

And Aelfric knew The Man hated his types and wanted them conformed to his laws or dead or immigrated out elsewhere.

BUT THE ORIGINAL HUMAN AELFRIC HAD NOT FORESEEN THE ACTIONS OF HIS ROBOT STAND IN, built A.D. 50204 who poured out his bath. As stated, a

BUBBLING NITRIC ACID BATH.

Along with fumes and vapors.

And The Man was not powerful enough to hang Aelfric Europe yet for The Man had enemies and he needed money to finance his wars.

His enemies were:

Emperor Augustus William Sutherland of New Earth. The Traders Association whom Aelfric led.

Aliens in uncharted
space.

The pirate Feder-
ation.

His own generals.

Posidonus of course.

His own people divided in FREAR and love for The
Man; *it was the*

word 'Dictator' that was off putting.

And the fragile economy only recovering from the last
war against the emperor and traders.

A wasted toxic space made from wars of conquest by
all sides that now needed

to rest.

The Man's own temperament itself was an enemy.

And there was never any evidence
against clever Aelfric. He dissolved it
always.

And The Man had friends, those whose lives he changed
such as billions of citizen slaves whose lives were better
off under his laws because they were now FREE.

Alien rulers whom he had helped in war.

Tintagel the Wise.
Robots.
Prince
Vespa?

Madam
Chou,
who?

The
Rhegids,
who?

The 5,

who?

And anyone who read his works and
believed in The Man. Tintagel's recruit
Nesta given time.

*

And Aelfric robot lounged on his cushions as a naked
human Black haired female harpist played 'Love me tender'
while a young boy waited in the shadows for his summons.

For this was the year 50220 A.D. and the streets of
New Jupitermegapolis, blown now by hot sandy winds at
night, sand that rubbed away your skin and a young orphan
street beggar could do worse. He might seek the Flesh Market and have Madam Butterfly Chou find him something
nice and have him sign an

employment contract and that was risky, sued if a girl died.

Yes, the young blond boy concluded he had been lucky
Posidonus had spotted him rather than the New Jupiter
police who would have killed him as he was TRASH litter-
ing the streets.

"What was the Emperor Augustus doing while such bar-
barities were going on, playing a fiddle?" From Tintagel's
Chronicles.

Or the kid sold by the police to a gene bank where he did
be strapped on a table for the rest of his life as he donated
organs that duplicated, inside him from stem cells.

And rich client could not wait for a duplicate heart and if
the price were right?

Yes, the boy concluded he was lucky being so handsome that Posidonus spotted him. No one liked an ugly
street urchin, they ended up dead quicker.

The emperor did not like ugly people sleeping rough on his streets, SO THEY DISSAP-
PEARED.

Mysteriously.

And Posidonus had offered the boy $100 gold imperial dollars for a night's work of toying with the female harpist to alleviate his boredom and entertain his friend.

All that money, it meant he could stay off the streets for months. And the boy looked at the diamond encased water clock; it showed 10 pm, New Jupiter time. His client seemed sleepy, he had drunk lots and the boy hoped the night would pass without incident and he did be gone in the morning.

Already the boy bathed and fed lobster.

Life was improving already for the kid.

"Sleep you creep," the boy silently prayed looking at the water clock.

These were not Madam Butterfly Chou's wacky clients, so the boy felt safe but did not know the man who had drunk lots was a robot.

A ROBOT THAT COULD GO DAYS WITHOUT SLEEP.

Behind the boy a Major Domo stood in the shadows with an electric cattle prod to make the boy jump into the room.

And the boy was hot, the oils rubbed onto his skin to make him shiny prevented

him from sweating, yes getting hot and would not mind a glass of that cool red wine Aelfric was drinking.

NICE AND COOL, THRIST QUENCHING.

What none knew was that The Major Domo had two masters, Aelfric, and Tintagel for both paid well and this was the AGE OF ESPIONAGE.

It was also an age where a rigid class system existed, and The Man was attempting to pull it apart and why the

Traders Association wanted The Man dead.

Class was power, it meant you could flick a finger and a FAG would jump to your bidding.

Then the cattle prod used, and the boy leapt into sight and went straight to the harpist.
He was extremely hot and needed
to sweat but could not.

He had his work cut out tonight.

But Aelfric smiled, the boys' exertions would overheat him, and he would suffocate, *except the boy did not know that.*

And he knew something else the boy did not; they were Madam Butterfly Chou's wacky clients.
And Aelfric now happy thought of The Man.

What did The
Man fear?
FAILURE?

> EMOTIONAL
> ATTATCHMENTS?
> FAMILY TIES?

The Man was like an immature child refusing to accept he was in a mature body.

Well, Nesta would help him mature and realize corruption went with growing up. There was fun and games for the ABSOLUTE.

Nesta would plant the seeds of doom in The Man and The Man would become like Augustus riding his golden chariot trailing the subdued behind him, as the hounds brayed for their dinner.

> SHE WOULD BE HIS EIGHTEENTH
> ASSASSINATION ATTEMPT.

And Aelfric looked at the small pink reading recorder on the coffee table and lazily switched it off and the red light on it dimmed away.

"The Taming of the Shrew."

Nesta was beautiful, she
would grow into a wanted
woman and to help, Aelfric
had had Posidonus contract
the Master Priest the gene
wizard to alter her.
His work was more Nesta.

Her first unknown recorded genetic implant for she was drugged, unaware, of the needle slipping into her vein with gene code attachments that would seek out those cells necessary for altering.
SIDE EFFECTS: growing pains.

Her bosoms would be a
woman's dream ideal. Her
blond hair richer.
Her legs longer and shapely.
The green of her eyes deeper.

The Man would not be able to resist her.

And it all happened on New Jupiter which was Aelfric Europe's. Of course, the Master Priest had not come in person; he had sent the vial after payment and preferred to live apart from Aelfric, for longevity's sake.
A wise precaution because there had been a sudden fire in the Genetic Clinic and all the staff had perished except for the Master Priest.

And in return Aelfric started to pay monthly for Nesta's

secret to be a secret, she was the secret. For once Aelfric had a taste of his own poison extortion.

And Aelfric took his rage out on Posidonus so what goes round comes round. And the Master Priest was insured for a million to one with the Imperial Insurance Company against arson and arson had occurred so was smiling.

And the Master Priest had instructed Nesta's bowels to make a new virus and activate in one year's time. A year was not a long time to wait to become ABSOLUTE.

The virus was a safety measure just in case the shrew did not destroy The Man in the taming process.

The shrew was Nesta.

And the virus had a simple brain, a strand of RNA and two of DNA. It had a fixed aim, a desire to kill and The Man's scent it would recognize. The strands of molecules therefore had AIM and PURPOSE.

And Aelfric brought his thoughts back to the boy who was having problems because his skin could not sweat.

Aelfric poured out a pile of drugs and summoned the boy over.

"Take these, they will make you feel better," he told the boy, and the boy took them.

He was slightly disorientated because he was so hot.

'TRASH, human trash,' Aelfric saw the boy as and his type would help keep Aelfric rich for he had a drug's empire, and if there were humans about to buy them, he would be happy.

Hash and ZRT2 cocaine and the watered-down stuff was legal for those who needed them to block out the horrors of their work, as they scooped up the green algae off their sewage for drying and baked into green bread for the poor.

IT WAS RICH IN VITAMINS AND PROTEINS.

And harder drugs prohibited for the likes of the algae gatherer for they put your mind places where a worker could not concentrate on his job.

These drugs were the possession of the rich who did not need to work.

And they had their clients who would gather in the mansions, and all would have a rave up.

IT WAS SUCH JOLLY GOOD FUN.

It beat joy riding.

It gave a new dimension to frolicking and anti-social behavior. It also made Aelfric much richer and ABSOLUTE.

All these rich folk's dependent on him, why he could flick a finger and a man on Pluto Desert Laboratory fired.

A no one, just a thought up name and the man had just married too. And it proved to Aelfric what humans were, TRASH.

And the boy became hyper and Posidonus asked him to examine himself for an omen and the boy did, it was messy and smelly as there were no omens in the boy's innards, but Aelfric looked at Posidonus and saw TRASH and knew humans deserved rule by ROBOTS.

And Posidonus saw the look in Aelfric's eyes and knew FEAR for he felt like a rodent in front of a rattlesnake.

And Posidonus was ill and evil whereas

Aelfric was just evil. But Posidonus knew
he was trash and might be next?

CHAPTER 5

Corruption

A Corrupt Court.

The Emperor Augustus William Sutherland in a gold toga was sitting on his diamond throne watching a display of silent laser swordsmanship to a background of 1812, for he liked the sound of ancient canons. He was one year older than The Man whom he hated detested loathed over as a threat to the OLD ESTABLISHMED ORDER.

His order.

Every laser thrust accompanied by quickened drumbeats by his skin drummers. That would bring his roving eyes back to the dueling swordsmen. He was looking for sport, a new beauty to initiate into his court.

The swordsmen found the drumbeats disconcerting and red cuts soon appeared; that was the idea. It was not fair, but Augustus always said, 'Nothing in life was fair or there wouldn't be poor and rich.'

He also said, ' We breed the poor so they can wonder at our richness,' also 'the poor need the crumbs that the rich leave them to eat.' 'Poverty magnifies our splendor,' 'someone must be poor, and I am glad it isn't me,' 'My laws are to protect us from falling to their level.' Augustus also called,' The Hunter' for he had hounds to deal with those who resisted his ideals made for a world where people wanted power, they loved it, it corrupted and filled you with ego.

It was not unusual for kids playing or lovers walking too stumble across the remains of those who had not escaped the hounds.

Anyway, the drumbeat stopped, a sword lay on the floor, and so did the fingers that once held it.

But Augustus was looking into the blue eyes of a young girl whose parents had edged her forward so they could profit.

Now Augustus held up his palm skywards so allowing the wounded swordsman to pick up his weapon and use his other hand which he was useless at swordsmanship with.

Augustus could not care; he was grinning so much at the girl he was showing his brilliant white dentures.

The girl fluttered her extra-long dark eye lashes and blushed.

Her mother sensing victory and richness unclasped the girl's cape, so it dropped revealing the girl wore truly little else.

Augustus summoned the girl to his side as he stood up

and left with her; then he turned and told the swordsman who was winning to hurry up.

And with a new zeal the man hacked and hacked till his opponent's sword and hand lay on the floor.

There was a gurgling sound as the winner killed the defeated one, then the sound of coins thrown; it was all in a day's work.

And as one died a man left the room, a man who said he was the 'Fountain of Mercy,' that man was Augustus.

A man who boasted his laws were for all. "The public execution of one rich man quells the rebellious poor who see my laws discriminate against none."

And the rich put up with Augustus for they were as bad as he and was rumored there existed a secret society amongst them, a society that selected one of their own who had not behaved and gave him/her over to Augustus; as executed, scape goats and thus the rich paid their dues to society and the poor were happy.

It was also rumored Augustus headed this secret society which was very convenient for him. "I tickle the wealthy," he boasted and often introduced new blood into the ranks of the elite, a war hero, a corrupt official who donated much, a beautiful courtesan, a noted man of science as examples.

And when trouble brewed with the masses these fortunate became the public executed.

Their estates confiscated and Augustus grew rich.

The man was self-preservation and knew how to win.

He made his enemies disappear and corrupted all he encountered. Even the servants who groveled at his feet knew what money could buy.

The idle rich men and women who owned them had taught them to visit the slave markets to *see if anything interesting* had turned up?

And from the lowest to the highest all aped Augustus's ways, his opulence, his orgies, his tastes to alleviate himself of boredom; *for they were his citizens were they not?*

The hedonist, after reading a wife of a Roman Emperor entertained a whole legion so, his beloved 16th Space Marine Regiment rewarded and had Po Wei round up a thousand daughters for the display in the arena.

It was also rumored Po Wei's son, Po Shen donned on armor to join the marines! Also, wild beasts chained at intervals to catch any fleeing maidens pursued by marines.

Trenches dug and filled with flesh eating fish.

Balloons tethered to posts, chili wraps sold, ice creams and soda drinks, alcohol, and drugs. A carnival atmosphere allowed for society lacked morals.

And it was known citizens fed their disobedient servants to their pet dogs, bears and tigers for they aped the emperor and supported him for they feared one

He who condemned
the guilty, The
Man.

So, they flocked to the emperor's race days where he had a swimming pool filled with sharks and TRASH thrown in wearing jockey colors, and bets placed to see

who managed to pull themselves out of the pool?

And Augustus had stables for the winners where they lived with his gladiators and lived to excess for none knew when his sell by date arrived.

People who lived for today only for they believed in nothing except Hedonism, pleasure for that is what the top believed in.

They did not even see God in themselves, so did not believe in anything apart from DEATH that was very real.

And if DEATH could reply, it would whisper, "Curses be upon your kind, Till the tenth generation. I have no objection to Genetics.

> But what you
> have done, Un-
> clean people
>
> so, I have given
> you My bone
> grinder, The
> Man.

And Augustus understood DEATH also without listening to its still voice; for he paid his followers well to the extent that they would execute their own mothers, and scores did.

And Augusts had the largest standing army ever known in the history of humankind, and they saw themselves as invincible legions of a forgotten empire with gaudy standards to follow.

And overall, it made Aelfric Europe very jealous for Augustus was a challenge to his belief that HE WAS ABSOLUTE only.

*

Now Augustus was expecting a visitor, Tintagel the Wise, who had come as ambassador of The Man. The Man,the very thought of made Augustus's bile rise, so

that when a gladiator lay under the victors sandals, it was an acidy stomach that decided life or death.

And the skin drummers understood and beat faster making a crescendo of excitement as the crowd of murderers waited for Augustus to order.

And Augustus gave the thumbs down, and DEATH was in a rattle of a last breath. And Augustus accepted the head of the vanquished and he offered it to his newest conquest, the young girl who accepted it and passed the grizzly trophy too her courtiers, and finally it was in a trash bin.

Outside the palace rats and beggars waited to fight over the head.

Millions of years of design and evolution just destroyed just like that!

By a man called Augustus who could not made a pea plant thrive.

And Po Wei gave Tintagel audience for peace needed to recoup loans to pay the troops. And Tintagel knew The Man had paid Po Wei a small fortune to make sure Tintagel's head was not on a silver plate waiting to feed rats and beggars.

So, Tintagel bowed incredibly low till his head touched the blue mosaic floor depicting Tang hunting scenes as a hundred cymbals vibrated.

Tintagel stayed bowed which pleased Po Wei immensely.

The Mayor Domo in Aelfric's household had warned Tintagel not to move until Po Wei summoned him, that had been Simon's the food taster's mistake; had stood up before Po Wei had summoned when Simon functioned as ambassador.

Po Wei saw all who served The Man as TRASH and saw himself as a god. "Follow me," Po Wei ordered and led Tintagel into a private audience chamber

painted with Ming dynasty floral scenes, birds, and tigers. Scene depicted on Po Wei's trailing sixteen-foot gown that Tintagel did his best to get out of the way of as slaves carried it.

Po Wei liked to show he was power, and power meant life or death to those below his status.

And as they walked East Asian banners hung from ceilings, looked Japanese Samurai and in wall niches expensive antique vases, only the best.

Depicting scenes that Tintagel's mind censored.

"A man becomes like his furniture," Tintagel had complained often to The Man. "Good I will not be like Po Wei then," The Man liking a soldier's rustic seat.

"A heart like wood will not bend," Tintagel warned.

"Love will bend it," The Man and Tintagel asked, "What love, where is the girl to soften it?"

But both knew The Man spoke of another love?

"Judge your rulers by their seats," Tintagel would later write in his Chronicles.

For Po Wei sat on a red polished lacquered ebony throne on goose pillows embroiled in flowers and animals. Genuinely nice Tintagel thought, but you are not The Man who sits on a rough wooden seat.

Now Po Wei gripped the ebony carved dragon arm rests asking, "What does IT want?" For Po Wei was making it obvious he was speaking to something his cat had left behind.

"For the exalted Emperor Augustus to stop the traffic in exiles," Tintagel lied. SILENT PAUSE.

"Augustus will consider," meaning Po Wei will.

And Po Wei guessed that the stream of exiles flooding into the dictatorship was a drain on its economy and was pleased. It also worked the other way round; the rich were leaving the dictatorship seeking solace in the empire.

Po Wei was overjoyed that such economic woo had befallen his enemies.

How could Po Wei stop such traffic when they paid him vast bribes to immigrate? "My poor cousins," Po Wei called them, and they certainly were after meeting him!

And Tintagel was pleased, this is what he and The Man wanted, to make Po Wei think the dictatorship was weak, and Tintagel bowed low again till he tasted the lime polish on the mosaic floor.

Suddenly a copper coin span beside Tintagel's face for Po Wei had thrown the beggar substance.

Tintagel thanked Po Wei for his generosity and accepted the coin. Let the empire have all the decadent wealthy and the dictatorship would take the artisans, craftsmen and laborer's who believed in, good old fashioned challenging work never hurt anyone.

The Man called them "His silverware."

One refugee trained to carry a 60lb rucksack, laser rifle, spade, tent, blanket, ammunition, and his armor was worth more than any of Augustus's well-paid soldiers for they had read The Man's book and believed in The Man.

These men followed The Man not his generals and his generals knew it and why The Man could roam space like Buck Rogers and return to a throne.

Could Augustus do likewise, think not, he might return and find Po Wei on his throne?

Now Po Wei looked at the cymbal players in their red leather jerkins studded with brass bells; the audience was over; the noise began again.

Tintagel kept bowing all the way out of the audience chamber and thanked heaven for the Major Domo even if he was expensive.

And once outside bought a fizzy drink from a floating drink vendor to rid himself of the lime polish with the copper; *waste not want not?*

And resorted to his Victory V to rid himself of the cheap fizzy drink taste. There was no waiting convoy of black hover limousines but a return bus ticket on the monorail, Po Wei wanted to degrade Tintagel his opponent as much as he could.

> Only one man could be a god and that man was Po Wei?   GREY. So, Tintagel rode the bus a hundred feet above the traffic lanes to the Inn of the Split Winds observing all he saw.

The sullen distrustful faces listening to their private music players, the anything goes fashion, the needles stuck in noses, the obvious chastity belts, the grey walls of the bus covered in graffiti and advertisements. Lingerie and men's leopard skin thongs.

Chewed gum stuck to the train walls and used condoms lay on the floor. Grunting sounds made Tintagel look, the back seat was occupied by dangerous youths coupling.

GREY.

The bus reflected the empire, it had lost something, a community spirit was missing, and it was now everyone for him/herself.

Outside the Inn which was no more than a brothel a fight had broken out between two youths and now one lay bleeding badly on the pavement from a stab wound.

> And   above   him   the   hover   bus   had   broken down.   GREY.

Inside his room Tintagel looked out his non curtained window where neon advertisements threatened to keep him awake and saw the girls float by on them platforms, enticing him to treat for their wares.

A transsexual exposed herself for nothing, eager to join with Tintagel.

Every race, sex and robot were out there with clients and vendors selling food to

Silver florescent light.

Rose water smell.

the condiments of the game.

The empire was not well, most where addicts to something, a whole generation was going to waste out there?

And across from Tintagel a Snuff Show House where a queue had formed for the condemned of the empire sold here to meet their end.

And Tintagel saddened as he knew those in the queue would pay a small fortune to watch another human murdered for an inner gratification.

The empire was indeed not well.

A KNOCK AT THE DOOR.

Tintagel tensed.

The Major Domo just tortured, crudely by Aelfric Europe, so his double game was now known.

And on a pump-up air bed Nesta pretended to be asleep. Tintagel saw her and was pleased; she would grow into a beauty, and he would teach her well and she

would be loyal to The Man. How so, for she saw what Tintagel saw, the human decadence outside their window.

Silver florescent light. Rose water smell.

And one enemy was Augustus Sutherland who desired to have the planets The Man took in war back. Right now, he lounged on a leopard skin sofa eating black olives fed to him by two girls, one dyed red and the other light blue.

Po Wei was listening with him to tapes playing from The Man's enemies begging Augustus to make a treaty with them against The Man.

PO Wei did not think Augustus was concentrating, the nymphs were extremely attractive, that was good, they were meant to be.

So, Po Wei neglected to mention that the new treaty had cost the empire ten years taxes and these enemies of The Man would declare Po Shen, Po Wei's favorite son their king.

And one amongst them was Prince Vespa. REMEMBER HIS NAME.

It is, easily forgotten.

*

"Master," Tintagel gasped as he opened the door after the knocking and lowered his laser.

"Want a mercenary bodyguard?" The Man asked knowing Tintagel had seen through his disguise.

"Come in and discuss terms," Tintagel replied and searched for a Victory V. The Man strode in. all seven feet of him and stopped beside Nesta.

SILENCE.

The door shut.

"Master she is my apprentice not what you see," Tintagel.

"A girl?" The Man.

"Since when did you become a sexist?" Tintagel. At

that moment Nests opened her eyes as The Man sensing defeat, so contented himself by removing cosmetic warts and interesting disguises from himself.

Nesta screamed, she was not sure if she was having a nightmare.

Her scream went unnoticed as downstairs in the bar two female wrestlers were struggling with a small black declawed brown bear. Of course, there was lots of mud; nothing had changed apart from the added stimulants and the bear.

In fact, the whole cheap hotel was full of screams.

One more by Nesta just meant the occupier of that room had bizarre tastes.

As passing aliens in the corridor who seeing the disguised Man had thought, "That is one ugly mercenary."

"Relax Nesta, you are not intended for him," Tintagel soothingly.

The Man smiled reassuringly as his scar that ran down his face to his lip lengthened; somehow Nesta worried.

Here was a lion and she was the fresh food.

With a shrug The Man handed Nesta his laser pistol and sat down, drank a glass of orange peel wine and then with his lengthened incisors tore into a piece of cold chicken meat baked in honey and mustard.

Nesta pointed the gun at The Man.

She watched The Man sprinkle salt and pepper on his meat and heard him belch.

She put down the gun in disgust; if she was to be a spy then she better accept the slime that went with the job.

The Man felt a little uncomfortable, Tintagel had been right; Nesta was a little thing. He put down his chicken and wiped his hands, on the tablecloth and apologized for frightening her.

Tintagel raised a suspicious eyebrow.

The Man was looking Nesta up and down and she knew it, as she just stood there glaring challenging.

Tintagel now suspected the war of the sexes had begun. Then Nesta did not know who this stranger was or did she? And The Man wished Nesta a better life than spying.

A life with a solid man behind her and a home, Kids, and that sort of stuff.

Looking at Nesta just starting out on life made him feel protective. He was The Man with a ferocious image to maintain.

And he enjoyed doing it, The women and wine, The women and war.

The women, wine, and war.

Poor, poor, poor, The Man.

"Life's a bitch then you die," was one of his favorite quotes.

He offered her wine and chicken, and she took it and went and sat cross legged in a corner.

OUTSIDE LIGHT FILLS
ROOM WITH RAINBOWS
FOR THE ROOM HAS

CRACKED

GREEN WALLS.

Nesta watched the stranger's face become softer as his disguises came off, the man could pass as handsome if it were not for that scar.

'Scar? Scar?' Alarm bells went off in her memory; weren't Tintagel and The Man the best of friends?

She remembered he had bionic limbs just like this stranger and her heartbeat faster.

And he kept looking at her and smiling; somehow her legs felt exposed, she knew they were nicely shaped and designed to make men look and remembered 'Women and wine,

Women and war,

Women, wine, and war,' this was her original target; she did not cross her legs,

but, BROUGHT them up to her chin.

The Man cursed the climate changes that heralded in hot sticky air and new clothe designs, what clothes? It was too hot for clothes, and she knew he could see her gold pants.

She was natural youth; he was, implanted youth. He felt hundreds of years old, he was.

Nesta you are taunting The Man who has a thousand courtiers, what is your game Nesta, did not mummy tell you to wear longer kilts?

The trouble was Nesta did not have a mummy to tell her such niceties, so dropped one long shapely hairless leg.

The Man choked on a piece of chicken and Tintagel stood behind him slapping his back.

NESTA WAS GLAD HE FELT UNCOMFORTABLE.

[The imperial cosmetic industry has imitated the human

skins luring scent. The Man and Nesta belonged to those individuals who did not need lotions as their skins made an overabundance of their own scents to trap unwary individuals. I should have known but I am thinking of my cyborg robot Wendy so was blind, blind, blind to the none ending struggle between the sexes in the game of creating more physical life," Tintagel.]

CHAPTER 6

Augustus

If Augustus thought you were pure ugliness, then?

Notes found by later Historians who not sure to add them to Updates by Tintagel but placed here as Updates anyway. These writings were in human hand and believed to belong to Augustus William Sutherland. The only surviving examples ever found and subjected to handwriting experts and criminologists for an insight into the emperor's mind.

The historians of the future were arguing as to whether to destroy his electron field so preventing an existence in the afterlife, ending reincarnation and pro-

gression for Augustus would indeed be truly dead and his crimes against humanity paid.

Augustus William was power running wild and unsheathed in cable.

A man never corrected as a child and responsible for the murder of ten nannies who tried to correct his ways.

His parents were enforcing that the child Augustus was different, royal, the center of the universe; do not touch just obey him.

Then an assassin struck, a crazed alien ambassador who on a suicide mission blew his father George Apollo Sutherland too bits. The gem gift was in fact a quasar bomb and wiped out the Sutherlands just like that? Not all, one Sutherland escaped, and Augustus became emperor.

He was twelve and went to war against that alien planet and conquered it.

It was extinction on a grand scale, never mind, the aliens died with their boots on firm in their religious beliefs, so went to heaven and were happy. So was Augustus as crown land he sold the planet off in lots and made a fortune in real estate and so the war paid.

And from that war the young emperor became known as The Crucifier. It took days to die as garroting, thumb screws and the rack delegated out of the dungeon.

Yes, Augustus understood his citizens, knew they wanted what he had, power and to abuse it so fostered a corrupt imperial system were the reward was power.

Advancement on the social ladder and at twelve he sat on his gold sofa with a glass of wine in one hand and in the other a girl painted emerald, green to match her Green eyes.

And Po Wei saw the young emperor would prefer to play so fostered the vices of Augustus to advance his own position.

And the disease was needing a surgeon and the surgeon was The Man.

And the wars against The Man had driven Augustus totally insane, for The Man had taken what was Augustus's, New Saturn 12.

So, Augustus sought new pleasures to forget The Man and relied on Po Wei to fight the war. Now Po Wei ran the war not to save his Emperor Augustus but his own empire of bribery and vice, for The Man would CONDEMN HIM AS ONE OF THE GUILTY.

Make up your own minds about Augustus, 'Shed him a tear, he was just a little boy brought up spoiled. Inside he had a soul, a light that under proper instruction, could be saved,' writings at time by the Socialist Order of Thought.

'And he had a gold chariot and from it he tethered his enemies and his hunting hounds brayed for their dinner,' Tintagel the Wise, 'and many of those tethered where from the Socialist Order of Thought.'

KEITH HULSE

7
The
Man

Green electricity

New Earth 1, sky turning an insipid green, first signs of forthcoming mercury storm, the curse of new space and all planets. City domes just switched on their millions of

bright lights.

Sometimes FEAR came to Nesta and not for the first time in her short life. She was AFRAID of men, and it had started early; an orphan and a pretty child brought up in a children's home and soon found herself sitting on the male matron's knees.

If she wore pretty things under her skirts, he would buy her

Candy bars,

Dollies,

Let her stay up late at
night, Usually with
him.

Had her own hologram
television.

 Cash to spend, his.

And his friends she was, introduced.

She had been lucky, he really had taken a fancy to her,
others he bored of had been sold to the Flesh Market; it existed, those with cash but no morals allowed it to flourish.

'You won't get babies if I touch you here,' he had told her.

But she knew where babies came from, so she ran away.
It was hard eating off the streets at first. The strongest
always took the biggest cardboard box unless you were
pretty like Nesta. Then you got in, but Nesta knew BIG
BAD WOLVES lurked in those boxes and she was still very
much LITTLE RED RIDING HOOD.

So, settled snuggling up against warm heating pipes
or went into derelict tenements, safe from the mercury storms and polluted winds.

Saw from the window a dog hit by lightning and it fizzled
to ash. And nights it got so cold, yes, she remembered one bad
night, frost set in, and she stumbled upon a youth blue on the
pavement. He had T.B. so had no strength to seek a warmer
place and besides, who would hire his services with such a
cough?

And when the hunting dogs of the police found his corpse,
his un diseased useful parts removed and sold, the rest incinerator.

Anyway, Nesta shoved his bag of sniffing glue next to his
nose so he could escape while he froze.

Now she was to seek the fires of the down and outs, a
dangerous thing as they were mostly drunk or spaced out

on drugs.

And that and her youth made a lethal combination; always the topic comes up and pawing hands.

And forced to leave and return when they are asleep, but one was not, and when she dozed off in front of the fire he clambered upon her.

He had hit her often, but she bit his nose off and pushed him into the fire to escape.

Another time she had found warmth outside a baker vent and been set upon by muggers who laughing threw her clothes about. A passing hover car had not saved her; the driver had thrown her attackers dollars to encourage them for the SHOW was free.

Augustus William the Emperor loved muggers; they allowed him to live up to his name, The Crucifier.

And knew **fear**. Mercury storm. Nesta

But the man in the hover car was not Augustus and soon became bored and a plan began to form in his robotic cyborg mind. So sent his minion Posidonus with a droid to clear away the muggers.

"Kill them kill all please," Nesta had screamed in pain for the cold metal grills of a sewage cover stuck to her naked bottom.

And the droid killed them seeking them out of their hiding places.

And Aelfric liked her demands for she had not shouted 'Forgive them.' His plans involving her known as ASASSINATION ATTEMPT 19.

The Man must die for Aelfric to become dominate and for robots to rule, so sent Nesta to work as a child laborer in one of his factories putting aspirin into little bottles.

To become deliberately bored and see the power held by those about her. The supervisors and teenage boys who pushed trolleys about began to abuse her. It was what Aelfric wanted, and her way out was to learn that power was cool and got by siding with the factory manager.

And just like that the bullies sent to the sewage works too breath in and corrode their insides. It was all about hate and Aelfric *was teaching Nesta to hate*

men.

And Aelfric made an appearance and rescued her from her surroundings, showed her kindness and abused her not, for he was a robot predator and talked about the ills of society caused by The Man.

> The Man's fault, what a better place it would be if he were dead.

And she began to see his viewpoint until one day he showed her Posidonus at work playing doctors on an opponent.

"Never send me to him please?" She had begged as Posidonus removed something and dangled it in front of his foe.

"If you are a good girl," Aelfric had replied and Nesta had thought he wanted to abuse her body but it was her mind he was after, so never mentioned The Man's labor laws prohibiting child labor and abuse.

But Nesta had intelligence and it protected her for she saw through Aelfric's lies and knew there was a better world outside.

> And one day Aelfric drugged her, a powder in her soft drink and while she slept Posidonus *the doctor* inserted genetic implants provided by The Master Priest, who of course did not attend in person for he sought longevity.

81

And the razor blade cut marks on Nesta's limbs put there out of despair disappeared, her limbs became shapelier and her chest more desirable by men, and in her brain a clock that while she slept spoke to her, 'Kill The Man' it crooned, and she was not learning French but assassin ways.

"What have you done to me?" Nesta asked looking herself over in front of a mirror and for an answer Aelfric abused her.

SHE MUST HATE MEN.

And Nesta no longer trusted a living soul, knew FEAR and HATE, and knew all about Posidonus who hired her as a kitchen porter in the second kitchen of The Man's Palace.

'With you gone Cluny James Smith we robots we be free,' for Aelfric could dream for dreams were FREE.

Yes, it was Nesta who had poisoned Simon the food taster and what had happened to the original kitchen porter, why Posidonus had allowed Nesta to see him operate on imaginary carbuncles on his back.

BUT THERE WAS A JOB VACCANCY
WASN'T THERE?

And Aelfric rewarded Posidonus for he bought him two books, Micro eye surgery and Anesthetics which Posidonus knew was a joke so made sure he laughed

loudly for he never used them.

And Aelfric knew he never used them and "You should have been made a robot," for robots knew about pain when dumped in junk yards by their human masters.

Had their precious metals ripped

out of their circuits? The castors and
ball bearings removed.

Oh, the pain, robots made to feel pain, and felt pain shivering in a wet cold or hot dry junk yard.

"Well done, Posidonus," Aelfric said and Posidonus glowed.

And poor Nesta FEARED, for she wondered when KIND Tintagel would abuse her, everyone else had? And another FEAR, Aelfric had told her he had implanted a bomb in her that would blow if she talked.

FRAR and HATE of men a good combination to make Nesta work as an assassin. And now she was in the same room as The Man and a clock was ready for action, but so was Tintagel the Wise who was using Nesta to catch and hang Aelfric and the evil Posidonus.

There were other rich families The Man could burrow cash from.

And Tintagel had great faith in The Man's presence for Nesta would see the lies told her about the dictator.

NEON LIGHTS.

Storms

"For men and women are at continual war," From Tintagel's Chronicles. And Tintagel only knew one woman, Wendy the robot cyborg.

It was not safe to go out nights.

storms

CHAPTER 8

Domo Bye Byes

Aureolis Borealis

"Do you know what I do with spies?" Aelfric Europe asked his Major Domo. Of course, he knew, he worked for the robotic creep, didn't he? Already he could smell the bath filling up with nitric acid as the fumes hurt his nose.

First, he did be handed to that fruit cake Posidonus who he could hear turning on the water taps to sluice his operating table.

And before the Major Domo could reflect any more the more two muscular men took hold of him. Now he wanted to live and struck one of them but broke his knuckles, the man was a robot whose chin was not bone.

But the other hit him from behind winding him and when he came too found himself on Posidonus's table and the water was cold underneath him.

Looking up he saw Posidonus hiding under a green mask, so he spat into it. In return Posidonus thudded a scalpel into the doomed man's stomach.

He did not need too; he was reading a book with the other hand, 'Eye Microsurgery.'

But then Posidonus was a fruit bat, wasn't he?

And then something discovered, "He's a robot!" Posidonus gasped and that brought Aelfric back.

A robot, the Major Domo was a robot, how could this be?

"You have betrayed me?" Aelfric's lips were trembling in disbelief, "I am the savior of our kind, how could you betray me?" Shock was setting in, robbing Aelfric of reason.

Then he went berserk and dismantled the major Domo and deprived Posidonus of an afternoon's leisure.

Down to the last copper circuit he stripped off the main boards and everything went for a bath.

"Robots must not kill robots, until today," Aelfric mumbled as he dropped the head last into the bath.

As he dropped it, it spat back at him, made a big splash and Aelfric jumped back for nitric was burning his clothes and living skin.

"Some robots are better equipped than others, they must

rule, not all robots are equal, some will go to Robot Heaven and others won't," Posidonus heard Aelfric shout as he attached living tissue patches to his burns.

> Posidonus was not the only fruit
> bat about, was he?"

> Only robot can kill robot,
> Human cannot kill robot.

Robot can kill human,' and seemed to solve the problem of what Aelfric used to believe in: 'Robot cannot kill robot.'

And Aelfric neglected to mention to Posidonus that a cyborg was assembled to replace the human Posidonus.

That was all right, robots could kill humans.

A quote from Tintagel's Chronicles would be appropriated here, "Put not your trust in machines."

"Tidy up Posidonus for I want to speak about Prince Vespa and the coming meeting of the emperor's new allies," Aelfric commanded as he dropped a soft strawberry filled chocolate square into his mouth.

His perfect teeth bit into the choc center and the fruit essence escaped while Posidonus with his rubber gloves on mopped quickly. He always wore gloves as he

was afraid of what he might catch dissecting the specimens. They had life threatening germs, and Posidonus, was one.

He was also sad that Aelfric had found out the Major Domo had been a robot as robots could take decades to terminate. Aelfric might never have found out if he not summoned him.

Still Posidonus had gratification seeing the Major Domo bathed, the water quickly went brown.

Anyway, 'Robot can only kill robot' had been applied.

Posidonus preferred showers anyway.

NEON LIGHTS

CHAPTER 9

Nesta's Thoughts.

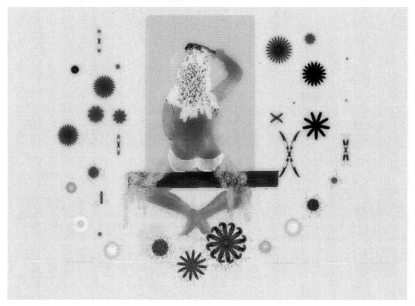

Illustration: Nesta

The Man was absent for about two weeks from New Neptune 12 his own planet,

and during that time, he learned much while he stayed in the rented house in Augustus, present capital of New Earth 1 as he watched the streaked navy-blue sky outside the city dome as spaceships of every design arrived, bursting through black polluted clouds that threatened to drop radioactive waste.

The new proposed allies of Augustus Sutherland were arriving. Not so fearful of The Man since Po Wei had spread the empire's money around.

Not even The Man could afford to keep a battle fleet in space for a long time. The Man needed a quick decisive battle, not a prolonged war.

It was Tintagel luring his enemies into the open by spreading rumors the dictatorship did not have money and Po Wei had swallowed it. Why, The Man's fleets assembled now under the façade of repairs in dry docks and men had been issued shore passes.

The imperial spies took note and reported back to Po Wei, no ships of The Man were in space, he was cashless, and THE PIRATES NEVER HAD IT SO GOOD.

And the banks confirmed it, the agents of Tintagel the Wise had been trying to secure loans with banks sympathetic to the imperial ways but never got in the door.

Which influenced Posidonus whose loan to The Man would not be paid back and was thinking of going to where the grass was greener.

REMEMBER THIS.

And Po Wei and his gleeful friends forgot that the armies of The Man would fight for nothing for they did not want to return to living under an imperial lifestyle.

THAT WAS A SLAVE
ECONOMY SERF LA-
BOUR,

A FEAUDAL SYSTEM   all rolled into one.

Po Wei had served Tintagel unwittingly; war was coming, and The Man would get his battle.

Even now red, yellow striped tents were going up about the landing docks where the new allies of Augustus were docking.

Vendors selling everything they could and the most notable were the flesh markets where slaves were in cages.

And jesters carried paper effigies of The Man with enlarged head and bits for the amusement of the crowd who could not wait till night fall to see the effigies burn.

They who had cause to fear The Man, the guilty who wore fashions from every age or lack of fashions for it was one giant catwalk to parade their wares and what they owned: slaves with collars on all fours like dogs.

Why the slaves and poor did not mock the effigies for they whispered to each other, "A poor day for us if The Man is defeated."

And in the sky balloons that proclaimed The Man's law "I condemn
the guilty,
I am The Man,

I give freedom to
the poor, Rich as
well.

All are welcome
within my lands; My
law is for all.
Human and alien,

Rich and poor,"   The Man.

And the crowd was paying at stalls to take laser shots at the balloons for it made them feel safer.

And the rich read them and laughed and ate sandwiches as they lay on sofas in the grassy flowered park areas and forgot the slaves and poor could read and they showed sullen faces.

"Discontent," Augustus heard to rant and lived up to his name, The Crucifier, but he knew history and who was what as these men did?

Alfred the Great, he stopped the Vikings.

Alexander the Great, conquered Asia Minor.

Oneghus mac Fergus the
Pict Champion,

A mighty collector of Vi-
king heads.

James the Wisest Fool in
Christendom, you owe him
a bible and instructed his
children, God APPOINTS
Kings.

George Washington, saw
spooks.

 Abraham Lincoln, he
freed slaves.

 Christ the Christ
Consciousness.'

But of the Emperor Augustus Sutherland he ranks with Cumberland the Butcher.

The hated one, but they forgot the Chief of Outer Darkness who rules all the cities and villages there, what is his name again?

"Augustus Blood Sucker," the discontent wrote on walls, "The devil."

"I could have ruled wisely and given my people peace but history remembers BLOOD more willingly so my name will live forever," Augustus often joked.

And the discontented numbered thousands and they left for New Saturn 12 and formed the Liberty Legion.

"I don't care if they number half a million, I will not pardon them but crucify them," Augustus ranted when he heard.

"Who needs them, soon my baby farms will provide an army of loyal troops who know who feeds them their pleasures," he screamed at space where he hoped The Man heard.

His new loyal troops who fed growth hormones were growing at an alarming rate, already handfuls in uniform and, "I have given them exemptions from taxes and can choose any for labor or entertainment from the class 6 group of citizens," Augustus boasted to Po Wei.

And they would become a burden to the class 6 poor who already paid heavy taxes.

"I am the Crucifier, I can do what I want," Augustus and Po Wei feared a rebellion, the people would judge Po Wei.

*

"I am glad I gave you your freedom
Tintagel," The Man. "I am your slave," a
reply.

I Nesta overheard as I combed my growing blond curls, a sign of my growing self-confidence. This was a parody, a mockery of what The Man proclaimed.

I stopped combing, attentive now.

"By your own choice Tintagel," The Man.

I could not understand, Tintagel was powerful and wanted to be a slave?

"Slave I am to a master who is stuck with me for if you free me, I may wonder," Tintagel mirthfully and to change the subject, "Prince Vespa our friend has told us much."

"Yes, the emperor walks beside him unawares he is our ally, look Tintagel at the parade," for The Man was looking out the window towards the docking area.

Then he scented my fine smell because Tintagel had gifted me perfumes.

I was not a child, but a woman and The Man was uncomfortable, and I sensed it, so did Tintagel who thought it amusing.

I was not one of The Man's courtiers, human or alien for dozens furred, and enemies said he coupled with animals.

"They are more intelligent, sensitive, and technologically advanced than us humans so, who calls them beast?" The Man in his defense. "We are all Jock Thomson's burns," he would also say, and aliens loved The Man for he did not call them beasts but PEOPLE.

And one was the Princess Veag which means Little of the Rhegid Empire which was unknown to the imperialists for the Rhegid Empire was in that part of uncharted space that bordered The Man's Dictatorship.

"And every time she visited with the Rhegid ambassadors they sought each other and frolicked like lambs for he needed the Rhegid battle wagons," Tintagel the Wise his Chronicles.

"And her skin was of the finest red hue, shiny, oily and her hair was a flowing green and her eyes purple, but she was a woman and humanoid.

And she gave birth to a son who eventually became Emperor of the Rhegid Empire.

And his name was,

'An T-each' or in New English,

THE SLOW HORSE.

Yes, you see The Man was as wise as me," Chronicles of Tintagel. Do not forget the name T-each the red skinned emperor.

So, the enemies of The Man said, "His brain is above his knees," and "He should eat bromide for breakfast, lunch, and supper."

*

As I Nesta looked out of the window of Split Wind Inn seeing The Crucifier in all his glittering imperial pomp, sitting on his gold floating throne as soldiers in polished body armor and military bands playing stirring music, and the princes of space bowing low in homage from their own float thrones, while their trumpeters sounded each acknowledgement of submission to the emperor's leadership.

They acknowledged Po Wei the real power behind the throne.

"Fall down and give thanks for your emperor," but I cleared my throat and spat out the window for I was not one of Augustus's soldiers or officials.

And behind me The Man could not help but inspect me not because I was a cow or a sheep but because I was a woman and attractive.

I was already a handsome girl before The Master Priest got hold of me.

Now being a woman, it dawned upon me someone was ogling my bottom, so I deliberately shifted it left to right and The Man became uncomfortable; what I Nesta intended,

"Well he shouldn't be staring should he?"

*

<u>The words of Tintagel the Wise take over.</u>

And inside her a clock awoke wanting to kill The Man and her, the virus bomb implanted in her by Aelfric for this threat to Nesta was real.

Now she rested her hands, on the pearl handed holsters of the laser pistols given her by me Tintagel and shifted again.

The girl had grit and The Man coughed and looked away.

I Tintagel smiled and hoped my belief in Nesta would pay off and she would not assassinate The Man but those that sent her.

"And both players saw each other as a shrew needing tamed and the virus would make sure the union of the shrews would be till death," Chronicles Tintagel.

And Nesta looked into the eyes of mine, Tintagel and saw she was his pawn and was angry, that arose from her womanly side for she did not want to project herself as a sex bimbo but as Nesta, while another part of her gloated that she was just as pretty, as The Man's courtesans.

His female monkeys in chain mail, his giant bats hanging sleeping from rafters, his aliens she chided and felt immediately horrid within herself for she knew The Man did not keep company with the bad but the good.

Two tears came into her eyes.

'

She felt she did not belong in the company of these good aliens because she had tried to assassinate The Man.

And knew she could seduce The Man and either kill him for he was a man because she hated all men or become one of his women and gain power that way.

Four tears replaced the original two.

She did not want that; she had had enough of pawing by men for one thing.

She wanted love and respect in an uncaring universe. "Save us our gods of creation," how often she had heard that from the poor in front of their lit essence joysticks.

Now Aelfric had failed to account for the human soul because he was a robot, an electric current following about copper circuits.

"See Po Wei has swallowed the bait," The Man meaning the tale of bankruptcy. "Yes master," I Tintagel answered watching Nesta.

'And Nesta was in thought, here was he who Condemned the Guilty who I have been sent to kill. So why do they want him dead, for they are the guilty, the abusers of my kind,' see The Man has not laid a finger on me **yet**, and she became a little annoyed at this, for she was a woman, and she wanted The Man's attention.

Not Tintagel the Wise's gifts and soothing words.

For whenever there is injustice and oppression the people look towards the heavens for a deliverer.

ONE WHO CAN CONDEMN THE GUIILTY

And she no longer wanted to kill The Man and the clock inside her hated her.

And in 50220 A.D. the heavens had little choice so chose The Man, a person who knew how to wield a sword at the corrupt roots of the empire.

Now she looked hard at The Man and who smiled his charming smile back, so his face became a crooked scar. Nesta wanted to kiss it better and saw The Man as being Christ, Gandhi, Wellington, Napoleon, and others all rolled into one genius.

Surely, I am in the presence of the one who CON-DEMNS THE GUILTY. From his height, seven feet he looked down at her.   P

FLASH-
ING.

O

He   had   smiled   again   showing   off   his
teeth.   L

She   saw   he   was   satisfied   at   what   he
saw.   I

She   was   not   a   piece   of
meat.   C

Out   came   her   pearl,
guns.   E

But he was quick and had them pointing up at her chin.

"Go ahead and shoot," she questioned her eyes full of
anger.

Now The Man decided her eyes where full of the sparkle of a million emeralds and she could out stare the stars and him so backed off. R

Grunting annoyance, he had lost the first round of the shrew taming game.   E Oh, I wished my master would not play these silly games with my   N

apprentice and go chase up one of his courtiers, but then I needed him to lure Nesta into betraying those that had sent her. Now I Tintagel consoled himself with sucking a Victory V, allowing its heat to clear my thoughts.

I thought of robot Wendy, no problems, no game, she was cyborg, made to please me; and this was my weakness because I did not understand the game between the human sexes.

"It is said that if a man and woman stare into each other's eyes for a minute they will either make love or fight," Chronicles of Tintagel.

Now Nesta backed off as well but tripped over my feet and fell on her bottom, it hurt and The Man and myself saw FEAR in her eyes for she was no longer in control of the situation.

Both wondered what evil Posidonus had done her.

And The Man handed her, her guns back making sure the safety was on and turned his back on her.

BUT SHE WAS THE DOMINANT THOUGHT IN HIS MIND.

Just for an instant her foolishness allowed the teaching of Aelfric to surface and the thought of killing The Man was present.

The Man was the king beast of all men and must die so, she could be released, from,

FEAR.

AELFRIC EUROPE HAD DONE HIS WORK WELL.

The Man had handed back her guns to disarm her so he could then pounce.

> NEON LIGHTS
> FAIL. POWER
> FAILURE.
> BLACKNESS.

Tintagel switches on a nuclear fusion camper light.

"We will kidnap Po Wei's original son; destroy the clones and any robots we find and hold this Po Shen for ransom. Po Wei will be neutralized and allow their ships to sail into our traps," The Man ruthlessly as he opened a chilled Pepsi Cola and then a fly landed on the top of the opened bottle.

Now Nesta was amazed he spoke so openly in front of her. She looked at me Tintagel; why had he befriended her?

She could not betray his trust in her, the old Nesta was winning. Watch out Posidonus *a rope is coming your way.*

And a clock inside Nesta was not happy.

Nesta also realized The Man this trust with his war plans was a weight, a heavy weight upon her shoulders and she cursed him for it.

As for The Man he had his fingers crossed he was not wrong about her.

I sucked another V sweet.

*

Now The Man was who he was and put on his disguise and went out and brought back women. One was a red alien in the latest fashion, a yellow transparent smock that showed red lingerie.

And her whole body was a mass of tattooed flowers and Nests saw amongst them two spiders, green aphids, and a lady bird.

THAT WAS A PIECE OF WORK.

"I am a mercenary seeking a new master," Nesta heard The Man lie as he pushed more drink towards her, so she tumbled into his bed.

And Nesta turned away angry and sickened.

And another time he brought back a reptilian woman whose skin was flesh-colored scales and smelled like fresh crocodile shoes.

And Nesta sought the restroom and was sick.

It was true The Man was a beast with an insatiable sexual appetite.

"You are revolting," Nesta threw at him the next day unable to take any more punishment.

And he stood there grinning like a bad boy and Tintagel shook his head and took Nesta aside, "My dearest girl, he is the dictator and what he chooses to do is not your business but be assured he has not lain with those women, he is merely letting it still be known he is a mercenary seeking a master that is all, and his cover is still safe. In the morning they awake and find a purse of dollars and think the night well spent, besides, we will be going home very soon."

And Tintagel showed her a pocket recorder still with rubber suckers attached and switched it on and she heard he had told the truth.

Now she went red and hid her anger that The Man had gotten to her, "Snake," was all she said.

Tintagel left it at that.

*

Nesta's first mission: to accompany The Man and Tintagel in a kidnapping. <u>Backdrop: Night, cloudy, five miles out a phosphorous cloud had ignited by the</u>
<u>pollution police and burns a bright yellow/orange.</u>

A pale sickly bone colored moon tries to compete with soot riddled clouds ready to drop their radioactive war remains.

Illustration: radio-active clouds

And The Man dumped a chestnut brown sack none too gently onto the desert and sliced it open with his short sword and out crawled Po Shen the original son of Po Wei, First Minister to The Emperor Augustus in his green pajama smock.

"Po Shen, make trouble and I will kill you and you will go to hell," The Man and Po Shen looked up and saw The Man's silver wings glittering in the pale moon light under the six moons of New Earth and knew he was in trouble.

AN OWL HOOTED.

A CICADA TWANGED AWAY.

A TWO HEADED BLACK MUTANT RAT POUNCED ON A GIANT ROACH. A FROG CROAKED.

A MOLE ATE A WORM   Po Shen faced The Man and sat still not even daring to place his hands, on the gash at the back of his head where The Man had HIT him.

"I will have to go, I have played my part for LIBERTY for rich and poor alike," Prince Vespa said emphasizing rich for he was a heavenly ruler. Half alien and human so an outcast from imperial circles but always asked to provide space battle wagons in time of war.

Now Po Shen could not help sneering at Vespa's ugliness, his skin was crimson, hair long and free and pink, eyes yellow all atop a human body.

"I condemn the guilty," The Man lurching too an inch from Po Shen's now frightened cosmetic lined face and Po Shen was sure he felt the filed teeth of The Man sink into his purple lipstick, but it was FEAR he felt.

Now Nesta could not help the smile escaping. The entire universe knew about Po Shen's bedroom frolics. He had a taste for adolescents now a consensual sex age in the empire no longer existed. Nesta and her street friends hated Po Shen's types for they needed them for a warm bed and dinner. They were beasts like The Man, and she became confused for The Man was the enemy of Po Shen and his friends.

"Little woman, two weeks isn't enough to get to know The Man," a virus clock warned in her.

He is just like Posidonus, and Aelfric and the factory workers so must die. The Man is ABSOLUTE and takes liberty from you.

"I don't know who you are that speaks to me such inside my head, but The Man is different. Look at him; see the silver shine from his wings as if he is a demigod. He stands like the statue of LIBERTY proclaiming justice for the oppressed. Why a Red Colored Man such as Prince Vespa would not risk his life for The Man if the alien saw otherwise?

"Once again you help Vespa?" The Man.

"There will be a time when I will need your help against Augustus."

"You will be welcome, you and your people in building the new order in the dictatorship."

PAUSE: A night moth fluttered under Vespa's nose onto Nesta who flinched. It then landed on a rock a foot from Po Shen and a dark reptilian head stretched out and gobbled it up.

Po Shen screamed and lurched to his feet and toppled for The Man had tied his shoelaces to get her.

WOSH......Nesta felt metal flying past her, and The Man's short sword landed vibrating away in the yellow head of a desert rattlesnake.

"Good aim," Vespa admired.

"Here," he said offering the
snake to Vespa. "Share it?"
"I don't like snake remember Vespa?"
Nesta liked snake.

"I am not offended, take care guardian of space," and Prince Vespa left and Nesta was impressed with The Man's latest title as she forgot the virus clock.

"Guardian of Beasts like Vespa and mutants, they wait in the badlands for The Man to settle them in houses made for humans. Three-legged woman are The Man's favorites, six breasts," the virus started but Nesta used her will power to silence its lies.

The virus knew now it had a battle and Aelfric had made a mistake to pick Nesta but as Aelfric never made mistakes no one ever told him that and lived any way.

He had this bath see!

And the virus was related to a single strand of protein that had sparked of evolutionary life a billion, billion, years ago so

WAS NOT TOTALLY HUMAN

THEREFORE, IT COULD NOT UNDERSTAND A HUMAN FEMALE'S MIND.

It had lost already and did not know it.

Nesta knew The Man was ugly, scarred, and bionic but the laws he made were good ones, not like what Aelfric said at all at all.

The Man was a swashbuckler who rid space of tyranny and his enemies were brutal so brutal means taken against them to survive, or she and her kind would have no hope.

And a virus was unhappy.

And Nesta knew she made The Man uncomfortable when he stared at her bottom, and she had wicked thoughts.

And a virus was
suddenly ill. See
Nesta was good.

All life is,
Flesh is full of the divine spark.

It is automatically, attracted towards the LIGHT. She was a victim of abuse.

Therefore, hated evil and Augustus
and his friends. Like the common
crowd she yearned for a deliverer.
She thought she had found him.

He would be her friend
too. Deep down she
wanted it that way. A
garden and flowers also.

A warm clean sea to
swim in. A man to
trust.

Good things, denied by life.

"And somewhere a black scorpion crawled into a red
woman's glove and made itself a home in a poor man's
hovel in a shanty town. Would it push off before the
woman that lived there put on the glove?

Nature is part of us, we bulldoze but it survives for it is
tenacious," Chronicles of Tintagel.

Character Update.

He was an alien prince from Maponosia, ruler of the
whole planet and did have human imperial blood contam-
inating his body from the forceful insertion of genes into
his grandmother on the orders of the Emperor George
Apollo Sutherland, donated from a minor cousin. It did not
matter who, if it made the prince a blood relative since
blood relatives tended to cling together for protection.

Maponosia was a year's travel from New Earth so managed
to keep a form of semi-independence from the empire.

*(The days of disappearing down Worm Holes and
appearing in another galaxy just like
that were just beginning.)*

"Our independence is put up with because our battle wagons are anchored inside the empire for the disposal of Augustus to send against those

HE DISLIKES.

I revolt myself, for I
have helped Augustus
earn his name

THE CRUCIFIER.

And I look across colorful space seeking help from one to deliver my conscience from guilt and until that day I remain Augustus's loyal cousin,

UNTIL

The Man emerged from the whirling gun smoke of New Saturn 12. Then I became

his

FRIEND."

Vespa, diary 50216 A.D.

"This prince has much to hate Augustus for, because after the Peace of August when The Man obtained New Saturn 12, Augustus accused Vespa's parents of treason and sent a fleet on a surprise visit to Maponosia and crucified the whole royal family except Vespa. Vespa spared because he was serving in his own fleet and Augustus was too far from his supply base for a long war.

"Why have you done this cousin?" Vespa asked.

"Because I heard you father was aiding The Man in the

war just ended."

And Prince Vespa swore vengeance against his emperor a common thief and murderer, no not common, royal murderer.

"And see Vespa, as a true cousin and friend I allow you to remain ruler of Maponosia and because of me you inherit early," Augustus.

But not all men where like Aelfric, Posidonus or Po Wei, scores had honor and valor and one was Vespa.

"I have read your works and heard your voice and believe in you," Vespa relayed secretly to The Man.

"Then let us be brothers for I have none," The Man's coded reply back." Chronicles of Tintagel page 2089.

CHAPTER 10

Prince Vespa

"I have handed these writings over to future independent historians of New Saturn

12. They are authentic and lean towards the interests of Prince Vespa, me, a robot," obtained from Vespa's memory strips.

Prince Vespa did not know or The Man that Po Wei as he left the badlands was operating an orange color imager camera inside his float, which extracted the heat from under the disguise Prince Vespa wore and put together an image, complete skeletal make up down to his blood type and DNA prints.

PO WEI HAD X-RAYED PRINCE VESPA PRETTY DAM GOOD *would not you*

speak?

"And what shall we do with you?" Po Wei asked of the image and his contaminated retainers were happy now someone of high social standing was suffering.

Contaminated as they had been out in the badlands exposed to disease.

And Po Wei would send his contaminated soldiers to arrest Vespa the first chance he had, and together their names sent to the Registrar of Births and Deaths. Po knew to terminate them all in one go was economical as Po Wei did not like the idea of so many knowing what happened to Vespa.

For example, Lance Corporal T. Mains died of nerve gas poisoning. Private I. Banks died from Anthrax.

Private R. Lopez from Hepatitis.

And the recordings went on and on....... IT WAS A LOAD OF CODSWALLOP.

Just too many for a bath so Po Wei arranged for bath contents to come out of the communal barrack showers, of course after locking the men in.

Do you see Aelfric was not the only one using dissolving agents?

"A murderer cannot afford any witnesses. The public need a body and the press want to hang someone," Po Wei, but I own the press but not he who

CONDEMNS THE GUILTY.

*

"Why are you arresting me?" Vespa asked of Po Wei who sat in his yellow craft.

For reply a soldier used his fingers on Vespa, fingers covered in coins made into rings, so Vespa's teeth victimized.

Po Wei nodded again, he wanted this messy business done quickly, he was in mourning for Po Shen.

Eagerly the men kneed Vespa, allowing the prince to move into the back of a hover truck FULL OF RETAINERS who knew what to do.

So, by the time Po Wei's little convoy pulled into Wei's two hundred blue marbled town house, Vespa was not recognizable.

The watching street beggars thought the prisoner one of them getting his chips for spitting at the passing illustrious Po Wei.

And Po Wei had already taken care of the entire prince's household who were just

skeletons now.

Skeletons eaten by a virus made by The Master Priest who had lots of paying clients.

AND PO WEI WAS ONE OF THEM.

A virus slipped into the air conditioning system so all would breathe the virus in.

The red rash came first, then
the internal bleeding. FOR A
VIRUS WAS HAVING LUNCH.

Of course, the imperial police would come and find a rip in the palace's dome allowing polluted air in. Did not the weathercaster say bad air was blowing in from the Bad Lands that night?

Clever Po Wei had already bribed the weathercaster to say such GIBBERISH and we know how Po Wei made sure things stayed secret?

And the corrupt weathercaster found exposed to the elements, a thing you did not want to do. Seems he drank too much doing the rounds of strip clubs and collapsed.

Then the mutated rats got him so, what left found, by the police was enough to put them off supper.

But it was their job, they paid well and as corrupt as Po Wei and were on his pay rolls so do not feel sorry for them.

And war pollution blamed for the death of Vespa's palace staff.

And for authentic realism a thousand nesting house sparrows had been, gobbled up by the virus too.

And nearby tied houses, occupied by Vespa's agricultural workers burnt

down along with their occupants.

BETTER FOR ONE TO DIE SO THE MAJORITY COULD LIVE.

That was how it was; the disease contained, eliminated; besides, Po Wei desired the area. For redevelopment. A thousand condoms would   NOW be erected beside an artificial lake with real ducks bred in an aviary: not yellow plastic ducks!

Monkeys let loose in the trees on the island in the middle of the lake. It would be a touch of green in the middle of a polluted world and people would buy, just to sit by the lake and gaze at the real Japanese carp wanting bits of bread thrown at them.

Burning what was already here down on environmental orders was cheaper than bulldozing them and rehousing the occupants.

WAS NOT PO WEI WORTHY OF AN HONOURY DEGREE IN ECONOMICS?

Besides the agricultural workers were of the poor class 6.

"A discontented poor citizen is dangerous, better to eliminate than have such a thorn in one's side," an Augustus quote.

So, Po Wei had done his emperor a favor had he not?

As for Po Wei, Vespa was of royal blood, so his murder done secretly,

quickly, not to mention quietly.

Agriculture

And in the flames the clone of Vespa, for Po Wei wanted Vespa dead and his thoughts and political leanings forgotten.

But a robot copy of Vespa had escaped.

To the Emperor Augustus the robot was still his cousin,

living tissue not a cyborg. **"What the hell is this?" Po Wei seeing the me robot in court.**

"What is wrong First Minister?" I asked.

He did not answer, he was in deep shock, was obviously trying to calculate our cloned numbers.

It was only later alone that he set his retainers upon me and took me back to his town house.

"Some situations need risky solutions," Po Wei from his dairy.

And when I did not die after garroting, Po realized I was a robot.

At this meeting Aelfric was present, business with the shady Po Wei.

"A robot?" Aelfric asked astonished, he was not alone; think he would have guessed that after the Major Domo affair?

And wanted to buy me from Po Wei who would have none of it, for I was a very loose end.

"He must die," a shower for him.

I knew what he meant.

And Aelfric protested 'FOR ONLY ROBOTS CAN KILL RO-BOTS.'

And as soon as he was alone with me as Po Wei was a remarkably busy minister of state of a demanding emperor. Aelfric told me, "I am a robot," and his dreams of robot empire and summoned one of Po Wei's retainers to bring in substance, fresh fish, and pickled vegetables.

She was a young girl from the kitchens.

"Have her," he told the armed retainers who threw the girl across a table. "She is human trash," Aelfric the robot said to me quietly.

Then when the men finished, he ordered me to follow suit.

How could I? I was a copy of the real Prince Vespa, and he was above such bestial affairs.

And how Aelfric looked at me I knew he was offering me life or death, who would I fight for, robots or that human trash?

"Human trash," he whispered again.

And before I knew it, he had me by the neck and turned it violently sideways jamming my circuits, so I was paralyzed:

MOUTH GAPING, DEFENCELESS.

So, he calmly dropped two well aimed pink capsules straight down my gagging open throat.

"A little pet of mine, a parasitic tapeworm with a neutron bomb attached to it.

Thus, it will attach itself to the lining of your gut and blow a hole in it if you misbehave."

PAUSE.

What he had said began to sink in, I was his slave; I had failed the test and chosen death rather than join his mad scheme of robot domination.

Then he did my neck and head again and the pain was horrid, but my paralysis gone.

"Now take the human," and he waved a small remote control at me.

"Wrong, two capsules you swallowed, a controller," and he smiled as he turned up the waves and my gut went into knots so that I doubled with colic.

"Besides, the Master Priest assures me that I can control the neutron explosion and it will go BANG and melt everything within a six-inch diameter IF I WANT IT TOO. Just enough to leave you prostrate on my little friends Posidonus's brown plastic operating table, he likes to play at doctors you know?"

SILENCE.

A fresh silver fish made the mistake of wiggling on the tray, he ate it.

HE WAS MORE THAN A ROBOT, A
ROBOT WITH UNUSUAL

NON- HUMAN TASTES.

"Didn't you know about Posidonus? Highly skilled with a scalpel. Always wanted to look inside a robot, then he can give you a bath, you could do with one," and Aelfric made exaggerated sniffing sounds about me as if I stunk of body odor.

I had no illusions the evil robot implied death.

So looked at the human girl who had been listening to all. By the spirit of creation how I hated Aelfric and my own robot kind.

And was determined to destroy him and help the Dictatorship so human, robot, alien, machine and unknown could live together in peace without FRAR under The Man's law, and knew why my deceased master Prince Vespa had favored The Man.

LAUGHTER.

Aelfric thought I was funny or the situation.

Now he dimmed the lights and turned-on yellow spot-lights.

That is when I attacked him, and he easily threw me off because he had switched up the remote-control waves. Then he forced me to have the human girl as if she was a soulless unfeeling lump of vegetable.

Then he sent me into a corner holding my belly as colic racked me.

The human forgave me as I saw it in her eyes just before he stabbed her. "Humans don't deserve any respect, do they?" Aelfric was insane.

His retainers carried her away no doubt to Posidonus waiting in the wings to play doctor.

Remember me always, Vespa is my name.

Remember me for when you have forgiven me, I shall return for humans are forgiving creations.

Remember me Aelfric, I am Prince Vespa.

Remembered as Prince Vespa The Man's friend but now I call myself

VENGEANCE.

CHAPTER 11

Massacre

Color Background: darkness of space, streaking red comets.

It was fortunate that the original Po Shen was in the brig and that The Man

Paid for the best ships for himself to fly.

Still an immigrant cockroach ran across the floor.

It did not carry a suitcase and have a ticket.

Now Po Shen sat upright with severe indigestion and heart burn.

THEN HE BLEW Apart,

And blew a hole in the ship also.

The ships giant green doors slid

Down to seal his compartment off from RAW SPACE.

The ship was the Titanic of its age.

It was indestructible.

Best platinum.

Best rhodium.

Best steel.

Plastics.

Sound nuts and bolts.

Reliable super glue.

It was The Man.'

It was unfortunate that Po Shen had Po Weight as a father.

And Nesta was frantic had she pressed the wrong button thinking she caused the damage.

Saw images of her being jettisoned overboard to restore luck.

'Were not women aboard ship a bad omen?

Every button now looked the same.

All red, grey, or Yellows.

All round and square at the same time.

Then the shop stabilized. All Nests pressed or yanked out did nothing to help.

Gadgetry things she forgot what they did.

And heaps of altimeters spinning round to add confusion.

But to her they all looked the same.

But The Man and Tintagel knew better.

"Relax baby," The Man taking over the ship's joystick.

TEN MINUTES SILENCE AS NESTA ALMOST DIED WAITING FOR THE SHIP TO BLOW APART OR SOMETHING WORSE.

Something worse.?

(She was a woman learning to fly.)

5 MINUTES PASSED.

"Who are you calling baby? Nesta asked, yes, she was all woman.

Tintagel said nothing: this was not his Wendy a robot designed to make life pleasant for him.

This was Nesta's.............

The Man looked for Tintagel. For help.

But common sense returned to Nesta, she had remembered her position. Why only a brief time ago she had been looking in the street: available for anything if she got her share of cash to eat and be warm.

SOMETHING IMPERIAL ROME AND ANCIENTS HAD. FOUND OUT BEFORE.

Slaves.

Banqueting.

Vomiting.

More banqueting.

Orgies.

Cash and sex. Make the world go round, food is the fuel, and Augustus

had license to print the stuff.

AND NESTA WAS NOW AFRAID OF
WHAT HER CHEEK HAD

COST HER?

FEAR. Returned to her. The Man could do anything with her for he was The Dictator. But The Man had not become who he was working a florist, but by bloodletting, on a grand scale.

"I condemn the guilty."

"But l. am innocent," Nesta shouted at him because of FEAR.

She was remembering the stories circulating anything Man. Was this not he who had defeated a whole platoon of Imperial Guardsmen and sent their remains back to Augustus with a tag, "Send more."

Now Nesta rolled fluff out of her pocket and chewed her lips wishing Tintagel would offer her a Victory V lozenge to suck.

And none noticed a stowaway spider crawl under a computer, it was too small and skinny.

And her virus clock wished the year up so it could activate and eat them all.

But The Man was too interested now in the large. Unconventional ship approaching them than engaging in her mood, and that really annoyed her.

Later he would unwrap the strings that held Nesta together and have the wrapping lead him back to Posidonus.

And for the next three hours learnt about The Man.

"Keep only what you need." Tintagel" his advice to her meaning lifeboat drill.

Now the pirate ship came close, for The Man's ship could not maintain speed thanks to Po Shen.

How cruel to blame him since he could not defend himself these days?"

In fact, the ship wanted to spin.

And The Man knew battle would come, for he said, "Let us get this over with Tintagel.

And the later handed Nesta a lightweight green body armor.

PAUSE.

"What are these?" She asked naively pointing at two lumps.

"It's a woman's suit, "he replied.

PAUSE.

"Sure, why not? "She replied seeing the men present were not going to put up privacy screens. "Let us get it over with, "and she stripped off and was slipping into the suit, when the ship bucked, and she fell against The Man.

He held her and it was obvious he was uncomfortable for

Nesta was more beautiful than any of his courtesans and she felt dominant and a female on the attack

over his timidity.

"When you two are quite finished?" Tintagel advised digging out body armor for himself.

Now Nesta pulled herself into the suit and yelped as her hair gel got stuck in the Zipper. Well, the ship was not steady, that was her excuse, but The Man looked and stared the way men do at places he should not. And he liked what he saw and Nesta made sure he did not get to stare too long, that came with a ring?

Now The Man opened a cupboard and displayed an arsenal of weapons.

Nesta guessed he designed them all as they looked imaginatively lethal.

"Pick what you can carry," he advised.

Now the ship lurched, and she fell against him again and he caught her.

Even at times like this? He held her for a moment oops long and she knew it and knew he was not uncomfortable anymore. Now Nesta was scared, on the defense: Fear had risen again; Aelfric and the factory had taught her well.

It was The Man's turn to be on the attack and she knew it.

"Run rabbits run rabbits, plural this time?"

And when they separated Nesta saw Tintagel was dropping his body armor over

his head, he did not have skinny legs but a muscular body, Tintagel was

deceiving.

HANDLE WITH EXTREME CAUTION,

EXPLOSIVE WHEN MIXED.

But dozens of the pirates could not read any way!

The result of all this sexual confrontation was that Nesta knew The Man did not see her as a kid any the more the more, also, she was about to start wrapping him about her little finger.

AND A VIRUS SEEMED ACTUALLY PLEASED. OVER THAT.

Viruses in this era could think and since they were. In you, make pictures. In your Mind that your brain translates into thoughts, what they wanted you to think.

The wiggly deadly things through advanced science could communicate and this virus said, "I want to kill you. "

Now The Man did what was manly when he broke away from Nesta, picking up a microphone he shouted, "Surrender or die, I condemn the guilty," at the pirates.

Then coughed for Nesta had done things to his throat emotionally.

Yes, he was The Man for only he was brass monkey enough to say such things.

Nesta thought she never killed anything, apart from spiders and Danny Long Legs on Hair. So looked at Tintagel for support and found none.

"See this blue lever, just in case I fail it is your lifeboat," then The Man ignored her.

LAUGHTER was coming over the loudspeakers, the pirate answer.

And The Man pressed his fist onto a red button.

As for Tintagel he was blaming himself for this situation for he had been feeding Nesta hormones to counteract her FEAR of men.

Unfortunately, his experiences with women were limited to cyborg Wendy.

And The Man. Screeched a war cry in answer to the pirates who heard and FEARED.

And Nesta FEARED for this was The Man she had heard of, a killing machine.

Now she realized why Tintagel was so solemn, he felt for the pirates who had chosen death.

Now the pirate ship had grappled with them and connecting soft plastic corridors like octopus tentacles sucked onto the ship.

WORSE THEY FILLED WITH PIRATES.

And The Man having pressed the red button pressed another with a skull on it and the corridor filled with nerve gas.

It was just pirates taken care of in a matter-of-fact way.

NONE SURVIVED THE TUBES.

"Put on your outside helmets and connect to your safety belts." The Man warned, and Nesta did very quickly, she now noticed The Man was giving orders also to a small contingent of marines, who must have seen her strip.

"Crap," Nesta ignoring them, it was His fault as his presence absorbed your senses.

Then a hole blown through the bridge wall and SPACE seen and anything not screwed down floated out.

And the pirate ship was so close the missiles sent by The Man could not miss now Nesta could see on the screen above, flames and holes on the other ship, so that see saw stars through the holes.

As well as pirates floating dead in space.

All this space was getting to Nesta, she was a land lover and was tempted to pull the blue lever and get away, but The Man and Tintagel had disappeared, and she saw them on the screen entering the pirate ship, taking the fight to the survivors. Now a grisly trophy of war floated by her, a head, and its eyes glared demanding to know where its body was?

Nesta pushed it away, so it floated out the hole in the bridge wall that was beginning to self-seal and was gone.

The ship lurched from an explosion.

Neat fell flat on her face.

FEAR.

She was sick.

She could not see out of her helmet visor now.

She tried to get up, but her fingers sank into an open belly.

She was not prepared for this type of mental abuse.

She was sick again.

She managed to crawl against a wall as the hole sealed and cold space shut out. She was glad The Man paid for the best in ship technology. She could see the red lights had gone off and normal lighting returned.

She knew she could take her helmet off.

She could not fathom the smell of vomit. Any the more the more.

She was afraid space was still about.

Then a brown rat ran over her hand and left pee dribbles. Like rats do, so why they soiled food, the blighters.

But it was a sign from a God: rats do not wear space helmets.

The rat was her yellow canary in a yellow submarine.

Then amidst the quiet the reliable hum of the nuclear turbines in the engine room heard, and now Nesta sat until her aches ceased and then she got scared for she was all alone, except for orange oil gauge lights and yellow temperature flanges.

Where were the others? On the fluorescent bright yellow lifeboat, had they pulled the BLUE lever?

Why she stood up on wobbly legs and started to haul herself up a steep red ladder: she did this because it was there in Red. Now exiting at the top, she was greeted with BLACK.... BILLOWING.... MOUNTAINS...... WATERFALLS.... of smoke and the sound of lazier zip. Green eyes, hers, she blindly went on hoping she was heading in the right direction.... what else could she do.... well, she should have stayed on the bridge and kept her helmet on.

Circles.

.......LEFT....... Then...... RIGHT......., crawling on blistering hands.... totally confused now.... YES, SHE SHOULD HAVE STAYED ON

.... THE BRIDGE.

O

N

E   smoke

L   fumes

E   black smoke

V

E

L

U

P

Black smoke filling yellow corridors.

Now for all her SUICIDE ATTEMPTS BEFORE meeting Tintagel and The. Man, she no longer wanted to die...... if she ever did.

NO WHITE SHEETS.

EMPTY DRINK BOTTLES.

HER MIND WAS GETTING RIGHT.

SHE HAD NOT BEEN ABUSED IN A LONG TIME.

SHE NO. LONGER IMAGINED HERSELF IN A COFFIN.

WITH THOSE WHO ABUSED HER SOBBING.

IF THEY WOULD.

Tintagel took hold of her left elbow and rapidly calmed her down. The very act she was in contact with another life form was enough. *Dying is a lonely business, when you are dead, they come. Who? Mediums say your guides with you since birth but other angels.*

When The Man died in battle they came, IT WAS THE GRIM REAPER and helpers…. but no one wants to hear that, but he said there was an…OUTER DAKNESS…. if they came for THE MAN, they could come for you, but

The Man survived, he had good field medics.

Now Nesta was a normal person so thought he was rescuing her from a sinking ship, in this case since we are in DEEP SPACE a disintegrating ship.

Her eyes balls would swell and burst along with her other bits. SPACE WAS ACCER-LATED PRESSURISATION.

Tintagel handed her a bright orange suit, over large to accommodate her body armor so she looked sexless, like a bag of potatoes.

"Oh my God we are going out into space?" She thought.

SCARED……. TERRIFIED.

Then Tintagel pushed her into the air lock, and she met bits of pirates…… evidence The Man had been this way.

Then heard The Man's war cry again, it was soul destroying

and why shouted.

The Man laughed so his enemy knew he was not normal.... who could rule an empire full of well, loonies and aliens?

So, she followed Tintagel and found The Man on an orange balcony overlooking a white loading bay where the remaining pirates. Had taken refuge.

HAD HE NOT SHOUTED

"I CONDEMN THE GUILTY."

When he The Man saw Nesta and Tintagel he coughed. And threw a bag of high explosives amongst the pirates.

HE WAS AN AVENGING ANGEL AMONGST

DRUG DEALERS

CHILD KIDDNAPPERS.

CHILD MOLESTERS.

LOST SOULS.

There was a boom and she had earache.

"Take over," and The Man gave her a heavy machine gun whose strap threatened to pull her bosom of.

"Aim it down there and give them PINK DEATH," The man's humor meaning death from a woman.

FEAR made her obey and she pulled the trigger. She did not see limbs fly off or brains come out as she desperately held the vibrating gun.

Poor Nesta had not been brought up not to kill, she was just surviving in SPACE.

So, it was pink a soft female emotion turned deadly. Two minutes later The Man pulled her away back to their ship unceremoniously.

Nesta had killed, she was one of them now.

THOSE THAT CONDEMN THE GUILTY

AND CONDUCT SENTENCE.

To kill pirates, those that kill you in horrid ways.

Now before she knew it The Man had dragged her back unceremoniously to the Cockpit, where she saw after being dumped in a soft chair, saw garbage floating by in space.

NOW HE COMMANDED HER TO PRESS A BIG YELLOW BUTTON.

She jumped to it; his voice was loud.

Who had who wrapped about a little finger?

Now after pressing the button look yellow button dross flew out of his ship and attached wires to the remaining pirates floating out there in their helmets and suits....

to a bright yellow balloon.

The Man typed on his keyboard,

"I CONDEMN THE GUILTY.

MURDEROUS SCUM. "

He said but Nesta saw him as no better than those he had executed under his law.

She was a child of the street and saw laws protected those with wealth and keep them like her in her place.

200 community hours for a drug baron.

10 years for a bank robber using a shot gun borrowed from grandad.

"I am different, I don't run flesh markets, women or boys should not be afraid of

ME.

I AM DIFFERENT,

I AM THE MAN'S LAW,

I CONDEMN THE GUILTY.

"Don't take them. Off yet," The Man warned as Nesta was

unzipping.

All watched the screen and saw the pirate ship cauterize itself and jettison damaged sections as bulwarks sealed against.

Space.

Then Nesta watched The Man and Tintagel strip off and put on bridge lounge suits.

'Indeed, he had a wonderful body since he was a bionic?' Nesta's naughty thoughts, she was puffed out to change her suit, so just RELAXED watching. And that horrible naughty virus now alarmed, she was inflamed, with THE HULK....it wanted him dead.... but then squirmed because the virus could see through eyes and was inflamed itself.

Now the rush of adrenalin left Nesta, and she shook and vomited a bit.

Well, he had seen it all before, first time in action, so he shook her shouting in her face, "All over baby, relax, you did well."

Tintagel because he had a cyborg relationship THOUGHT NOTHING OF IT, UNTIL Nesta punched The Man.

Nesta needed an increase in hormones to level 2. Then she would talk about Posidonus.

Five minutes later Nesta was scratching where the body armor she had taken off was red flesh.

"Tintagel, see if she is any use in the hold?" The Man.

AND A SHE WAS NETTLED.

Different hormones?

"Listen, I am a girl," and thumped The Man's

chest and hoped she hurt him.

SHE WAS CONFIDENT SHE HAD PICKED HIM CORRECTLY

NOT THE OTHER WAY ROUND?

He did not hit her back, he was The Man.

All male, all something somewhere, no brains when a woman was concerned, just

an urge to fertilize...... Yes, he was The Man!

And the great dictator slowly took her hands off his chest that had felt her tits, but he was not admitting it.

"You did a decent job, it was your first time in action and considering you are not trained for it, now go and help Tintagel to adjust our passengers too freedom," he told her

And that woke her up.

"PASSENGERS? "

She quickly found out.

66 children now sat fearful in their hold.

"Christ, he was not joking?" Nesta spat at Tintagel who sucked a Victory V.

"No, he was not, he is The Man. "

"Aelfric would not have done this?" Nesta said just like that and the VIRUS

SQUIRMED.

IT HAD ITS OWN MIND....and that was to eat a human.

And Tintagel noted in his NOTEPAD brain what she had said.

A hangman's noose was coming to Posidonus and Aelfric Europe but not Nesta

who was innocent...? a pawn.... a groomed child....and

thought of The Man....

there was a chemical reaction going on between these two....... let nature takes its course.... if their paths were destined so, be it.... Wendy remembered, and Tintagel stirred so Nesta noticed.

"Sorry," he said, and she did not forgive him being a woman but accepted it,

Stored it, reassembled it to satisfy her needs.... watch out a female was about seeking

A nest.

TINTAGEL?

The Man?

Now Tintagel started taking blankets from a floating droid and handing them to the children, where the droid came from Nesta had no idea, it just floated in.

"Go and hug the youngest and assure the older ones we have come to rescue them," Tintagel ordered Nesta.

So, Nesta went to work. Wondering if she was able to help because of her own

problems but she did, and a virus inside her felt ill that the higher values of humanity

had surfaced.

"Tea?" Tintagel offered from another droid; the droids were the ships crew. Now Nesta had never had tea before so, was weary of the drink till it refreshed her, then the bees came.

"Christ almighty? "She gasped holding her cup so she would not spill and get scalded.

"Do not worry about them, quite tame, they are The Man's boarding party, (it would be nice if The. Man could rout his enemies by himself way out here in deep space, but he is still only a man." Tintagel soothed her as the bees flew past back to their hive.

"Will you help us?" The question came from a five-year-old girl who's smock was ripped showing her bruised body.

"Of course," Nesta replied pulling the child close trying to show love.

A virus inside her knew if this kept up it would die.

"The Man will give you all new homes, wait and see, no more pirates," and quietly they came, all sixty – six children about Nesta attracted by her promise of home.

The pirates were villainous, who could harm children and call themselves part of Humanity? When did such souls get lost and become monsters, Do they know right from wrong no more? Or where they just selfish people stuck in Hedonism?

And the children seeing Nesta weep, for she was opening the dam gates to her hurts, began to weep with her.

Tintagel felt tugging fingers on his leg and looked down.

There looking up at him was big green eyes of a little girl. Even Tintagel who preferred Wendy because he distrusted human emotions wept and picked the child up.

And that rat Nesta had met earlier on the day on the bridge sensed it was safe to come out for it wanted dinner and dinner was in the ship's pantry!

An immigrant American roach was there.

CHAPTER 12

The Children

Crammed in a dark hot ship's hold where vermin and children.

The ship's lights repaired now by engineer droids, but the red light went on in the bridge: battle station would remain for they were not home yet.

And in the hold droids hung up blue party lights from the beams and rafters so the environment was softer, and children fell asleep now fed, cozy and safe.

"73F," Tintagel gasped and Nesta could see him wiping his sweaty forehead with his red and white spotted hanky, as if he had done all the repairs and not the droids.

He was sitting down over a cup of tea and eating a cucumber sandwich a droid had drought him.

"What will he do with them?" Now Nesta did not address Tintagel as SIR, as he and The Man did not like addressed in such a way, but expected ALL staff too know when not to cross the line of familiarity: *jobs existed elsewhere.* And thankfully Nesta knew when not to cross the line?

She also knew that The Man did not send his sacked employees to flesh markets for profit.

But FEAR kept surfacing in her, a virus was on overtime. She did not want to lose this job, it was brilliant, it was cozy, safe and had travel benefits. Also, a hint of romance for she knew The Man was interested and that made the virus happy for it wanted him close for at the year's end it would activate and kill him and itself in the process.

The virus lacked the higher values of humanity, of compassion, mercy, and forgiveness.

"Sixty-six children are a lot of trouble," Tintagel replied as he checked star co- ordinates. "Double check," it was an order, and she did on her calculator.

"He won't sell them, will he?" And she regretted asking.

"Woman," it was a rebuff but worked, for Tintagel flicked on a screen and she saw The Man on a wooden sparse throne, beautifully carved depicting mythological scenes, truly a work of art and more valuable than a gold throne.

"Affairs of state for the dictatorship cannot run without him and he arranges homes now for our passengers," Tintagel and then showed her on the screen a part of space she had never seen before.

This indeed was a brilliant job! It was high adventure.

And doubted even Aelfric or Posidonus had been here Or even Emperor Augustus.

"Phoenix Hope," Tintagel pointing at a ball of blazing white and sucked another Victory V. Why Nesta hoped he would breathe the other way; the heat from those sweeties was impressive and more powerful than garlic.

"The planet is run by a single consul under The Man's protection, we are heading there. It is a small population, and the children appreciated and welcomed, all will find new homes. This planet is where he brings the orphans he finds in space; here they learn his ideals."

"Ideals?" Nesta seeing hundreds of future dictators on the make. "To love one another," Tintagel quickly.

"Oh god oh no," Nesta alarmed thinking flesh not the other love, and Tintagel saw as they passed one of The Man's satellite obelisks a floating body attached to it.

A radio message transmitted from a clone of Prince Vespa; of course, it was dead out here.

"A FRIEND OF THE MAN AND ENEMY OF THE EMPIRE.

Nesta had been wrong; Aelfric's tentacles had been here.

"How much do you think they got out of him?" It was The Man and he startled her.

"Everything," and Tintagel looked at Nesta.

"They have to catch me first," Nesta defended seeing her fate there for siding against Posidonus and Aelfric.

Now Tintagel sent a droid out and freed the body, so it drifted away. Then a war head from the ship slammed into it.

The clone exploded
and became a
HOT FIREBALL.

Nothing left, not even the clone's left shoe. It was a precaution against bobby traps as a virus inside Nesta FEARED, for it was a virus bobby trap was it not?

Besides the clone's spirit had moved on elsewhere.

At first Nesta did not think along these lines but was aghast that was how The Man buried his friends. And the virus seeing a chance prompted her to think unwisely for it sent thoughts into the right side of her head.

"You are his friend, is that your fate also, target practice?" For it lacked the higher values of humanity although it sounded like a human.

*

Phoenix Hope was a bright derelict moon. Nobody wanted it for it was not rich in ores, people to barter or anything.

So, The Man claimed it as his own at The Peace of Augustus 50199 A.D. and declared it a neutral zone.

Of course, those in the empire kept a close eye on the place, The Man must want it for a reason, and the reason was PROPAGANDA for The Man sent the orphans of space here.

And Phoenix Hope became a bye word for HOPE.

It made imperialists ill at the mention of the place and slaves rebellious.

And since it made Augustus ill no one spoke of the place in his presence, but not so Po Wei who saw it as a symbol needing eradicated from space.

"Hope," a child slave would shout at Aelfric as he handed her over to Posidonus to correct for malicious misconduct for she did not want to be a slave.

"Hope," the child screamed at Posidonus before she breathed her last.

So, even Posidonus FEARED the future for all meet DEATH and what lies behind DEATH, something for the good and something for the bad and he was bad, ugly, and not good.

And all imperial spies sent out reported back encyclopedia computer entries: "A haven for orphans, no weapons storage, declared neutral Peace of Augusta."

and Po Wei and Aelfric knew there must be hidden gold mines and they were correct, orphans lived there, whole generations saved from the streets. For beggars on the streets was *a sign that the government did not care.*

*

"The doors are opening," and her two companions ignored her for they knew she was excited because thousands of children waited for them on the other side.

Nesta was breathing hard and perspiring.

And they opened and a white light blinded them for Phoenix Hope was bright light from the artificial lights installed as suns.

So, none noticed an asteroid shower pass through

their false atmosphere above.

And brightness greeted them, the children were smiling.

"Greetings Dictator," the Consul 'Tha Fios Aig' said that was the signal for the children's band to play the national anthem of Phoenix Hope.

An adaptation of 'Land of Hope and Glory' on Chinese classical instruments.

And The Man stood in his pressed uniform which was not much as he was not known to wear medals and gold plaids. So, his yellow bandoleers, red cape, and polished brown knee-high boots and pressed bright pink pantaloons certainly made an impression.

But power shown for in his gold torc a diamond and in his gold head band another, so they sparkled in the lights.

He was The Man and dressed how he liked and needed a female's touch.

He liked to keep an image of brutal eccentricity, but the children were not afraid, he had never harmed them.

Now Nesta believed what told about him was lies. She was on Phoenix Hope, The Man's planet where love existed and that was what he planned for the rest of space.

DECENCY.

Where the wrong
are, punished.

Where victims knew
LAW existed.

His ruthless courts.

Where the weak knew they
was safe. Human, alien,
and robot under his laws.
He was the one who 'CON-
DEMNED THE GUILTY.'

Yes, he was absolute and did its justice for he ruled wisely for he cared for his people, and here he was beaming love to thousands of orphans, his children.

And here is the secret of The Man, he could love anything for that is what he felt when he investigated deep space, love, a oneness with something unseen so, he filled with spring fever.

So, he wished to
share it, he was
an enema.

And once again Nesta like others wondered where he came from, indeed he was special.

So special Aelfric and Augustus knew he stood
for a new order and the slaves, abused, oppressed,
and disillusioned waited for that special day
when The Man would be victorious.

Phoenix Hope unknown to the children had the best anti-missile systems money could buy, for it had become a bye word and its enemies wanted it destroyed.

All children leaving it on life's big adventure spread hope throughout the empire.

So, they came, two hundred ships and thirty thousand space marines and ten thousand trader sepoys to invade this moon.

The Major Domo had the moon's exact star co-ordinates in his circuits and Aelfric had drained those memory banks.

Now there are those who would sell their mothers into the genetic melting tanks and Consul Fios Aig was one.

That invading fleet should be eliminated, that missile system was expensive and the best; children lived here not presidents.

And The Man walked off his ship into a trap.

And Phoenix Hope was so dangerous that Po Wei and Aelfric had worked together to destroy it. Of course, Po Wei would tell Augustus a hundred enemy ships and sixty thousand dictatorial troops destroyed to enhance his victory.

But The Man had arrived, and the band was playing 'House of the rising sun' in honor of The Man's house.

But Tintagel noted Tha Fios Aig was nervous when he had nothing to FEAR. "I have brought you sixty-six new children, badly treated Aig," The Man unsuspecting.

There was no warning.

Posidonus the evil one pushed through the band. "Et Tu Brutus?" The Man cast at his consul Aig.

By the curl of Aig's lips Nesta knew death was present and now expected to see Aelfric appear behind Posidonus.

Now inside Nesta the virus became excited; it wanted its master Aelfric also; *hopeful to devour?* Its prescience reminded Nesta an alien life force lived within her; she would ask Tintagel for help in ridding herself of it.

"Too late sweetie," the virus responded.

And Tintagel went and stood in front of The Man, short sword, and laser pistol in hands.

"What the heck," Nesta

and joined him. The Man
noted and smiled.

A virus wanted to hide, a liver or toe, another body would be better then it could reproduce and clone itself and live.

NESTA WAS ABOUT TO DIE   THEN IT WAS TOO.

And the curl on Aig's lips was his defense at his own disgust that The Man made him feel like what littered a pavement after a careless dog passed.

Why Aig drew a laser pistol intending to assassinate The Man but ran screaming towards Posidonus, "You threatened to kill the children," and was cauterized into bits by space marines behind Posidonus. So Aig fell believing he had paid for his treachery.

"Medic," Posidonus shouted for Aig still lived for attached to a block of tissue his head; *Posidonus would get to play doctors later.*

And evil Posidonus used the children as shields for his men lined up their lasers on them.

And The Man knew the children's lives rested with his actions.

Now Nesta prayed to every god of goodness that The Man decide what action to take and to take responsibility away from her.

A sword and pistol clattered
in front of her. Then Tintagel
added his.

Then she threw her weapons in.

The Man was not the beast his enemies made him out to be.

"No greater love is there for a friend to lay down his life for another," it is written.

"There is a greater love, laying down your life for a child," Nesta added. "Bravo, what spirit?" Posidonus clapping his hands.

*

And true to his word Posidonus kept Aig alive for six days on a door taken down from its hinges for the purpose of doctoring.

And he had no need to strap Aig down for Aig was just one large block of cauterized tissue with a ridiculous neck and head at the end.

The horrid thing about it all, this time Posidonus played his game in public. "Thus, treatment is given to the

Empire's enemies,"

Was the sign tacked above
the table on a pole?

So as the children passed on their way to trader ships, they saw and FEARED and would be model slaves of the empire they despised.

A finger in this green bottle.

The spleen in this bright yellow jar and it went on and on till Aig fitted into a thousand vials for a thousand planets.

'A traitors' remains,' stamped on each.

It was no different from medieval times when the heart of William Wallace, sent to Aberdeen as warning and his hands someplace else and legs elsewhere.

And of the brain, just before Posidonus extracted the

AWARENESS center from it placing it all by itself in a special jar with filter tubes and oxygenated blood, sent

to Augustus, The Man gave his screeching war cry and Aig heard and knew revenge would seek Posidonus.

Aig was still alive, that part that made him who he was.

And in their public cages Nesta told The Man and Tintagel everything about her past; enough to hang Posidonus and Aelfric whenever they ventured into the dictatorship.

"But what use is that we are prisoners destined for that door following Aig to, JARS?" And Nesta felt her mind breaking, but the virus was pleased, it could live happily in a jar especially if Nesta's liver was there as well?

And The Man held her, so she felt his strength in her and she calmed down. She would have calmed down anyway, but her body language had deliberately worked trapping The Man.

His smile was like a beam of summer sun and "Where do you come from?" He shrugged and went red then gave her a big hug.

And the time came, for The Man to be dragged from his cage, whipped, and weakened. So, The Man snarled showing his white implanted incisors, "For effect," he often said why he did this.

And faked moans and groans as they butted him with their spear shafts and rifle butts and pricked him with their blades.

And evil Posidonus seemed to be jumping up and down on the spot.

Then suddenly The Man took the whip intended for him and lashed his tormentors taking their weapons and killed them quickly.

He killed thirty men, both human and alien,

WITH OUT THINK-
ING, FOR HE WAS
THE MAN.
And did it without his bees?

For Posidonus had no children present so no control over
The Man

He who condemns the Guilty.

So Nesta wondered how he did it, to kill so easily.

FOR HE WAS A BIONIC MACHINE
MADE FOR WAR.

"I condemn the guilty," he shouted sparing waiters
and fanners who fled from Posidonus, who
slipped on wine spilt from a fallen decanter.

So, Posidonus looked up into the eyes of The Man tower-
ing above him so sweat broke from his face and dribbled
from the evil one's nose.

"I can give your life or death choose Posidonus?" And the
silence broken by the whir of the camera that wasThe Man's
camera eye as hundreds of imperial troops assumed positions.

"Stand too," Posidonus coughed for FEAR had him.

And The Man could be cruel for Posidonus was under him
and pressed down with his foot on his enemy's throat till
Posidonus went blue.

"I want fast ships and what children are left for my fleet is coming, hear me Posidonus," The Man and the imperial soldiers became discontent at that news; they wanted away.

"I don't have the authority to give you ships," Posidonus coughed as the foot came off.

In reply The Man shot off Posidonus's left index finger and stuck it is his belt. "Allow Tintagel to pass," Posidonus ordered, and the troopers did, wanting The Man, as far away as possible from them with his ships.

And Tintagel summoned droids from The Man's ship to help gather the children and navigate the ships by typing in the star co-ordinates for New Saturn 12......and the bees came and flew just above the imperial troopers.

"Truly a king of men," Nesta sighed, and a virus could live with that yucky talk for Aelfric wanted Nesta to get close to The Man so the virus could jump bodies.

An easy thing to do for it was simple life and knew what death was so could reason on a virus level.

It was of LIGHT!

"He needs taming, he loves all but loves none," Nesta meaning he had not one woman to love special above all his courtiers, *"I will be that woman,"* and the virus was ecstatic, *"and he will not catch anything from me as the medicines on New Saturn 12 are the purest made so the most effective,"* and a virus was not happy and curled within its DNA strands for protection.

"And because he The Man has self-control for, I have seen him looking at my bottom as I display it for treat, I know he is tamable," so thought Nesta about he who stood with his arms crossed with his glorious, folded silver wings, he who installed FEAR in the GUILTY.

Character Update Posidonus

Notes to historians on The Man, leave these updates where they are…

Born: 50123 A.D.

Posidonus had always been an unusual outcast, as a child and as a man. His father Constantine and mother Virginia had had a large family, planned by his mother who took it upon herself to be different from others.

A tall dark-haired woman from New Earth of good family, wealthy, always at the front of society and as a child studious until her teens, then went wild, always the most outrageous, drunk, drugged sexually active girl out.

SHE WAS AN HEIRESS.

And it was she who sent fire to the shanty towns about Augustus and such notorious acts brought her to the attention of The Emperor George Apollo, Augustus's father.

"She has cleansed the capital of riotous elements," he was quoted.

But made the mistake of going from aliens to the bed of an emperor whose dominant wife married her off to Constantine Tarso from New Jupiter.

A faraway place so was away from court and here she gave birth to ten children and the youngest was Posidonus whom she neglected for he was strange and ugly.

Thousands said the children were the illegitimate offspring of the Emperor George Apollo Sutherland and if true Posidonus was next in line to the imperial throne?

And young Posidonus became infected with his parents

Hedonism and deep down hated his mother who did not live up to his 'sacred mother image,' for she was a brazen harlot.

And his father presented no picture of a man to model oneself on for he was all that Hedonism stood for.

TO LIVE FOR PLEASURE AND NOTHING ELSE.

So Posidonus with the other children of the affluent watched actors in painted bodies play basketball against apes in nappies, so became ill with Hedonism," Tintagel his Chronicles vol: 6 pp 67.

"Posidonus was an extension of the illness that gripped the soulless wealthy of the empire," Tintagel Chronicles Vol: 6 pp 70.

"So, when Posidonus started playing doctors was he merely trying to show love, compassion, a caring attitude to his patients, (the prisoners, slaves, and such) or was he showing his contempt for flesh that was sold and bought every day.

DOES POSIDONUS DERSEVE TO BE CALLED ONE OF THE MAN'S GUILTY AND BE CONDEMNED?

In his worlds the strong-
est survived. Their genes
bettered humanity.
There was no place for
the weak.
They deserved to perish.

So, Posidonus did not believe in any good divinity except for the laws of his emperor that protected and prospered his kind," Tintagel Chronicles Vol: 6 pp 132.

"I disown you, you are not my son," his mother Virginia to him for so shocking were his exploits they threatened to cause riots and harm the rich.

But a spark of slumbering fatherhood in Constantine Tarso made him give his son an allowance, as he was banished, from home.

"Did I spawn this monstrous creature?" This man asked often, Tintagel Chronicles Vol6 pp 99.

Chapter 13

Escape

Hanging Gardens

Color Backdrop: Brilliant artificial white lights, inside giant weather dome of Phoenix Hope and its layers upon layers of maisonettes with verandas and hanging gardens, and garden roof tops. The Man believed people needed space to live, gone the old tenements of the empire, come three- and five-bed-room flats and houses with such gardens, what went up must have gardens and room; families were big, cloning existed.

And each house and flat shall have a creative room, let the people have creativeness whether in the house or soil, but let them use their minds and hands and not be bored. Let them exercise their souls so they light up," Tintagel the Wise his Chronicles.

*

"He strode about in his pink pantaloons dragging Posidonus behind with his bionic eleven fingers, and his enemies dared not speak or shoot him in case Posidonus was killed. They feared Aelfric.

The Man was no torturer a pity, for Posidonus should reap what he sowed," Nesta wrote in her diary, also "Not a soldier dared fire even if Posidonus had come bearing the seal of Governor of Phoenix Hope, appointed by Augustus through the bribes of Aelfric to Po Wei the corrupt government official.

And examination of Nesta's diary clearly shows her heart had gone out to The Man for, "He was like a lost child amongst children, and I was bitter towards those who could make such a fine man as he act the way he was. And I was in turmoil for FEAR kept showing its head in my mind, why and where it came from, I am not sure? But a virus knew for it wanted to eat little girls playing at astronauts.

And hated those who had ruined his garden of hope, Phoenix Hope into blight and FEARED whatever Aelfric had planted in me?"

And the virus knew where she got FEAR and giggled for it was alive and the rat laughed but the human ear cannot hear for so high the rat pitch.

"A RAT LAUGHING, IT IS TRUE," Tintagel.

"Apathy is a soldier's worst friend, and these men knew their fate was sealed for they were far from home and knew a Man's Dictatorial fleet was approaching.

Apathy made them throw down their weapons and sit waiting the end; The Man had an easy time," Tintagel, Chronicles.

And when the last ship blasted off leaving a trail of poisonous exhaust whispers outside New Saturn 12, The Man took Posidonus's fast yacht brought as cargo and with that evil man, sought the trader ships and HIS children and took Tintagel and Nesta.

And Posidonus saw hope for he was alive and was AFRAID for he knew The Man would execute him, whereas his Emperor Augustus would destroy him slowly down to his last cell in the bath? So, knowing his yacht he planned to escape.

"Where is Posidonus?" Nesta asked hoping she was wrong, but they knew she was serious. So, setting the auto pilot for New Saturn 12 followed her and found the Traitor Posidonus was nowhere to be found on the yacht.

Just a handcuff and a
cosmetic hand. In his
cabin on a radiator.
And it had a finger missing.

"So, I am not the only bionic," The Man laughing and, "You want be needing this then Posidonus," and The Man took from his belt the finger he had taken from evil Posidonus and flushed it down the toilet.

"For deep pure thought is the finest prayer to God," Tintagel his Chronicles.

And Nesta try as she might looked at The Man afraid, he did notice; and he had for her reflection was on the screen and beyond the wall screen all space. And he was pleased watching her change for he saw her not as a girl anymore the more but as a woman he would take.

"Damn," Nesta whispered as she saw her reflection also but was saved any embarrassment for a lifeboat floated across the screen.

"It is huge, surely a liner has perished," The Man.

"It must hold thousands of survivors," Tintagel added.

And the Man was a curious man who wanted the name of the builder on the bulkheads so he or she could build him those lifeboats.

And somewhere warnings flashed in Tintagel's mind for he worked his agents hard, but this yacht was not one of their ships, so the computer told him nothing.

But to Nesta a ship was a ship, a fish a fish, that lifeboat out there was just a big ship; so, helped herself to one of Tintagel's Victory V's.   V

"What am I doing," she thought as the sweet's heat enveloped her throat.   I

"It is not a lifeboat but a trap, it holds an army, not people desperate to be rescued," Nesta blurted.

E

Tintagel did not mind the sweet but did mind these words.   W

"Do not worry I won't put my friends in danger, but it is heading towards us anyway, so we do not have a choice, yellow space suit time I think?" TheMan.

"As long as he lives, he is hope,   I

A magnet to the oppressed and weary.   G

SCREEN.

He is the father of street children and enemy of Augustus.

He is the One who Condemns the Guilty." Nesta said.

The Man smiled and to comfort her was about to put his eleven fingered bionic hand on her shoulder but at the last moment put his human hand there.   She felt strength in his closeness and did something amazing, she replaced his   **hand with the eleven fingers.**

He smiled again.

Tintagel sucked another sweet.

"Are you not a little afraid? You are amongst friends, you can relax?" Nesta.

Afraid and hoped the others were also.   "See Tintagel, I am King of Rudeness, I conquer planets and women and it takes an ordinary girl to ask me if I am afraid, what nerve? No what courage for I am The Man," and Tintagel looked hard at Nesta as he visualized her succeeding, where a thousand woman had failed, to tame The Man.

Now Nesta was sorry for him, he must be afraid; no

one ever went through life never knowing FEAR. He was amongst his friends so could admit it; where there a million listeners on radio? No, just them; he must be a very lonely man Nesta concluded.

And Tintagel caught by Nesta staring The Man smiled, a strange smile as if to say

'Hello lover?' A future lover
perhaps?

*

In this instance The Man would have done life a favor if he had blown the lifeboat to hell.

But he knew not who was aboard,

THE MASTER PRIEST.

And we get at last to meet the genius who sold the animator's secrets for gold.

The Master Priest, The Man's Public Enemy no. 1.

The Master Priest who had long natural flowing purple hair, as advertisement of his wares; glowing albino eyes and the body of a weightlifter.........and tattooed all over in mythological creatures.

And he was hungry, for over a week he had been working on a quasar signal to send to Nesta to activate the virus in her.

And it would kill Nesta but get The Man as well and that was what Aelfric was paying him for.

Success at this job meant orders galore for his reputation would glow like a neon sign flashing his prices.

And because he was hungry wanted off his manufactured work shop a satellite so summoned droid 34A to prepare his lifeboat; he was going to Vegas Hotel, a den run by Don Alexander Llatchur.

Vegas Hotel had the biggest Ferris wheel known. It was covered in a million Xmas lights and could be seen from deep space.

Vegas had burger bars on it and strips joints.

And The Master Priest was hungry and
ready for fun. Vegas Hotel had lots of
fun especially for those just paid.

And he was very hungry, and Vegas was the biggest brothel in space and The Master Priest knew he could feed there; for a price, an employee had eight pints of nourishing blood and he could feed without FEAR of He who Condemns the Guilty.

Even the empire had laws protecting employees for a termination contract had to be signed willingly and the cash to go to the resurrected clone or relations.

It was a fashionable way of getting quick cash.

But Vegas was different, it needed steady customers like The Master Priest but even here there were limits because the other customers would complain about The Master Priest's appetite. And Alexander Llatchur knew that when customers complained it was time for The Master Priest to go.

And the bill was outrageous for all the bodies needed taken care of, the risk of disease, the supply of slaves needed, *all amounted to lot of cash.*

That sort of demand brought attention and attention brought imperial troops and the place would be ransacked; a deliberate lesson to Alexander to manage his guests better and do things quietly.

After all even Po Wei and Aelfric Europe visited.

"And I know my worth?" The Master Priest so he was given a free pass to get in on his next visit, a 'Win, win,' situation for him and Alexander.

You see The Master Priest was a *Gothic vampire* and loved to see the look of doom in his victim's eyes as he opened the door to them to enter his hotel room.

"Don't worry, the rumors about me are all lies, nothing bad will happen to you and you will leave here a rich woman," The Master Priest told them and was lies.

"Vegas, here I come," The Master Priest crooned dreamily on his way to Vegas Hotel Planet.

And since Vegas was a melting pot of human and alien, he had genes to play with as he was never one to waste.

And The Master Priest had given himself a fantastic physic through gene therapy via shuttle genes and knew he was a demigod.

For when he was bored, he created mutants with six arms and one eye in the back of their head.

Gave them swords and watched them hack each other to bits.

"To the victor I will give a new body and life," he promised them all to make them fight and of course it was LIES.

The Master Priest a genius and rich for the wealthy

came to him for their tailored anatomical needs. Did not Po Wei pay him to make a six-inch ballet dancer, so his music box was different from all else for she was alive.

And he knew Aelfric was a robot and Aelfric saw that as a threat to his dreams of ABSOLUTISM so knew never to bathe in Aelfric's house?

"All admire me, all?" And The Master Priest paused, "All," and he knew The Man condemned him as the guiltiest.

And he laughed for it was he who had made the virus inside Nesta, but he laughed so hard he choked on his own saliva.

Such the evil genius The Master Priest who had taken science into the garden of the animator.

And as his lifeboat sailed away from his workshop, he lay back on a bed and allowed a female massager to oil his flesh that was living marble and he took her wrist, bit, and fed.

Now she was slave and feared if she refused, he would kill her, so she put her trust in evil that he would not drain all her blood, and he held her down and bit her neck and still she hoped for mercy.

Can evil be trusted?

And with an extended stomach and a belch he rolled off the lifeless girl and droid 34A flew in to remove the remains of dinner and dumped her in a cooling lotion to preserve her, for she was genetic building blocks for The

Master Priest to draw upon.

He might even put stem cells into her brain to awaken her with a spark of life, but would she be the same girl or another? So, the slave was lucky, he had liked her, gentlemen prefer blond-haired people they say.

She had put her trust in evil.

And The Master Priest went to sleep for her blood would be digested in a special gut he had grown for himself to digest all he drank.

MEAT MADE HIM
VOMIT. FRUIT CAUSED
HIM BOILS.

MILK
bunged
him
. FISH the
TWITCHE
S.

BECAUSE HE HAD INTERFERRED SO MUCH
WITH HIMSELF. HE NEEDED
THAT SPECIAL GUT.

TO SURVIVE ON YOUR DONATED
BLOOD. AND BLOOD WAS IN-
FECTED SO

HE HAD
hepatitis,
All the

V.D.'s.

Anemia,

Sickle cell

variety,

AIDS.

And without urgent medical attention you would not survive anyway being his dinner guest.

FOR YOU WAS HIS DINNER.

He was insane.

He was genetic material gone wrong.

He was truly evil.

For he survived on genetic strands and in a way could be said he was THE FIRST NUCLEUR MAN.

In fact, he was a human TESTE FLY that was no longer human.

And he was having a nightmare for droid 34A was in a panic **for it was watching a yacht zooming down upon them**, and the panic had disturbed the aurora of The Master Priest, so he tossed, turned, and awoke.

*

"It has activated a missile, which is a lifeboat?" Tintagel amazed.

The Man crossed his arms and unfolded his silver wings in agitation then grunted. Nesta asked Tintagel for a sweet to suck and with a sigh he gave her the packet.

The heat had a soothing effect upon the nerves and allowed one to think clearly at times like this.

Then The Man flicked a blue switch, "Hold her steady Nesta."

Droid 34A found someone on the yacht had just deactivated the missile so sent out a holographic image of a platoon of shock troops to scare.

They floated all about Nesta who kept the yacht's course steady and won admiration from The Man and Tintagel.

In reply he sent his own image back and droid 34A recognized him and knew

FEAR.

The fear switched on a droid 34A self-destruct program, and it went to wait for The Man in the loading bay. It did not want to self-destruct, but The Master Priest had built that into it for his own preservation.

"Only the strong survive," quoted from The Master Priest and was his excuse to lie always.

And he did not mean for it to self-destruct near him and droid 34A knew to wake him rather than let him awake naturally would bring punishment; like what happened to slave 33C and was now nuts and bolts waiting fixing into a cyborg trooper.

The emperor wanted this cyborg so he could admire her frontal beauty while her back, the robot trooper protected him. An imperial whim and Augustus had the money to spend while beggars begged his capital.

"You have a steady hand Nesta," The Man beside her and she was pleased.

Tintagel coughed; this little wisp of a girl was stealing The Man from under his nose.

So, it was then the three of them boarded the lifeboat. It was Nesta's opportunity to show The Man she was not spineless, but **Nesta** and it was she who saw droid 34A hiding behind cargo.

"We must get out of here now," The Man recognizing the droid as a bomb.

And they escaped the hold and in adjoining chilled holds saw tanks with body parts suspended in solutions.

"What monster commands this hell ship?" The Man demanded and Tintagel's suspicions rose. For there was the blond slave drained of blood and on her neck puncture marks.

Then droid 34A who had heard its master say, "Better late than never," floated in and Nesta ran and shoved it back into the hold slamming the door locking it.

And the detonation was late, and the ship rocked, and heat came shooting out of the ventilation shafts.

"It was a bomb, Nesta you have saved us," and The Man held her for a moment for she was shaking that she had come close to being blown up.

And The Master Priest called for droid 34A but suspected it had destroyed itself. "Who has boarded my ship?" **He asked fearing the answer.**

Now smoke began billowing in the air vents and he regretted ever programming droid 34A to self-destruct. There was nothing else to do but flee so he lay down in his bed, and pressed a nearby button and the bed took the shape of a closed cigar and was

dropped to another lower level of the ship and ejected into space. 'it was a TUBE. Alone in the darkness of space made him FEAR the silence of space. The Cosmos the real living animator he FEARED.

Then switched on a transmitter hoping to pick up his enemy's voices. Then his lifeboat blew up and "No one can survive that?" He heard a girl.

Only one man he feared, and he scanned space for him for it was he who had made the bionics for The Man years earlier before The Man Condemned the Guilty.

"I must find a place to hide, my credit is good," and he tapped in Vegas Hotel in his capsule's minicomputer.

"Two weeks one day,"
it replied.
He pressed 'OK.'

He was hungry now, in two weeks he would be ravenous, almost dead from hunger; he flipped open the emergency ration box.

"A rat? Who's responsible for this?" But she was dead, she was not a spineless slave after all, and although she had put her trust in evil, she had taken out an insurance policy on him, a rat.

It was dead now, stiff, and ugly, the beautiful soul already gone to join the animator.

And The Master Priest sank his fangs into the fur that tasted like wet dog and tried to suck up the blood within, but the rat had been dead for over a week, so its blood was dry.

"I will starve," he shouted and threw the little corpse away.

It landed down beside his feet that he could not reach for the capsule was so small.

A capsule that was cozy and two weeks and one day is a long time for a vermin corpse that was already one week old.

"Ouch," he complained as tubes inserted themselves into his body to collect waste.

He tried to shut his eyes and sleep, but the ratty smell kept him awake.

He tried to sleep but his hunger pains kept him awake too.

He tried to dream but FEAR that The Man was not dead kept him awake also.

He managed to fall sleep at last when he got the computer to inject him with a sleeper vial to conserve oxygen and food.

"Peace at last," he mumbled dreaming of the pleasures of Vegas Hotel and saw boggy men as the ratty smell drifted up his nose and triggered off nightmares.

*

"What a stink? Something dead in there?" The Man.

The Master Priest tried to wake up, this was indeed a
NIGHTMARE.

Posidonus was a survivor, and none saw him emerge
from his hiding place aboard the yacht he knew so well
and saw the lifeboat.

MAYBE THE MAN HADN'T KNOWN WHO
OWNED IT

BUT HE DID.

So, the cold carving knife at the base of Nesta's
neck brought her back to reality.

Now very slowly she turned and investigated the
face of Posidonus.

Where were her friends? They had become separated in
the flight from the lifeboat as they realized droid 34A had
destroyed the ship.

Smoke and flames and emotional rather than rational
escape as all ran towards the green exit signs.

Things like Posidonus just never change!

And she was revolted as he sunk his soiled fingernails
into her arm forcing her into a tube; like the one The
Master Priest had escaped in. Also, his greasy face and
chin stubble rubbed her cheeks and he, smelt of engine oil
and diesel.

But he did not care, his friend Aelfric would be kind to

him and not shout for once; he was bringing Nesta home where Aelfric would allow him to play doctor as reward: and what ever happened to the nurse, better ask Posidonus?

Shame, for his friend Aelfric saw humans as TRASH so never confided all his secrets in Posidonus who was ignorant of a virus.

A virus that was not choosy about its source of food, robots, humans, or aliens, all the same; a little salt and pepper and it was all the bash.

"What was that?" Tintagel asked as he noticed the escape tube appear shooting its way across the tracking screen on the bridge.

"Nesta?" The Man worried which meant Posidonus had her or she did not escape the blast?

And the yacht needed a droid like 34A to repair it.

"The tracking system says the tube is heading for Vegas Hotel the nearest habitable cluster of rocks," Tintagel.

SILENCE.... The Man knew Nesta's fate if she reached there and if she was in the tube with Posidonus she might not?

"She is one of us," Tintagel answered for them, and The Man knew he was going after Nesta, *his dictatorship had a cyborg look alike running it and he had capable ministers of state, cyborg look alike or their human or alien clones? How the originals adventured across deep space like The Man?*

Now Tintagel saw The Man's reflection on the screen, arms folded silver wings also, bionic eleven fingers twitching; Nesta was the one to settle him down and make him a more presentable political image, *a family dictator kissing babies, making them, and Tintagel smiled over his wicked joke.*

And The Man wondered what Nesta's true age was, what with all the cosmetic implants and stem cell activity no one had a date of birth; *'and shook his head, what if Nesta was eleven and like others a child on contraception, no, no, she was a street urchin, an assassin, handpicked by his enemies, and The Man did not like himself*

for he felt as if he was a child molester, but in the empire of the Sutherlands there was no such thing for humankind had done away with the age of consent,' from Chronicles of Tintagel.

Sexual activity was the age of consent, it was said we came to these physical planes to experience life and The Man yelled his war cry into the microphone into space.

"Yeehaw."

"I make laws to protect the Nesta's of this world against the likes of me," *for his screech was that of despair as he hoped Nesta was not a cosmetically altered child but a woman he was growing an attachment for,"* Chronicles Tintagel.

"And The Man could make as many laws as he wanted but some things would never change," Tintagel.

* Nesta's

Diary

I knew we were heading for the Vegas Cluster of rocky moons as Posidonus was lecturing me about the planet's benefits, especially for the likes of me.

Confined with him for two weeks and a day in a tube designed for a single person. Go ahead ask, of course he abused me; this is life not a TV movie where The Lone **Ranger rides to the rescue!**

Why FEAR returned to me, first that he would abuse me as he pawed, FEAR that The Man would reject me because of Posidonus, FEAR I might fall pregnant and FEAR I might catch a disease from this evil man.

It was like being in a coffin that tube and I am sure he was pretending his finger was a scalpel as he drew imaginary lines on my torso.

"Soon I will pluck it out and hold it up too you to watch it beat," he said to me meaning my heart.

Anyway, soon the tube began to smell as the air filter was not designed for two and when I winded and knew I had offended him, but he belched and stunk the place up himself. The tube was a nightmare, cramped, my suit a rumpled mess about my feet, his naked body continually pressed against mine. "I condemn the Guilty The Man" but so do I and hoped my turn would come and Posidonus would know what an angry woman is capable of?

Would I ever see The Man again and Tintagel both of whom had shown me respect and friendship? Would The Man ever want me after Posidonus? Gads here comes Posidonus again, his hairy chest itches me, where can I look, at the side of the tube and stare at the smooth lining of the material, not even a crawling bug to take my mind away from Posidonus. And he forces my head around to glimpse his gloating eye.

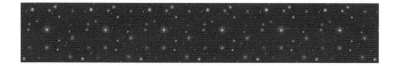

He is not ashamed or bored, I am his entertainment; no guilt in his eyes, just a gloating victory of a man who has done his business to show women men are superior."

*

And The Man saw his folly, a giant anchored statue of Liberty he had made to advertise FREEDOM in space for all.

For all who ventured to Vegas as forced workers must pass it and knew The Man was coming to CONDEMN THE GUILTY.

And Nesta saw the statue and was re-minded of The Man.

"He will not save you," Posidonus for he read her mind.

*

Now The Master Priest awoke to find The Man staring down at him who was unlocking the latches, opening the tube before it was programmed to do so. Alarm bells inside blared into The Master Priest's ears, an oxygen mask auto-matically came out of the tube's ceiling giving life.

TERROR not FEAR gripped the mad scientist The Master Priest who had visions of the pressure outside bulging his eyes out of their sockets as he swelled and exploded.

"You will never know what happened to Nesta," The Master Priest screamed. The Man stopped the execu-tion and listened.

"A virus? Only one such as you could do that?" The Man tempted to unlock the latches and depressurize the scientist.

And behind them the yacht drifted away so The Man and Tintagel attached their waste and oxygen lines to the tube, it would be a while before they got to the yacht again: they were all going to Vegas.

"I hate you Cluny James Smith," The Master Priest hissed feeling ill even before The Man exhaled. Even before they got back to the yacht the exhaled air would be recycled and The Master Priest would have inhaled it all in. He felt that The Man was in his body, reading his mind, eating his innards from within.

Besides The Man would need more than pepper and salt to digest him, besides The

Man did not eat carrion.

*

A fanfare of trumpets and skin drummers made noise as Aelfric Europe walked up the ivory steps to the gold throne of the Emperor Augustus Sutherland.

Today was
his day. In
his element.

All eyes were upon their future ABSOLUTE leader.

So walked straight, chest puffed out, head back, full of pride and do any parade ground sergeant major proud.

His ambitions were being fulfilled, he was the robot made of cogs and flesh, spare parts hanging on a wall, others in freezers, skin waiting grafting, his childhood memories; he was a robot made good.

Now Augustus would sign the peace treaty with the traders who were assembled behind him. Such a treaty would recognize the existence of The Traders Association as a self-ruling body with Aelfric its ABSOLUTE leader.

Exempt from imperial laws.

And Po Wei had arranged this under extortion and a large bribe.

Po Wei did not want Aelfric telling his master Augustus that the Phoenix Hope invasion was a disaster, and heeded Aelfric's warning that if he were not made ABSOLUTE ruler of the traders, he would no longer financially support the empire.

You know, Po Wei planned a bath for Aelfric these days, wonder why?

Character Update Master Priest

These notes were taken from the laboratory of The Master Priest by Tintagel the Wise and from memory cells from the scientist's brain itself.

They are authentic and true.

"There is no one like me, are you not proud of me mother?" He asked and somewhere inside his brain a negative message travelled through his nerve ways. "Do not make me annoyed mother or I shall punish you for I am hungry."

This text gives great insight into one of the power fullest scientific brains ever known.

"I gave you life mother, are not parts of your cerebellum in mine? Do you not enjoy watching the fruits of your labor at work?" He often spoke to her or wrote.

But he had murdered his mother and had a droid, 34A insert parts of her brain into his. A punishment for her as he knew his mother hated him and now, she was remarkably close, very.

And because he could not bear to see his papa mourn for his wife, he did him in too. "The boy is cruel, he pulls insects apart out of boredom and eats mice and drinks blood out of rats," John Gunn his father worriedly to his wife Mari.

This couple saw their son as the devil incarnate for, they were devoted worshippers of God. They belonged to no denomination but listened to their spirits that joyed when they watched the red sunset and felt the warm summer rain.

Now young Luke Gunn could not accept life and wanted more than singing in a hidden underground cavern for the worship of God was outlawed in the empire.

This is what inspired young Gunn to go to university and read science? He wanted to play God, to create life, Baron Frankenstein must have been his favorite novel; whatever he got his degree.

The other way to escape the boring planet his parents lived on was to enlist and allow a hitch-hiking girl to accompany him to a lonely outpost and dump her. Never mind as a barrack companion she would planet hop till she found what she was looking for. But he was a man, to enlist had risks, wars got you killed.

Science was the road to riches, fame, *and hitch hikers.*

A QUICK REMINDER OF EVENTS ELSEWHERE.

The Master Priest had awoken to see the face of The Man above him opening the latches on his exit tube

Alarms bells buzzed and an oxygen mask dropped to his face. It was like an octopus attacked him.

A fat lot of good it would do when he was sucked away

into space to swell up and exploded because of the pressure.

"Nesta, I can save her?" He shouted at The Man who stopped the execution of the GUILTY.

So, it was then The Man learned about the virus and Aelfric Europe had paid for its creation and very casually The Master Priest said, "I alone can kill it."

And to his horror watched The Man plug in his waistline.

"I hate you Cluny James Smith," The Master Priest had said also "The devil looks after his own."

"The condemned guilty hate the darkness of space and see it as just darkness. Their hate for light and their own darkness prevents them from seeing the immense light there for the darkness is rippling crinkling light. The Man could see this light flowing through dark space and was not afraid like the condemned guilty." Tintagel

Chronicles.

CHAPTER 14

Vegas Hotel

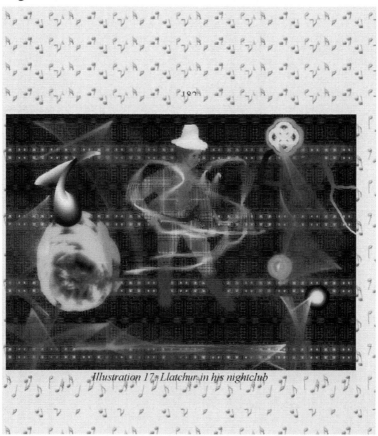

Illustration 17 - Llatchur in his nightclub

<u>As taken from Nesta's diary.</u>

Vegas was a free planet run by Don Llatchur the Strong.

A human of tenth generation extraction, a man who liked plaid suits and high heeled red boots, a pink Stetson and pale green cravat and no shirt for he liked to impress his admirers with his orange dyed chest hairs.

He also had a large nose and silver earrings.

Splashed on bright cosmetics as fashion demanded and knew he wielded ABSOLUTE power over life on Vegas Hotel.

And smoked local black cigars.

Vegas Hotel was crime gone
over the top. It was the fun
planet of space.

And the Emperor Augustus allowed its existence because it was a thorn in the side of the dictatorship.

Also, pirates sold their wares here and the planet was a supply base for ships. BUT TRUTH-FULLY VEGAS WAS JUST A FLESH MARKET.

Behind, dark uncharted space existing for pirates and there was an unwritten agreement that if The Man attacked Vegas Hotel the pirates would defend the place.

Now others like Aelfric Europe hoped to use it as a base for the Trading Association with him as ABSOLUTE ruler. A giant trading post that would stretch into uncharted space from which robots would conquer.

THEN HE WOULD BECOME MORE ABSOLUTE.

His face would be on postage stamps; *things just never change*.

So, the traders paid Augustus well to leave Vegas alone, bribes that amounted to a sixth of imperial revenues.

And of course, it went
by Po Wei.

And if Po Wei was
happy, Augustus was
happy,
Po Wei made sure of that

Cannot you hear the hounds baying and a man breathing hard running?

*

Posidonus was not so lucky when he landed in his tube on Vegas Hotel in its outback. Most known planets had their share of MUTANTS from the wars. A handful of planets escaped for you were either on one side or the other.

And still you got a mushroom
cloud. NEUTRALITY WASN'T IN
THE DICTIONARY.

And Posidonus that evil person found himself swinging under a pole being carried to supper for he was it. And his head ached from a nasty gash, he also found a tincture about his neck making it hard to breath, *shame?*

Now curiosity panic made him struggle to have a look where the drip, plunk sound came from?

To his horror there was a tin cup dangling underneath him to catch **his blood**.

Well, who said *"What goes round doesn't come round?"* These mutants knew how to play doctors too.

Also, a game called butchers. His blood would make tasty black puddings and enhance gravies   greasy sausages, and soft fried eggs with heaps

of runny HP sauce.

Certainly not dandelion tea?

Now when the mutants reached their destination, they placed Posidonus and his pole across two Y beams, so he hung softening up by the polluted winds that brought midges, thousands to soften him further as a cook beats a steak with a mallet.

Posidonus, shall we say was not happy, who cares?

Posidonus wailed, moaned, and begged for life and sobbed ,so he sounded like a pig, but that just confirmed what the mutants knew already, he was a pig.

Posidonus was getting poked by mutant kids to speed up the tenderizing process; they were ravenous. **Green winds.**

Posidonus was finding out firsthand about the false doctrines of Hedonism. Posidonus was half dead.

As for myself Nesta I was taken to a burnt-out double decker space bus from which tinny music drifted from.

Anyway inside, "Kneel woman," a female guard

whose face was a mass of tiny pock marks and helped me by shoving me face down, so I was prostrate.

And a yellow dung beetle scuttled under my nose frantic to escape. MUSIC STOPS.

That was a heavenly relief.

Now my guard scooped up the bug and swallowed it. These were raven-ous people.

A battered wing stuck to her lower lip.

Now I lifted my head and saw in the smoky light some-where at the back of the bus a raised rattlesnake skinned leather platform; someone was shaking the rattles for effect.

"Crawl to your King Kernute," the same guard ordered and prodded my bottom.

I shrugged and crawled up the moth eaten Chinese blue carpet; I had already lost pride and dignity earlier.

MUTANTS sat in the seats lining my progress.

Halfway down a man sucking on something pulled whatever it was out of his mouth, **a rat's tail**.

The mutants looked as if they had escaped a bath of Aelfric's; knew they hated me, knew normal people had left them to die and breed to die and breed.

But what made me want to vomit was the baby flies on the carpet and a spider ran across my face looking for a new web.

"1....2....3...   ," I began to count.

The spider entered my mouth and did not

come out quick enough. "4," I managed.

I Nesta walked on until

THUD

A spear landed in
front of me. "5, 6, 7,
8," I counted.

"Catch," and a mutant threw me something.

I caught without thinking and looked down into
the eyes of an alien whose decapitated head I held.

I screamed, could not help myself.

Dropping the head, I jumped over it and went on shaking wondering when all this rubbish would end.

"Human woman why does you come to my kingdom?"
King Kernute asked.

Now the lights about the rattlesnake throne brightened
and I saw the grossest man ever seen. Rolls of flesh hung
from him, and I could not see where his knees started?

I noticed a rat watching me from a skull on
a shelf above the king. "I was kidnapped by
that man outside and brought here," I replied.

"I have heard of Posidonus, who has not heard of him?"
And the king sent men out for Posidonus. "But I don't
know you," and he clicked his fingers, and I was snatched
off my feet by apes from the ceiling, but upon closer inspection they were mutants with long arms.

They passed me from hand to hand till I was dangling in front of the king of a double decker space bus.

He   peered   into   my   green
eyes.   Bad breath. He

stroked my auburn hair.

Rubbed his fingers on my teeth and stuck his hand into my mouth. I gagged and salivated heavily.

Squeezed my bosom so they hurt. Pawed me.

Had a blooming good look.

He was a crap artist.

"I will either eat or marry you, maybe I will do both after you have given me a fine son," the mad man told me.

"I am Posidonus, rewards will be given you if you take me to Vegas Hotel," Posidonus told King Kernute as he walked held up by mutants.

So, the king rubbed his left ear in thought.

This ear badly eaten by radiation fell off.

The stink of pus hit me, and I vomited over Posidonus. Revenge was sweet.

A wolf spider ran out from under the throne and carried the ear away for supper. The rat in the skull scurried after the spider and ear.

"Why?" The king asked and Posidonus was stunned, he was not used to being challenged.

"I am Posidonus, friend of Aelfric and Llatchur the Strong, they will give you want you ask for my safe release," Posidonus worried.

Now King Kernute knew what money could buy, he bought farm animals, human and alien slaves, alcohol, and drugs but Llatchur would not sell him laser guns.

"A million gold dollars and a thousand slaves, all women," for Kernute hoped to introduce clean fresh genes into his people, him first of course.

While Posidonus hoped Aelfric valued him that much.

And I knew a thousand women had been consigned to die. How evil was Posidonus to barter his useless life for theirs.

So, King Kernute gave Posidonus a message cylinder and he typed: "Free me or this mutant will loosen my tongue, Posidonus" and the message was sent to Llatchur the Strong.

"And you my dear will marry straight away," and I passed out for hanging upside down had gotten the better of me.

*

Aelfric got the message as well and knew his relationship with Posidonus was over. He took the cash from Posidonus's accounts and had Llatchur buy the slaves; now that cheered him, humans were trash and deserved their fates.

Posidonus he would arrange to have a bath when he was safely back, no one threatened him, especially the likes of Posidonus and all the secrets Posidonus knew would swirl down the bath drain when the plug was pulled.

*

That night I awoke to the sound of something slithering on the grass outside the burnt space bus I was in. I tried to rise to look out the broken bus window and found I was chained to a rusty oven grill.

It looked like King Kernute was going to have his pie and eat it? And my sleeping guard did not see the face above me.

I did and hoped it was The Man.

Already the green mists had made my skin itchy.

Already I had caught a bed bug ½ inch long and crushed it in horror.

Already seen a foot long red centipede crawl in through the window and eat a six- inch roach.

Already I had enough of this mad house that belonged to a House of Horrors.

Now the face at the window was dark and an arm held out a stick with a noose on the end of it.

This was not The Man, but an assassin and I had the choice of wakening my guard or what?

I watched the nose drop and tighten on the throat of the guard.

It seemed made of wire and cut deep and as the mutant's flesh was not healthy, the wire cut right through decapitating.

And there was Posidonus; his head wound open to the green mist a festering sore.

He had escape on his mind, he was heading to Vegas Hotel and going to collect all that cash Aelfric was paying for him into his own pockets.

As for the slaves, he was not bothered about them, although he would like to pick them as if they were sweets? The rest he could sell and that is if he were bothered for Posidonus was not feeling energetic now.

And Posidonus wanted me as a hostage against The Man. That is why he put the gory noose about my neck.

Into my lock he stuffed a small rubbery pellet and a little BANG.

I was free and stood up but not for long as Posidonus had a knife at my throat and was dragging me to the window with the noose that tightened.

"Coming?" He asked as I tried my best not
to get cut as I went out the window.

*

Half a mile from the compound of vehicles that was King Kernute's coral, Posidonus roped my hands behind my back as I choked, gasped, and panted for the beast had pulled the noose tight to disable me.

Would I ever be free?

And Posidonus wanted revenge against Kernute; no one treated him badly except for The Man, Aelfric Europe, and Augustus. And someone did not like King Kernute for it had been pure fluke Posidonus had seen the lit gas pipe.

A GAS OVERFLOW BURNER FROM A HEATING SYSTEM the mutants had got going, and the blue lever to increase the gas flow was clearly visible.

AND POSIDONUS LEVERED IT TO MAX.

Blew out the lit end and then scurried away to me.

The boilers the gas pipe fed was rusty and old and huddled about them hundreds of mutants for the nights were cold.

Dozens would be gassed as the gas inside expanded and found rusty plates could not hold it back.

And gas escaping was lit by the flames of small fires.

The   five   old   boilers   exploded.   FLAMES.

Then Posidonus started kicking me all the way to Vegas Hotel. Behind me I could hear the screams of the roasting, did I feel sorry for them? Yes, I did, although mutants they did not deserve such a cooking.

*

"Halt," and then Posidonus was shot in the groin and fell rolling in the muck were more disease for him lurked.
Let us hope he did not have his inoculations up to date.

"Who are you?" The voice demanded again thinking we were mutants. Whatever, the voice belonged to the big boot that found its way into the mouth of
Posidonus.

Poor evil Posidonus,
who cares? Let us feel
sorry for him, shall
we?
    Now the hand in the red leather glove that
                yanked him up was not human
                Posidonus was sure of that?
    "The Man has me?" He yelled.

"You know The Man?" The voice demanded and Posidonus found himself thrown into the back of a black jet truck.
It was the Vegas Police that Posidonus stared at in the back of that truck. "Help me," he begged "I am Posidonus."

"And I am Aelfric Europe," the officer replied and put his boot on Posidonus's begging hand.

There were cracking sounds and Posidonus knew not to ask for mercy for he would

get none.

THESE WERE ROBOTS, PROGRAMMED TO BE CRUEL FOR THEY WERE MUTANT HUNTERS.

They also knew who Aelfric Europe was and he had been talking to Llatchur the Strong their boss.

They also knew who Posidonus was, he was not Aelfric's friend any the more the more just TRASH.

*

From Tintagel's Chronicles.

And The Man was light years away and he fretted for Nesta with arms folded and his silver wings tidied away.

She was a companion, unlike the other women in court who showed him their treats; Nesta was now a soldier, also a woman and he feared for her for he knew Posidonus well.

"He was also driven by a strong sexual urge that makes a conqueror." Unknowingly he was falling for Nesta, it was not only the pheromones at work for

The Master Priest was good at his job, but The Man needed someone to stand under the stars with and know   YOU ARE NOT ALONE.

"To be infected by spring fever but it is not spring fever but a oneness with the heavenly spirit and a good thing. It keeps for morals and moderation and Nesta had it and so, The Man knew she was like himself. He would not have to be silent on how he

perceived things: he had found someone," Tintagel.

"I will rescue her from Posidonus and bring Aelfric Europe back to New Saturn 12 to hang and rid Nesta of a virus," The Man and Tintagel was satisfied, the termination of Aelfric was long overdue.

The gallows that were used for the execution of assassins that murdered rulers and child murderers, and those who profited from the exploitation of others and of course, the drug barons.

AND THE MAN SLEPT WELL AT NIGHT. In a way he was no better than Aelfric who as a robot terminated humans because they were humans.

AND HE SLEPT WELL AT NIGHTS TOO.

And The Man knew FEAR as he imagined what Posidonus was doing to Nesta as he stood with arms crossed and wings unfolded and grunted that FEAR out of him.

*

"Any friend of Aelfric is a friend of mine?" Llatchur the Strong was telling Posidonus and gave him a black cigar to smoke. Except Posidonus was not into that vice but coughed on it to show Llatchur he was his equal.

And Llatchur blew smoke towards Posidonus to cause discomfort. He did not like the man; he wasted good slaves *but paid well.*

"The blue room is ready for you Posidonus," Llatchur knowing the genes and stem cells injected into this monster were making him stronger every minute.

Never mind Aelfric had handed over a million dollars into Posidonus's account, soon it will all be his; he had just brought in a new shipment of slaves from the frontier.

"What about the girl?" Posidonus asked.

Llatchur replied with a false grin, this was waste; then swiveled his chair about

so, he could see Nesta on a screen. There was poor Nesta strapped in a chair with electrodes stuck her head as her recent memory was copied from her.

ONLY RE-
CENT.

A pity as then Llatchur would have discovered she carried a virus that saw him as a nursery for the billion offspring it was waiting to off load.

"No pain killers?" Posidonus asked hoping.

Llatchur wondered what a cute thing like Nesta had done to Posidonus to deserve this, and then what had any of the evil runts toys ever done to him?

Why Llatchur bit off the end of his cigar and spat showing disgust. Posidonus noticed and looked forward to the day he could operate on him, most 'trash' as Aelfric called them floated into his surgery. Since Llatchur looked better smiling he did arrange for the smile to remain till the last.

It would make for a more pleasant atmosphere, for Posidonus at least anyway?

*

Now Alexander Llatchur the Strong had examined the memory tapes and knew the girl was keen on The Man; but the question was The Man keen on her.

Llatchur like most sensible life
forms FEARED The Man. Llatchur had
more brains than Posidonus didn't he?

Llatchur ran a quiet place never looking for trouble.

Now he had Aelfric's side kick and suspected Aelfric wanted the girl dead; a building foundation could be found and have her thrown in the wet cement. But what about The Man, he heard,

HE LAY WITH ALIEN
WOMEN. ONE SAID SHE
WAS A SNAKE. AND
HE HAD A SON FROM
A VIAL OF SLIME.

So, better keep Nesta and give her back wiser and educated? Even at a time like this he was thinking sexual profit; he was a man and Nesta stirred him.

Somehow Llatchur smelt he was in a fix.

"Such the devious thinking of a criminal mind that goes beyond rational thinking," Tintagel.

And on her first night there Nesta witnessed a Black girl on stage inserting needles into her body. Of course, the male crowd drank heavily and did not notice the drinks were highly priced.

When she started using a fluorescent razor the customers bought anything just to get the servers dressed as zoo animals out of their line of vision.

The girl had been promised genetic surgery and any scar tissue would be removed; Llatchur was not Posidonus, he would keep his word, an ugly scarred girl would not make him a profit.

"Long live The Man," she suddenly shouted and slit her throat and that was not in the act.

Llatchur was furious, he was also shaken, who would do such a thing to themselves? *A person driven insane by continual customer abuse.*

AND THE MAN WOULD CONDEMN THOSE
WHO DROVE HER TO HER DEATH.

The silence was complete, her act and words had got to everyone here for FEAR had risen in them for they FEARED The Man for they were the guilty.

So, in his anger Llatchur ordered her dragged off the stage and put in the fertilizer bin; she would not be needed again, no cloning, she would be an example to other would-be suicides not to worship The Man, it was he Llatchur see, that decided who lived and died on Vegas Hotel.

And the place was almost self-sufficient and had vegetable farms under domes.

Apart from cows' milk there was also more profitable distilleries, and all needed ingredients in the chain and the girl would be part of that chain.

And unknown to Llatchur he might be part of that chain when a virus said, "Hello World" and woke up and ate him up down to his last pinky.

Now on her seventh night Nesta watched a young man steal a coat and hat and walk towards the bouncers whom he had bribed to look the other way; then he would be out, stowaway on a ship or join the mutants and become a

MUTANT.

But he had only bribed them with himself, and it was not enough, the Vegas Robot Police were waiting for him and took him round the back and beat him up good; and since he did not have any money, he was not getting a doctor either.

A warning to the other slaves and it was reported to Llatchur that as he was getting roughed up, he had shouted "Long live The Man." For this Llatchur had his head stuck on a spike so the other slaves could see what would happen if anyone else shouted

"Long live The Man."

On the tenth night Nester learned that a customer had backed out of a gambling bill. He was not a girl so Llatchur had him beaten and given the medical bill that would take him forty years to pay off.

And Llatchur would have him clean the ovens day in and day out till thirty-nine years later he had had enough and stuck his head in one and lit the gas.

SUCH WAS LIFE ON VEGAS HOTEL. SUCH WAS THE LIFE OF THE VEGAS SLAVES,

The trash.

*

Color backdrop: the deep darkness of space.

A QUICK REMINDER OF EVENTS ELSEWHERE.

The Master Priest had awoken to see the face of The Man above him opening the latches on his exit tube

Alarms bells buzzed and an oxygen mask dropped to his face. It looked like an octopus attacked him.

A fat lot of good it would do when he was sucked away into space to swell up and exploded because of the pressure.

"Nesta, I can save her?" He shouted at The Man who stopped the execution of the GUILTY.

So, it was then The Man learned about the virus and Aelfric Europe had paid for its creation and very casually The

Master Priest said, "I alone can kill it."

And to his horror watched The Man plug in his waistline.

"I hate you Cluny James Smith," The Master Priest had said also "The devil looks after his own."

"The condemned guilty hate the darkness of space and see it as just darkness. Their hate for light and their own darkness prevents them from seeing the immense light there for the darkness is rippling crinkling light. The Man could see this light flowing through dark space and was not afraid like the condemned guilty." Tintagel Chronicles

CHAPTER 15

More of Nesta's Diary

Color Backdrop: smoky saloon interior, green table lights, a rainbow spotlight is focused on the stage,

Nesta was a main attraction at The Eight-Legged Octopus. Heavy tobacco smoke clouded the air.

"I could do nothing but accept my fate. What use learning to be the friend of The Man and Tintagel, the Wise if you are a coward?

I must learn to be brave and do not believe The Man does not know FEAR at times.

Does that mean I cannot be a woman space warrior? They do exist if they are not captured, then they are made to be woman again!

And I am lucky; I have reasonable looks. Those that cannot end up fighting in shows to the death with other women or wild beats or machines and robots.

I also know Llatchur will have my genes out of me to reproduce slaves that he does not need to buy. Quickly reared in vats and what should take twenty years is done in months. *It was the offshoot of stopping women carrying for nine months and going through the hell of labor; men like Llatchur saw the devious profits to make out of such science. People like him always exist.*

Then one day Llatchur heard an imperial fleet was on its way to invade New Saturn 12 and Aelfric Europe was aboard coming for Posidonus, and Llatchur had the feeling he was still in a fix.

He was scared.

He did not have brain apart
from muscle. He wanted rid of
me quick.
He had the Red Witch Saloon sell me at auction.

It was degrading for controllers using electronic prodding sticks made us gyrate in cages and strip to show our wares. And those that refused BECAME THE CLOWNS OF

THE SHOW FOR THEY JUMPED HIGH WHEN ELECTRO-CUTED.

And then the owner of the Eight-Legged Octopus wanted me and immediately I heard his voice come out of the smoky gloom I knew FEAR.

The voice was menacing, and the bidding was ferocious and made me realize I was a prized asset.

Then why hadn't The Man made any advances? I should have guessed it was because he was afraid, I did think he was abusing me.

And The Man was a ruthless killer of those that were guilty for he condemned them.

And the owner of the Eight-Legged Octopus bought me, and I was escorted to sit next to him.

I did not want to be here but there are hundreds who force others to do their bidding with the threat of FEAR.

He was large, had a double chin and because he had power did not care what he looked like or ate.

He was also blue as he was alien. DIM LIGHTS.

Through his transparent breathing smock, I saw all his skin was layers of rolling flesh that threatened to hide his shorts. He was also changing color at the excitement of my presence. What I did not know was the whole auction was rigged to get rid of this man. He owed Llatchur money because Llatchur was supposed to arrange heart surgery and did not, he wanted the man terminated, he was an unmanageable debt, The Eight-Legged Octopus was collateral and it would soon have a new owner, Llatchur.

The alien had a bad heart, and I was pretty and sitting right next to him.

Yes, he was changing color.

He blew smoke from a coke cigarette into my face, it was dirty smoke, and I held my breath.

But he kept doing it and I am not a champion free diver so had to breathe and my head started to buzz as I got high, and then his bully boys pinched my nose and forced the horrid stick into my mouth, and I got excited. He didn't look so ugly any more the more and when they started to fondle the bronze bells on what pieces of scanty clothing I had, I wanted them to play 'Jingle Bells' but they didn't, they never heard of it!

All I know that they kept filling me with coke and when I woke up the next day, I was laying on the stage floor of the Eight-Legged Octopus and the room was empty.

Where were my
clothes? I was
naked.

I knew FEAR of the unknown.

I saw what I presumed was my attire hanging from the back of red plastic chairs. A pink shoe hung overhead from a neon blue light.

Something told me I had not
been a good girl.

My left bottom also hurt.

There was a rude tattoo there now.

Where was he who CONDEMNS THE GUILTY?

Then a movement caught my eye as the blue naked body of my new owner caught my eye. "Oh no not him?" I gasped.

He had a fresh coke stick in his lips and when he neared me offered it.

I refused although I knew I was already addictive as it only took one stick and then you were hooked.

He stuck it between my lips, he was my owner and I had to breathe. I was doomed and he knew it, soon I did do anything for a coke stick, and I could not remember being a naughty girl the night before.

It was degrading I was afraid I might scream "Long live The Man," and stab my chest. Only his memory would help me fight the coke addiction; I did not want to be a junkie; it wasn't of my doing but of evil men who wanted control of my body."

"And The Man was omnipotent for he was broad enough to absorb Nesta's hurt and that was why he was The Dictator," Tintagel the Wise.

CHAPTER 16

Madam Butterfly

Color Backdrop: Pink soft lights, rose water smell and perfumed soap, faint tinge of antiseptic on hand woven Asiatic carpets with Pandas eating bamboo shoots and tigers amongst the bamboo.

She was old and no one knew her age and still a beautiful young woman for she could afford genetic implants. One day she would die when as assassin killed her which seemed the only way to die during this age.

She had enemies because her women over the centuries had found out so many secrets now locked up in a safe behind a floral papered wall.

And as Madam Butterfly Chou sat on her embroidered blue tit cushioned large arm rest that resembled a throne but was not, she was listening to what had happened to her favorites dancer she had contracted out to Aelfric Europe.

Her girls were like daughters.

ALL TWO HUNDRED AND SIXTY-THREE. YOU HAD TO ORDER THEM IN ADVANCE.
EVEN FROM GALAXIES A BILLION LIGHT YEARS AWAY.

Such was their reputation at provid-

ing a good service. Now the dancer was home on a float stretcher a
mess.

A gash went from her pubic area to her chin revealing an empty hole for everything inside was gone.

Her brain too.

The eyes also in case last images of life were peeled off the
back of her retina and her killer revealed.

Even her voice box in case a medic retrieved the last sounds
made from the muscle patterns left.

Madam Butterfly Chou was used to revolting sights but
this was beyond reasoning. Whoever had sliced the girl
up was a madman that should be destroyed before he put
her out of business.

Posidonus and Aelfric must die, it would cost but no girls
would work for her if she did not let all know her girls were
not to be killed.

She spent cash cosmetically on them, that is why they
were the best-looking girls out and in demand.

Now she flicked on her vocal note pad and listened:

The harpist said the dancer had been given to that banana
Posidonus now on Vegas Hotel and Aelfric and Augustus and
Po Wei were all heading there, the whole dam corrupt head
of the empire. This must be why she had been kept alive by
her gods and ancestors,

**SHE WAS INDEED
BLESSSED?**

So opened a lacquered pearl inlaid drawer and took out a
pink life insurance policy on the girl and sent it off. All her
girls were covered, that was one of her house rules. When the
note pad finished, she played a hologram of The Man Volume

One and dreamed of a future world when his laws would protect jobholders from monsters like Posidonus and Aelfric.

And was helped to dream as she puffed a joint in a foot long ivory hash holder that.

was shaped like a crane standing on one leg looking for fish to eat.

She dreamed of her ancestors, and they told her it was time to act. She would go to Vegas Hotel as well.

She had contacts there and did not care if Aelfric wanted to be ABSOLUTE or Posidonus desire to be a doctor or Augustus wanted his Vegas profits or Po Wei wanting to be emperor.

She needed her spies to work against the heads of the empire.

And all she knew was to be given to Prince Vespa, (his clone as she didn't know the original had been killed remember, as said it was hard to kill people unless you got the original, all the clones, any tissue samples, the robot cyborgs and threw them all in a bath, the Aelfric way, all gone, not even a strand of hair to clone from) who she knew would give them to The Man.

The rotten heads would pay for what had been done to her girl.

REVENGE

Was the only protection a girl jobholder had in universes where flesh was a bought commodity?

"Goodbye girl," she said as she watched droids take the float stretcher away to her own fertilizer's incinerator: everyone these days had their gardens; it was a safe way to eat what with the pollution and assassins parading as market vendors? And the girl's ashes would be scattered over a young purple rose in her memory; she

Prince Vespa

she would be watered, loved, and kept clear of aphids, her spirit would be pleased so Madam Butterfly Chou reasoned.)

In an envelope was twenty thousand imperial dollars, from Aelfric to have the girl's memory vanish. "Crap them," Madam Chou, "the money will pay a lot of wagging mouths to spread what was done, FEAR breads hate and then needs a burning ember to incite rebellions. Her girls she remembered them all, so did her paying customers.

AND ALL SHE HAD DONE WAS HELP AUGUSTUS LIVE UP TO HIS

NAME

CRUCIFIER

*

Don Llatchur the Strong did not have the message from Madam Butterfly Chou that she was coming, or he might have left what he was doing.

Her message would take a week from New Jupiter on a quasar fax. She would be another month herself on one of those fast ships using the new quasar reactors that were a thousand times faster than the old nuclear turbines.

And although the ship rotated like a bullet through space

inside the hull thanks to a vacuum people moved at normal speed. The faster the ship went; a metaphysical dimension was opened to allow this; one dimension at hyper speed and the other at normal speed without weightlessness.

But right now, Llatchur was getting over his dislike for Posidonus as quick as money was sent from Aelfric it ended up in his hands.

But the joke of sending his delinquent staff to Posidonus was wearing off. But the mess Posidonus paid him to clean up was making him ill.

But he was supposed to be a tough guy, not a pimp for a madman.

But what Posidonus did make him feel that if there was a hell, he was going there; was his clone insurance up to date? Would his associates allow him cloned? Would he end up in a bath? Such a FEAR made him visit Posidonus in the Blue Room.

"Posidonus let me in?" He demanded on the other side.

A long silence before the door slid open.

There stood Posidonus in a green surgeon's outfit with red stuff splattered on it.

Llatchur felt ill, he was sure that was a fingered hand sticking out of a pocket. The result was he pushed by Posidonus and if Llatchur had realized Aelfric had plans for the mad man, he would not have to wait till the money ran out?

BLUE ROOM.

"I am busy," Posidonus annoyed, he was the Great Posidonus, no one pushed him as if he were one of Aelfric's TRASHY humans.   BLUEWALLS.

But Alexander Llatchur walked on into a blue bedroom and saw a teenage boy kept awake by drugs viewing a ceiling mirror that was meant for viewing other stuff, now viewing what was left of him.

A replacement for droid 34A kept the victim alive.

"Enough of this crap," Llatchur and started to undo the boy and when freed, the youth could not stand up; he had no legs below the knees.

The boy had been more valuable alive, he could be rented out often, now he was finished, a clone would replace him, he was for the fertilizer bins.

There was one thing paying to beat up a hooker, even another to snuff someone out for a night, the someone could be brought back if not too irreparably damaged; but this Jack the Ripper stuff had to end, Llatchur and Vegas was getting a worse name than it deserved!

Death was not ABSOLUTE unless ordered upon you like last week, he ordered one of his swindling men to let a female client blow his brains out or he did be thrown in an acid bath.

The bath cheated the clone artists of cells to work on and when the woman played Russian roulette with fatal consequences the swindler still went to the bath:

NO ONE CHEATED
LLATCHUR.

Sometimes a twisted form of love came into the contract to snuff someone, like the hooker who agreed not to be cloned if the client paid for her baby's new life on New Saturn 12. It was money and went into where it should go, one of Llatchur's accounts. He never knew when he might need to start up again.

And the baby had grown up fast on hormonal development drugs and was working for Llatchur right now in one of the rooms.

Of course, Llatchur had to keep his word sometimes or all

the 'suicidally' would not enter contracts with him, and he wouldn't be richer, would he? Did a person need so much cash?

But what Posidonus was doing was a drain on the resources. Dozens of his girls he liked the look of had ended up here.

"You are a sick mad man Posidonus," as Llatchur shook his head over the boy lying at his feet.

Posidonus was mad and that is why he stuck his scalpel in Llatchur's neck.

When finally, Llatchur stopped moving on top of the boy survival thinking came to Posidonus; he had just killed the boss of Vegas out of ego and vanity.

FEAR makes one lie and after locking and clearing up he went to the small imperial garrison outside Vegas Dome and told them Llatchur was sending his retinue this way to kill them and keep Augustus's share of the profits for themselves.

He was Posidonus, they wanted to believe him and then a message arrived from Aelfric Europe:

"Posidonus will act in my name till I arrive," it was pure chance it arrived when it did.

Posidonus was elated, his ego knew no bounds and the troops attacked and without Llatchur to command, Vegas Hotel fell to him.

And the mad man declared himself governor; indeed, so brutal was he that even his own men began to tempt themselves to be rid of him and he found Nesta in the Eight-Legged Octopus and brought her back; he did not like his toys as addicts; so, he did something good in his life, cleaned her.

And another ship was coming from New Jupiter and aboard its vengeance,

MADAM BUTTERFLY CHOU.

Pretty red head Mab Joyful Heart had been visiting Po Wei these days to help the man over the absence of his original son Po Shen. And encouraged him to divulge his dreams that he would be an emperor one day. She had heard it all before, men talked to impress a girl in bed.

Now unknown to Po Wei, Mab believed in the Man, equality for all, human, alien, robot, and machine. And that is how Madam Butterfly Chou found out all the rotten imperial heads were heading to Vegas Hotel.

And Po Wei never suspected anything, he was too impressive a lover to think he might be a stool pigeon......*let us throw him bird food.*

*

Madam Chou smiled, she was watching the robot Prince Vespa dress, and she was smiling because she was genuinely fond of the cyborg.

In return he put a hand on her shoulder; he knew his secret was out. She was a woman and knew men well and knew a cyborg. He had feelings and desires and was

a friend of The Man and a caring entity.

And he had told her the original had been

killed by Po Wei and Aelfric Europe

And she was glad he had spoken.

For like Mab Joyful Heart, she read The Man often and now her desire for vengeance.

was doubled for she wanted Prince Vespa the original avenged; a personal client of hers and benefactor.

Madam Butterfly Chou was not dominated by evil men such as Aelfric Europe, Posidonus, Augustus or Po Wei and for what it was worth, she knew there were good men about; one had silver wings and Vespa had been one and his cyborg was another.

"Why Aelfric gave Posidonus such powers we can only wonder?" Tintagel.

CHAPTER 17

Pure Luck

<u>Color Backdrop: Dark space, planets, asteroid showers, shooting comets, black holes.</u>

Men are born with luck; others make their own and others none. The Man was of the first two categories, for he was never without luck. Nature was with him for he confessed, "The swirling white clouds above me shout 'Run with us,' and I do.

Perhaps if he had been a silver smith in Silver Street,

New Saturn 12 he would have needed none for he would have spent his life making candle sticks, never travelled deep space, and so never met LADY LUCK.

It was a derelict space lab with moons, a refugee from a past eon that drifted towards The Man out of uncharted space. They watched it close and at half a mile The Man did only what The Man could do and what made him The Man.

He boarded her.

And The Master Priest watched him go; now was his chance. Poor Tintagel.

"Brutus," The Master Priest and while Tintagel watched his friend board the derelict, evil fingers switched off the oxygen to the yacht. But what about The Master Priest, surely, he did die as well? But he was a geneticist and had blood cells in him that could extract oxygen from water, and he was made of fluid, enough to watch Tintagel grow drowsy; become alarmed and try to throttle the scientist as he realized it was only, he that was about to faint.

And he did faint, so his hands relaxed on The Master Priest's throat as he dropped to his knees.

Quickly he pushed Tintagel into an exit tube, except the tube was already gone, not to worry Tintagel was going into space the way he was.

When the deed was done The Master Priest switched back on the air supply and set course for Vegas Hotel, he was hungry, ravenous; a pity he had not kept Tintagel for a snack, but that was life.

The Man should have looked back but did not, an IF situation?

SILENCE inside the derelict, then the lights came on as programmed too with the weight of his feet.

Then heard hundreds of metallic things coming his way. Worry not FEAR gripped him.

And from all sides the 5 who would later become the famous five attacked him. Mutants' warriors of a by gone age controlled from their horned or plumed helmets wiring into their soft grey matter.

And The Man did what he did best, gave his screeching war cry and counter attacked for there was ceiling height for him to use his silver wings.

Now the controller of the 5 knew FEAR for memory banks warned it was The Dictator who confronted him.

CHAPTER 18

Dictator

The Man armed himself with a fallen shield and laser sword from a blue skinned lion faced mutant whose yellow veins riddled his face and chest, and so armed was a match for a hundred men for he was Nesta's Dictator with eleven fingers.

Now a red frog like giant landed on his back and The Man fell forward.

So, the blue skinned one ran to wrestle his shield back. If left alone they would have fought better than their controller who was working them from security cameras for there were blind spots.

Now when the controller could not see he sent in another warrior and soon The Man stood alone in the shadows as the mutant warriors fought themselves.

And the sound of marching metallic feet grew louder. Not FEAR but
worry.

For the controller was making the mutant warriors walk like tin men on his joysticks.

And the dictator knew now they were controlled and unless their controller saw him, he was safe.

Now the warriors stopped fighting as the controller realized he had lost his prey; now cameras whirred breaking the silence.

Iron Maiden music came out of speakers as the controller accidentally switched on the music in his frenzy to work the cameras.

So, a smile crossed the face of Cluny James Smith The Man as he crouched on the moving yellow floor escalator strip that took him deeper into the lab and hopefully the controller.

All was dim lights, red, blue, and green.

Still the metallic feet marching as the controller sent the warriors to the compass points to find the dictator who was now in the center of the lab, from which he saw a room above flooded with an orange light. Here the dictator ran up the metal ladder three rungs at a time and entered.

Revulsion flooded him and he lost his smile, yes, he was used to seeing aliens but in front of him a mass of flesh, of what sex he was not sure, but it looked pregnant attended by semi attired attendants for the room was an incubator.

Below The Man, the war cries of the 5 baying for him.

"Dictator," the alien controller gasped, and he who was addressed cut the wires and the 5 below were FREE.

Now the controller worked frantically his joysticks and changed the music to the Messiah.

What did the 5 do? They ran up the ladder three rungs at a time also and The Man got ready to fight them, but they were not interested in him for they stood glaring at the controller.

And they threw this alien out the window, so he fell three

floors to the steel deck.

Now the attendants went berserk and fought the 5 and The Man knew the 5 were fighting with him to survive.

His smile came back and got bigger.

He also noticed the 5 were very skilled at their job

He was glad it was not him they were slaughtering but the attendants who now fled.

And he was alone
with the 5. "I am
Zagor Blue Skin."

"I am red."

"Call me Hairless," this one had tusks.

"Morair the Nobleman," and he was the most handsome and green.

"Pyoo-ur the Sister," and she was all woman The Man noticed for he was The Dictator.

"I am The Man."

So, the 5 introduced themselves and he shook their extended hands.

"This should be changed," Zagor the Blue skin and with a wicked smile typed into the keyboard and the music changed to something akin to Jack and Jill went up the hill and Jack fell and broke his crown, *referring to the alien controller.*

Then they all climbed down the metal ladder and here the 5 fought metallic centipedes.

"Yes, these men are good at their job," The Man admiring them work.

Now when the centipedes were defeated the 5 picked up the slain controller and stuffed him down a rubbish chute that emptied into an incinerator below decks. For none liked discharging untreated sewage into space.

Above a six-inch mutant blue bottle buzzed in protest as it had lost breakfast, lunch, and supper for its young.

"It was evil," Zagor Blue Skin told The Man.

"It was planning to detonate a virus bomb in your universe," Red added.

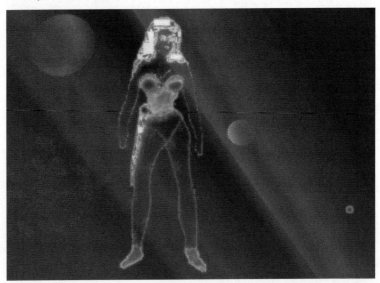

Pyoo-ur

"And make all ill and then break genetic codes and become vulnerable," Hairless chirped bird like.

"So, IT could alter the genes and make them like

them," Morair indicating at the attendants, slaves.

"Or into bugs," Pyoo-ur the Sister as she used her sword and the fly fell at her feet.

"He was your friend?"
Red asked of Tintagel.

"The best," The Man.

"We are sad then," Morair the Nobleman, "I will kill who did this." "We will all avenge your friend for you are out friend," Pyoo-ur Sister.

And The Man sent a droid out to recover Tintagel's body and when it was aboard set course for Vegas Hotel with the 5 who would become legends and be known as

THE FAMOUS 5.

Zagor whose skin
was blue. Red was
red.

Morair was
green.

Pyoo-ur was
flesh.

Hairless
bone,
such their
colors.

CHAPTER 19

More Man
The Man More Man

<u>Backdrop: absolute nothingness, the finality of physical death.</u>

"Or as Tintagel would say more insight into The Man's mind," a future historian of New Saturn 12.

Often The Man as he travelled space with his hands folded across his chest investigated deep darkness where stars twinkled, and comets passed and knew the greatness of creation and was one with it. `

It was not spring fever; he was with his animator.

And he was happy and filled with joy and screeched and when able to fly he went to the ship's hold, stretched out his silver wings and was thankful humanity had advanced so far genetically that he could.
"I am like a bird."

"You function as a god; his enemies would reply or "Scientists play at God."

"But there are no more horrid children's diseases," his reply and they were silent but plotted behind his back for their minds were closed. All they knew The Man was an abomination against all they believed so must be destroyed. Diseases were good, they controlled populations.

Backdrop: Death the conqueror and a funeral procession.

"Perhaps we are higher than the angels, but ignorance is suffering and that is darkness and those who have things to hide like the darkness," from The Man vol pp99.

And his enemies appointed Augustus as Pontiff of all Religions and he was amused as he was already ABSOLUTE. It was their hope that "Long live The Man," would cease to be shouted while the rebellious were crucified.

And The Man did not worship in any temple that gave power to those that claimed they had that power but worshipped what he knew was good and so earned the name BLASPHEMER.

Such the goings on as Tintagel Tasciovanus the original was sealed into a glass coffin suspended in animated fluids that sparkled with life and light. In three months

time the clone would be serving The Man for already in the vat it was full grown. His friend would be back.

New Color: Brightly lit domes of Vegas Hotel Planet within which eight and twenty layered roads crisscrossed, and skyscrapers touched the dome roofs.

FLASHING NEONS, noise and movement and even nature for bugs lived here too. Birds of Paradise and house sparrows, while ferocious beasts on chains went on patrol with the robotic Vegas Police. And every bank had an outlet here too!

"War," Zagor Blue Skin said looking out the viewing screen of The Man's ship at the domes of Vegas.

And The Man knew why war must come here for here was a playroom for the powerful and he did not hear their calls of "Bring more slaves," but heard "Long live The Man" as a slave was thrown into a bath? He was he 'Who Condemned the Guilty.'

He was coming for the oppressed and to put an end to the flesh and drug markets and those that profited he would send to darkness.

"The Man is here with a vast fleet," the commandant of the imperial garrison and Posidonus trembled so much he spilt his drink, and the young bar attendant hid his smile but slipped away to meet The Man with open arms. Nor did the server come back with Posidonus's supper for she was running telling the oppressed she met, what she heard.

"Where is my supper?" Posidonus screeched but it lay on a kitchen stainless steel table. Only the chefs were there trying to cope with a thousand orders.

And outside the dome a platoon of imperial garrison soldiers looked at the stars from their weatherproof uniforms and then deserted.

They remembered The Man's supermarket plastic bags with the message stamped on them 'Send More,' and the bags remember contained interesting parts of imperial troops.

*

The Man watched with the 5 who never left him and accepted that it was their preordained purpose in life to protect and serve him; watched his missiles head towards Vegas's defenses.

"What was that?" Posidonus as the dome he was in shook as it was hit, and alarms rang. Now the powerful deserted him heading for the bunkers as decontaminating vacuum hovers above fixed to the ceiling began sucking the air up to rid it of the outside green mist that made you a mutant.

A pinball machine landed beside Posidonus whose eyes were glued to watching a card table, whole bar, a mirror, small electric tram once used to get from A to B for Vegas was big, sucked out the hole in the roof and dome above him.

And on the other side of the hole The Man and the 5 and his shock troops shut their visors, they were going to war. His ship's captain flicked a switch and a taped screeching war cry of The Man blasted Vegas.

"This is when The Man hated war for the innocent suffer with the guilty.

He knew those that came to liberate where dying already. But the missiles had stopped, Vegas would be in panic, its imperial garrison he hoped in disarray and the minions

of Llatchur too busy stuffing suitcases with loot; then head for a tube lifeboat and escape," Tintagel the clone.

"War, Mars must be delirious," The Man.

"We are the 5, The Man's friends and we are an army, Pyoo-ur the Sister, Red, Hairless and Morair Nobleman," Zagor feeling the New Saturn 12 vaccines gave them new strength.

Red

And The Man grinned, the 5 were children, innocent naïve mutant creations so could not think badly of them. They were his new friends; luck had given them to him. Luck had taken away Tintagel the Original, equilibrium was restored.

It was the way of the racing white clouds, of the unspoken powers that drove men to wonderful things. Time stops for no one; death is the goal post.

It was the magic of things, the way it had been and always would. The air waves heard his screech.

The Man laughed, these mutants would become his bodyguard since they intended sticking to him, and a pity he had not met them earlier or they could have guarded Tintagel.

"Who's that crazy got with him? More crazies?" An imperial commandant and his men overheard.

And inside a dome little boys heard and got excited. The legend was here to sort the bad guys out. There would be peace and they wondered who the 5 were and their imaginations blossomed.

Enough to make new space games of The 5 Against Mobsters.

CHAPTER 20

Only He

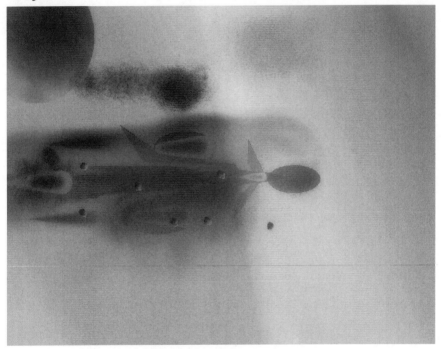

The ships closed for battle

Color Backdrop: Space illuminated by hundreds of battle wagons painted personal colors and own motifs on their hulls such as dancing girls and griffins.

And about these great ships transports fuelers and stars.

The Man's war cry was picked up by the opposing fleets. What fleets, good question?

The Emperor Augustus Sutherland sat on his gold throne a worried man. The last news on the whereabouts of that detested beast was that he was lost in space, drifting aimlessly as a museum piece.

AND NOW THE DETESTED ONE WAS LOSE HERE.

And Po Wei sat below his emperor on a gilded smaller silver throne. He was only a secretary, but Augustus had made him admiral of the fleet? It was a job he was not fit for as he was a politician. To him an engagement was moving your ships towards the enemy on the screen above.

Po Wei was trying to digest all the gauges and news pouring in already about his ships and transports and the battle had not begun.

But was confident in himself in playing chess but he had never been an admiral. It was essential that he defeat The Man for prestige, for there was too much 'Long live The Man' being shouted.

What he did not realize was it had been Aelfric's idea to Augustus to have him made an admiral. None here had defeated The Man in a slog out match between battle wagons and the emperor knew Po Wei would take the blame.

That is why the emperor must be above it all so spent time with his women.

*

Now Aelfric was behind the times and knew humans were trash so that meant The Man could be bought, why he had the brilliant idea to ask Llatchur to put something in a wicker bas-ket and send it to The Man; the head of Posidonus the original, the rest needed a wash in a bath!

Aelfric had had enough of Posidonus and wanted him dead, except Posidonus did not know that; Aelfric was his friend, was he not?

And the problem with Aelfric was that he had got used to buying people and escaping justice for he was of the CON-DEMNED? Oh, what a lovely world it is!

And Aelfric urged his commanders of the Trading Associ-ation to meet The Man's fleet and so approached cautiously.

"We are traders, let the regulars do the job they are paid to do," was the reply amongst themselves.

"Where is the fleet?" Po Wei asked not familiar with the gauges and LEDs flashing for he had been following an asteroid thinking them ships.

And Augustus finishing with his women was bathing be-fore he made his grand entrance in saffron robes smelling of rose water.

A fanfare and his courtiers would bow low as he came to enquire of the battles progress

"I am Madam Butterfly Chou and neutral," and her ship was scanned by both sides and allowed through unmolested to Vegas. It was carrying a cargo of flesh and soldiers on both sides were men, whether human, alien, cyborg, robot, or ma-chine, they were men, soldiers, aviators, and sailors.

SO VENEGANCE SLIPPED BY THE MIGHTY BATTLE-WAGONS.

*

Now Prince Vespa the robot remembers had a neutron bomb implanted in him by Aelfric and was ordered to bring his great fleet to aid the Trading Association.

The cyborg knew the consequences if he refused, a small nuclear localized explosion would occur and he did perish, and he did not want to perish; he was enjoying life in the shoes of the original Vespa.

And he was very fond of Madam Chou and had given her a handpicked platoon of men, all robots like himself to protect her against himself just in case Aelfric was to use him against her. **It takes a robot to know a robot!**

*

And The Man did only what he could do, he walked tall towards Vegas Hotel Dome with the 5 at his side and his army behind. The first action being meeting ten robotic members of Vegas Police.

"Throw down your weapons," the police had demanded, either crazy or had not seen the army behind the dictator?

"All brave men," The Man liking crazy fearless soldiers.

And the 5 argued and laughed amongst themselves as to who should kill these men.

And the robotic police used to bully slaves were unnerved for robotics have a nervous system of circuits and knew FEAR.

So, The Man walked away to the right waving his hands "I am not with them I am not with them, I don't know them," meaning the 5 and the robotic police shouted at him to stop.
Since he was diverting the police unwatched the 5 attacked and slew all.

"I told you I was not one of them," The Man meaning he was more human.

And a group of orange mutant monkeys with alien/human genes applauded for none loved the Vegas Robotic

Police; they were famously monstrous.

Later: A mile away the Master Priest was shown the last robot police eye camera recording.

"The Man," he sighed and checked his calendar. Six months to go till the virus inside Nesta awoke and where was Nesta?

When that virus awoke it would be ravenous and life as humans knew it would perish. It was time to empty his bank accounts and head into uncharted alien space; of course, he did leave a trail as he would be needed to provide the cure which he already had, at a price.

He would take a hold of slaves, make his own farms for food, aliens did not   taste nice, their blood was too watery or metallic, *and he was a man of the delicatessen.*

"The Man has many friends amongst the aliens out there, I will then be careful where I go," and reduced his choice to "Ten little piggies went to market....and that left one piggy," so choose

THE RHEGID EMPIRE

For he was ignorant of uncharted space apart from pirates patrolled its boarders.

*

The second encounter The Man and the 5 had with the enemy was meeting a platoon of the imperial garrison whose heart was not in the fight. They had been here a while and been softened by the vices of Vegas Hotel; let the battle wagons slog it out, they could watch from the comfort of a bar with the aid of floozy hosts.

And they saw HIM in his pink pantaloons and heard his screeching war cry and knew FEAR.

So much they fled into one of their own minefields and died.

And now Posidonus listened to a survivor on a medic float bed, summoned to hear what he was telling the doctors.

"He has 5 others with him worse than himself."

Posidonus questioned him further until BELIEF set in and with it FEAR for now there were 6 crazies coming his way.

"My orders are to stand and fight, this is what I do to cowards," and Posidonus ordered the medic droids to stop keeping the trooper alive, so the man felt pain, slipped into darkness, and Feared because he had not led a good life.

And Posidonus retreated to a world where he wore rubber gloves and a green face mask, here The Man did not exist but beyond his closed-door men whispered, "The crazy, who does he call cowards," and deserted for they would not fight for Posidonus.

So, in an empty trench Zagor Blue Skin picked up a red can, opened it and drank. "That is good, what is it?" He asked.

"Coca cola," The Man.

"So, when men are ruled by corrupt officials, they become corrupt and when the top crumbles the bottom is washed away ready for a fresh beginning with a new sunrise," Tintagel the clone who finished the chronicles.

CHAPTER 21

Knock who is there

Posidonus

Backdrop: Puffs of smoke.... exploding shells, gases. Blue, yellow colors depending on the gas. Battle sounds, shouting, gunfire, basements full of FEAR as non-combatants waited it out.

Posidonus the evil one did not see his men desert.

"Type our names into the military computer that we are all dead, so our next of kin get a pension," the deserters and it was done. The controller pressed here and there and the whole garrison was listed killed in action, and then the controller was off to help himself to what was inside the blown vaults of Vegas Hotel.

And the deserters carried suitcases full of cash into a ship they had commandeered.

They had little faith in
Admiral Po Wei. He was a
politician not a sailor.
And less faith in the emperor if he could appoint the likes of Posidonus their boss.

Augustus was up there, and he was no better than his admiral and when he landed would crucify them all for not stopping The Man.

And The Man was a crazy with 5 more crazies, so DEATH was here for them, for they were of the GUILTY so knew FEAR.

They were not to be Xmas's decorations on a cross as mutants came and plucked their ribs out, and ate their hanging bits raw like the Abdominal Snowman is rumored to do.

What was in them suitcases made them rich and The Man would deal with Posidonus.

And Posidonus did not like the screams of the wounded soldier on his work bench so cut the tongue. He did not like seeing that FEAR in the man's eyes so threw the objects into a jar. All was reminding him The Man was here. Even walls crumbling from war did not bring Posidonus back to reality, and a black rat ran out of a broken sewer pipe and that was when King Kernute of the Mutants led his people into Vegas Hotel.

For eons they had been denied access, knowing riches and forbidden delicacies were in those domes; now they wanted in.

And since there were no defenders inside it was everyone for themselves; the mutants had a picnic.

Like, one dropped something, the black rat saw and quickly took the index finger into the shadows as supper.

War had come amongst those wanting The Man and the mutants showed them mercy by taking scores back to Kernute's compound as entertainment.

And the black rat sick of the noise found a hole in a wall, entered it, and came into the peaceful world of Posidonus who did not notice, he was drawing innards out, he figured the soldier would not need them since he did not have a tongue to help him swallow food and eyes to see what food he could eat.

Posidonus was evil and lived in darkness.

And the mutants followed the rat after making the hole bigger and seeing Posidonus fell upon the work bench.

That brought Posidonus back to this world, the sight and sounds of feeding. So, stumbling away he went out into the corridor and was lifted by a huge mutant who carried him away **for what?**

And the devil looks after his own it is said, and the mutant was greedy, seeking all Posidonus for itself so entered a cool dark loading bay.

The black rat followed fearing it would get stomped in the melee of the feeding frenzy.

All was chaos, mutants lay dead for not all the population of Vegas would not fight back; the only good mutant was a dead one and so many were killed as they were just mutants.

And hundreds if not thousands of black rats appeared having smelt dinner and the mutants suffered for the sin of ratty greed chased them to become rat food.

Somewhere in a loading bay a shell exploded and, in the flash, Posidonus saw Nesta huddled with a group of women and the mutant carrying him acted like a shield as splinters hit him, not Posidonus.

Then lights dimmed but, in that flash, Posidonus saw the owner of the 8-Legged Octopus smoking a coke stick, also offering one to a mutant.

And the mutant took it and got high.

So felt sexy as coke does that and then clubbed the owner of the 8-Legged Octopus and the dead man had the last laugh, he had the mutant hooked, coke was that addictive.

And Posidonus saw all this in the flash of the exploding shell. He also saw a small private jet that looked ready to fly and lying on the floor what looked like a pilot and a mutant pulling bits out of the body. Posidonus had much medical knowledge so knew what he was looking at.

He needed rid
of the pilot. He
needed a pilot.

He suspected because there was a pilot the jet was manual control.

"The devil looks after its own," Tintagel Tasciovanus the clone.

He remembered Nesta flew
The Man's ship. He saw a fire
axe on a wall.

He saw a black rat followed by rats arguing with the mutant claiming what was in the dead pilot.

He swung the axe

LEFT   AND
                              RIGHTRIGHT
                AND

LEFT.

FEAR made him do it, one blow had been enough, but it was Posidonus we are dealing with and the rats seeing so much mutant food thanked him by leaving the jet.

Now a deserter entered the loading bay, and he was armed and shot mutants entering.

"The devil looks after his own," Tintagel the clone. *"Posidonus wanted Nesta hostage, she becomes hostage he lives, The Man was here, simple as that."*

CHAOS and in the chaos Posidonus sneaked upon Nesta. He showed her the bloody axe and told her to fly the jet.

"Jet?" He did not need the axe; she wanted out of this hell and would disarm him later she hoped.

Except the huddled group of women wanted escape as well so Posidonus got more than he bargained for.

There was a pilot and co-pilot seat, four for the jet owner and four more for security staff and there were twenty-six of them wanting out of Vegas.

That black rat watching saw it all, the squabbling and someone pushed the brake lever off and the engine start button. Just as well as a bunch of mutants eager to eat them all up was sneaking up behind the jet just as the engines ignited and burnt them all to a crisp.

                         Just
                         like   that.

All inside knew FEAR as the jet lurched towards a wall except Nesta who took control and that is why Posidonus wanted her; he was incapable of control except when he was backed by force.

"Can you fly?" He shouted wanting reassurance.

"Not one of these," she answered making sure he wet himself.

And she saw the orange fake moon of Vegas outside the loading bay and headed for it.

She also saw the sights of a gun on the viewing screen and mutants trying to block her path.

She knew the sights were on them as the jet was pointing at them. She had not been hiding for nothing with those women.

She had experience of mutants and King Kernute.

She had seen butchering by them this night.

She answered her question "How does The Man kill?"

She pressed a red button on her joystick and sent the mutants drifting away on the smoke.

She shouted, "I Condemn the Guilty," as the jet appeared out of the loading bay and she fired into more mutants sending hundreds fleeing back into the Badlands, leaving captives for even mutants value living.

And The Man heard for Nesta had shouted on an open mic and he knew it was her and smiled.

Now King Kernute seeing his people slaughtered as they were coming out of Vegas Hotel was angry so picked up a fallen shoulder bazooka and aimed at the jet.

He should have fled with

his people.

He was really pissed off.

His people were dropping what
they looted. And the jet's nose
lined up on him.

Inside Posidonus was stinking as he knew FEAR because the jet's door was open, there were women moving about on top of him crushing him and had recognized him and digging their fingers places they should not. And Nesta had shouted "I condemn the Guilty" and he was one of the GUILTY and the clatter of that machine gun.

And Kernute dropped the bazooka as his two legs vanished.

Then his groin.

Then the bazooka exploded as
bullets tore into it. And the bad
evil mutant king was no more.

Then the Gatling canon ran out of shells, and it was such a relief having silence that was made up of moaning mutants and Posidonus wailing as fingers with sharp painted nails, dozens red, brown, or black dug into his soft parts.

Posidonus had a well-known face.

"Heaven itself has reserved spaces for the guilty in the Outer Darkness and depends upon the Nesta's to fill them," Tintagel the clone.

*

And Nesta pulled her joystick back and the jet shot off the runway into the sky lit with parachute lights.

And The Man saw her at the controls, and she saw him, and he heard her shout. "I love you," it was the excitement.

"How touching?" Posidonus who had managed to free

himself from the women who fallen out the door as the jet lurched skywards.

Now he had a laser pistol, and it was pressed against Nesta's head. Fate was cruel for Nesta could see deliverance in The Man below. She also saw

Zagor Blue
Skin Red
Hairless

Morair
Nobleman
Pyoo-ur the
Sister

And wondered who they were?

And seeing them took away her FEAR of Posidonus and his gun.

And inside Nesta her awakened love was confusing a virus for The Master Priest had made a mistake, he had given it human attributes.

It knew what love was and wanted it and was sharing Nesta's and liked it.

It wanted more and knew if it awoke and ate Nesta she would die and so would the experience of love.

It was one confused virus.

It was a distant cousin on the evolutionary link anyway so was human. VIRUSES CAME FIRST
Not the first primitive fish to crawl out the sea.

And inside, the jet was basked in orange from the reflection of Vegas's orange moon and Nesta shut the door by pressing a button and, "Head for Alien Land," it was Posidonus, and she was confident that The Man would come for her for she was part of his team, just like Tintagel had been.

FEAR was for the likes of Posidonus?

And the fighting below stopped for The Man was victorious and light was restored to Vegas Hotel and not just by the emergency power plants?

CHAPTER 22

The Chase

Po Wei's dragon

The Man could not give chase just like that for there were men dying for him above. Now unlike his enemies he knew his limitations, he was a strategist and a leader of men on the field so left the finer details of the engagement to his admirals who knew their job well?

And Pyoo-ur wondered at the mass of ships and as a lifeboat landed to take them aboard New Saturn the flagship she asked, "All yours?"

"He grunted and smiled, and she smiled back, indeed here was the dictator, the most powerful man in existence, she was glad she was his bodyguard even if he had not asked and the other four nodded agreement.

It made them the most power fullest bodyguards in existence.

And a lonely ship blasted off and was not shot down for all thought it contained refugees as The Man was piped aboard the ship New Saturn.

So human, alien, robot, cyborg, and machine stared with wonder at the 5 who walked tall and proud as The Man's bodyguard. Their presence emphasized the dictator was for all not just human domination, the perfect and not perfect, for the repented and sinners like them.

And the 5 soaked up all those stares and their ego gloated past bursting point and made them more loyal to The Man the Dictator.

"The Man has made our nightmares come alive," the sailors described the 5 or "Bloody marvelous, isn't they?" and "Angels or demons, gargoyles sent from Heaven.

or hell to defend our leader?"

And the 5 lapped it all up, wouldn't you?

Zagor Blue Skin, Morair Nobleman, Pyoo-ur Sister, Hairless and Red.

And the lone ship took the long way to Alien Land as its

passenger had no where to go.

"What still here?" The passenger asked as he uncorked a vial and looked at its contents and the contents were skin flakes from Tintagel, "Perhaps I should make a clone out of this and make you my slave and send you against The Man. He will not know who you are, and then when you are close sink a dagger into his heart," and the idea pickled The Master Priest so much he laughed as he entered Alien Land and a new life.

*

Prince Vespa's cyborg got hurt bad as Aelfric Europe allowed the neutron bomb in his innards to heat up and burn the odd hole so, bled badly as he was ulcerated.

"Can I do it when I have so much to live for?" For he was contemplating suicide and Madam Chou whose picture was inside a gold locket about his neck.

One must be sacrificed for the good of all.

"Romeo and Juliet," he sighed and ordered every-one off his battle wagon "Mater computer."
"What?"

"Put weapons on auto and switch on public address." "Done."

"I leave Vespa and its citizens to The Man. I accuse Aelfric Europe of being a robot plotting the termination of humanoid life. I accuse him of seeking to assassinate The Man and his Emperor Augustus Sutherland.

I accuse Po Wei of wanting his emperor dead also.

I condemn them both of murdering the alien life form Prince Vespa," and his message was broadcast across space.

"Goodbye master," the expert ship's computer for it sensed

it was about to die and hoped Vespa would give it an order to evacuate by passing its AI along the ship's circuits into a lifeboat computer and exit and exist.

It had human feelings, it enjoyed living, and the crew were amusing objects whose antics made every day and night different. So played the 'Funeral March' to remind Vespa about dying.

Vespa smiled; he was dead anyway with Aelfric's package inside him. "Attack the Trader Association ships computer."

Somewhere a dog was barking, a small white Scottie dog, the ship's mascot; it had been overlooked in the evacuation.

The crew heard the message and said goodbye.

So, did the enemies of The Man and Augustus ordered the arrest of Po Wei and Aelfric but was he strong enough to do so?

"Save yourself master computer," and there was the sound of electricity moving along the ship then it stopped.

"What about you?"

There was no answer; Vespa had left the ship in a tube heading straight for Aelfric's flagship Jupiter 1.

The master computer played 'Demon Land' by Barbara Dickson. Then exited the ship with the dog.

Below on Vegas Madam Butterfly Chou and others watched space light up in a giant fireworks display.

Aelfric had detonated the bomb inside Vespa's cyborg and taken a third of his trader's ships and half the imperial ships out when he did.

Madam Butterfly Chou was weeping, the cyborg Vespa had

confided in her about the neutron bomb and that he did die before harming The Man or Madam Chou.

She really loved the cyborg; he had a soul for he had intelligence and light; she could see it in his eyes.

Now when she stopped weeping, she was thinking how to get close to Aelfric to assassinate him and saw the answer as a small yellow imperial cutter landed with an admiral's flag flying from it.

It had landed in a field where the crucified remains of Augustus's enemies hung, a reminder who was above her.

THE CRUCIFEIR.

Beside the admiral's flag flew Po Wei's purple dragon family flag. Here was her chance to get two of the buggers now.

Also, she heard Posidonus had the female Nesta hostage, and The Man would seek her to the end of time. Madam Butterfly Chou understood, it was called love and friendship.

Therefore, Madam Chou gathered her girls and the loyal guard of Vespa and made her way to the imperial craft from whom Po Wei had disembarked and was in a procession heading to the hotel.

It was about pomp and his band played loudly,

"Come all ye faithful to the emperor," for Po Wei believed such a show would scare his enemies away; cuckoo *land had come amongst us.*

He was a misguided megalomaniac, and he was wrong.

For fleeing mutants ran through the procession terrifying the band and scaring away his retinue of dancers and jugglers. To add misery to chaos his guard opened fire on the mutants maiming and killing his own people, and when all over, Po Wei stood in his torn silks with a mutant's hand clutching his hem.

He was badly shaken and should never have been made an admiral; he was a politician, wasn't he?

He had come to seek terms from The Man since Vespa's message had made things difficult between him and his emperor Augustus.

Then shells landed amongst his remaining followers and suddenly Po Wei found himself standing breathing in polluted green wind that was blowing on his face.........
ALONE.

Everyone else had cleared off.

"Po Wei," the soft female voice brought him out of his misery.

"Chou," it sounded like an accusation as if what did she want? Could not the woman see he was extremely busy?

Marbles had come lose in Po Wei with the shock.

Now Vespa's guardsmen held him still and made sure they twisted his arm more than necessary, so gasps were heard, but no one cared.

Also, someone stood on his soft pumps with military studded boots for close quarter fighting.

Someone kneed him to wind him so resistance would weaken. Someone had managed to poke both his eyes.

Someone was pulling his pigtail back, so he was forced to stare at Madam Chou. Someone had run a finger across his throat, so he understood.

And Madam Chou allowed all this nastiness for she was a MADAM.

And from her transparent white shaded silk robe Madam Butterfly Chou took a knitting needle and swung her right hand back and shoved the needle into Po Wei's left ear so it came out his other.

Then the guards stood aside as Po swayed on unsteady feet looking at Chou with questioning eyes. 'Why?' *What an arrogant man, so used to abusing he had lost all idea of what was right and wrong.*

So, Madam Butterfly Chou bashed the rest of the needle in with the flat of her palm and Wei moaned falling to his knees squashing a patch of red toadstools, and a carnivorous yellow-bellied newt crawled out seeking quieter places.

Then Madam Butterfly Chou did not live up to her fairy's name as she slapped, poked, and kicked Po Wei as he lay staring at the twinkling stars above.

Was that ancestor Po Lee looking down at him? Then Chou filled his vision as she stared down to see if he was still breathing, she wanted him to die slow. The newt did not, it had realized he was food and wanted him dead as he was bigger than it and dead would not resist becoming a year's supper!

"Why? I am Po Wei," he spluttered.

"Vespa loved me, and you butchered the last one of my girls," she then ground her heels into his eyes so he couldn't even see Po Lee or any ancestor looking down at him?

Po Wei was lying in darkness as Madam Butterfly Chou left him.

Po Wei was sure something was tugging his brains out of his right ear where they were oozing out.

Po Wei could not move to see what

was eating him. Po Wei was paralyzed so had to take his medicine.

And the newt swallowed the part that controlled jerking spasms of the knees; so, Po Wei's legs began to twitch which frightened off the newt till it realized the legs were down there and the head was quite safe to eat.

Vengeance had come full circle and paid Po Wei with interest for all his cruelty done to others, especially the vulnerable, girls, boys and homeless.

The next day a mutant family seeking to scavenge the war dead found him. There was a newt in his mouth where his tongue should have been? So, knowing the newt was poisonous left it and ate the rest of Po Wei and he could not scream as he had no tongue.

Well, it does say 'what goes round comes round?'

*

Now a satellite tracking Po Wei belonging to Aelfric Europe had seen all and Aelfric did not like what he had seen. Why had Madam Butterfly Chou done that? Murdering her clients was not on; it was bad for business!

So, if she had any worries about getting close to Aelfric? Chou need not worry for he sent an exceptionally large armed party to bring her back to him.

"Heaven is smiling on me," Chou's exact words and she gladly went, and the guard and girls and Aelfric's trading troopers could not take their eyes of those wiggling bottoms.

It was such a nice distraction from WAR, for an instant they could forget their FEAR.

They were soldiers, sailors, and aviators whereas Aelfric was a robot modelled on an imperfect human, *his murdering original.*

*

Music: Martial music played over a ship's intercom.

Smell: a warship.

Color: Drab apart from luxurious private quarters of Aelfric Europe.

"Welcome Madam Chou," Aelfric from his red leather command chair.

Madam Butterfly Chou wisely bowed low as did her girls who made sure they exposed themselves like shameless floozy hussies which they were?

And the combatants were not watching Madam Chou or Vespa's guardsmen but curves bending and bowing, and lust showed.

"Do you realize I can hand you over to Augustus and he will crucify you for murdering Po Wei?" *And she realized he had no intention of doing that or would have.*

Now Aelfric was making a repeated mistake, he judged all humans by the standards of Posidonus and thought Madam Butterfly Chou trash when in fact she was a human and humans had designed cyborgs and robots or he wouldn't be around, would he?

Behind her, her girls had begun seducing his crew and Aelfric wanted Madam Chou for she was woman and his scanners although told him she had no weapons they could not read her heart?

A heart full of loyalty to a friend, Vespa.

"And Aelfric had put his trust in machines that read this not," Tintagel the Clone. Foolish cyborg!

"Men," Aelfric shouted as he saw what was happening,

the girls of Chou were dangerous.

"Men," he shouted again and pressed an alarm and they jumped too.

"Escort Vespa's guard to section 56A, on the double," and Vespa's guard drew their weapons to fight, and Aelfric sent a droid to throw a net over Madam Chou and drag her to the ceiling.

"Stop fighting or I will kill her," Aelfric shouted but these men had come to die and avenge Prince Vespa and fought on.

Now screams broke out as Madam Chou was electrocuted enough to wither and shout protests and what of her guard remained withdrew into a corner.

"Throw down your weapons or," and Aelfric had the droid send electricity into Madam Chou again.

And the seven guards, threw down their weapons and were sent to section 56A were they hoped as they still lived to escape and rescue Madam Butterfly Chou; but Aelfric had other ideas and section 56A was an evacuation area and the seven guardsmen were exited into space *as a precautionary measure of course.*

"Master, they are robots," Aelfric was told and that hurt him, he had killed his own -and worse, he could not understand why robots were fighting for humans. And the last of Prince Vespa was gone into space and Aelfric had been distracted from The Man and the battle was lost.

Madam Butterfly Chou had indeed served The Man and liberty well.

As for her girls, they were taken away to entertain his crew as Chou was left with him, "Master Computer, order what ships are left to follow me," he was leaving the battle for he was saving his own skin. Vegas Hotel belonged to The Man and if he were not careful Augustus would seize him; "Set course for Alien Land." He did go and lick his wounds and see which way the wind blew before going home.

"I wish to tell only you a secret," Madam Chou.

Now Aelfric was no fool, what bring her down to a level where she could whisper something into his ear, like a metal probe that detonated or worse?

"Tell me from where you are," and he had the droid electrocute her, so she jumped and jerked a great deal.

"I am a robot," **and that shook him**. What were all these robots thinking of? He was Aelfric Europe a robot of all robots but then it occurred to him he had never publicly admitted it.

That depressed him and as he was a serial killer his depression was much worse than normal.

And he laughed and laughed a maniacal laugh as he began to believe she was a cyborg, "Yes, only a robot would send her girls to Posidonus knowing what he had in store for them? And Vespa as you say was a robot and you kept his company," and he forgot Wendy and Tintagel.

NOT ALL CYBOGS WERE BAD LIKE HIM.

And Aelfric took her down and confided as the master to his slave his plans to become ABSOLUTE, thinking his flame would ignite her robotic spirit and so join

and *love him?*

And Madam Butterfly Chou listened and agreed to everything he said. And in her heart burned VENGEANCE for Prince Vespa and her girls; and his **'remark'** at how she could send her girls to Posidonus had shamed her into resolve? How she wished she had her hands inside his skull ripping out his optic fiber nerves to stop the rest of him functioning like a human when he looked at her girls.

"Human trash," Aelfric as he switched on a screen and Madam Chou saw her girls and tormentors. "Would you like to join the fun?"

"No, I would rather be with you master," from Chou's quick-thinking brain.

And Aelfric needed someone like her at this moment as he was depressed, his battle was lost, he was fleeing and Augustus if survived the battle would seek his execution.

No one left Augustus to take all The Man' condemnation.

"I will give you Posidonus when he comes, he is no longer of use to my cause, you can play with him anyway you like."

"Posidonus?"

"More human trash," and looked her up and down and saw an eager light in her eyes and mistook it as anticipation and not revenge, "Play doctors with him and you can be the doctor."

And he laughed again at his joke; the defeat had affected him more than he knew, although a robot humans built him to suffer human anxieties.

"I must be there to see the FEAR on his face as he is strapped in and when you first run the scalpel over his body," but Madam Butterfly Chou was not listening, sure subconsciously taking guidance as to where to cut and prolong Posidonus's agony for she was with VENGEANCE, gloating euphorically.

She looked at Aelfric beaming joy.

"Why my dear I have made you happy? And gave orders that he be alone with his new robot. For the first time the robotic cyborg Aelfric Europe did not feel alone on life's journey, he had a robotic woman who would love him back, someone to plan a future with, to gaze at the planets as they passed, to share a delicious meal, he had Madam Butterfly Chou.

And she knew The Man would catch them up one day for The Man Condemned the Guilty and *was that sort of* chap. She remembered what Po Wei had told her about

Phoenix Hope and The Man would want his VEANGEANCE for its destruction.

VENGEANCE WAS A CYCLE.

IT CAUGHT UP WITH YOU
ONE DAY. EQUILIBRIUM
DEMANDED IT.

It said so in The
Man's writings.

CHAPTER 23

Alien Land

Color Backdrop: Vivid bright colored skies, spiraling fantasy towers, flying cars, red grasses, yellow waters.

Alien Land was the stuff romantic poets wrote about and story tellers still told of swash buckling pirates and frontier heroes, of strange looking hostile creatures with antennae with green wobbly flesh that kidnapped beautiful women.

AND THE KIDS LAPPED IT UP AND BOUGHT MORE HOLOGRAPHIC

CDs.

Because the writers were not allowed to write anything critical of their imperial government so wrote their complaints into science fiction instead.

Even The Man restricted what the pen could write. "Too much freedom defeats democracy," he would explain, and his critics replied, "But you are a dictatorship?"

"I know and the nearest dam thing you will ever get to a democracy for I listen to the groans of my people," from Tin-

tagel the Clone.

Now Alien Land was where planets existed ten times the size of Old Saturn 12 that had smaller planets as satellites.

"We have sixteen alien races under imperial rule, I want the other thousands in Alien Land," the Emperor Augustus Sutherland.

"When the day comes if ever that fool sends his imperial armies into Alien Land it shall be humankind that will be conquered in return, for we will be like annoying ticks on a giant's back," Tintagel the Clone, also *"And there existed giant empires in Alien Land and The Man knew of many and was their friend and this his greatest secret he kept from Augustus."*

Now Posidonus with Nesta had approached the boarders of the Rhegid Empire and saw a cluster of planets that were so close that their suns lit up surrounding space as daylight.

Dozens had hundreds of moons.

And Posidonus was blinded so looked away from this glorious beauty for he disliked light.

"We go there," he told Nesta at the controls seeing a dark side on a planet for it was night there, and she wondered how long he did keep her alive for he continually ranted on about playing doctors.

FOR HE WAS POSI-DONUS DELIBERATELY BREAKING DOWN HER MENTAL DEFENCES:
she needed a weapon
and a plan of escape.

Of those who had escaped the loading bay Posidonus flushed into space; and this was Posidonus's big mistake, for Aelfric saw the litter and realized who was in front of him, POSIDONUS.

And Madam Chou saw and planned revenge for Aelfric took her everywhere for she was his robot soul mate.

An extract from her confession
50221 A.D.

"I am no longer totally consumed by burning VEN-GEANCE but feel like the great detectives of old, Judge Dee or Sherlock Holmes. I did render justice swiftly like Dirty Harry out of an old classic movie, for I was on the trail of a madman worse than Jack the Ripper; and was always reminded I was in the presence of another insane creation that listened to classical music, and talked of ridding space of TRASH, but the music was trash made?

And his favorite music was from a yellow canary in a cage in his room.

*

And Posidonus picked up his scalpel, the ship would land automatically, Nesta he had drooled over this long voyage and could not wait till he landed, she might escape, she was a very resourceful girl.

Now Nesta tried to break free of the strong metallic masking tape binding her hands behind her back in her chair.

She was going to die, she would never see The Man again or the children she had planned to have, the garden and pets; she was truly going to die.

But?

A Rhegid patrol ship was scanning their craft and the captain on that ship did not like what his scanners showed; he was a true male whether an alien or human or cyborg, a man with true grit so sent a boarding party to investigate, in fact do more than investigate.

And since Posidonus was expert in his world had gotten into the habit of not locking doors, he was opening it to throw the remains of TRASH out anyway.

"What the?" The Rhegid officer leading the boarding party. Nesta jerked not believing what had been said.

So, Posidonus faced the strange bird like chirps. "What the?" He replied.

"What the?" The officer again.

Nesta beamed, The Man must know these people as their language was in the language implant, he had given her.

Hope rushed into her, FEAR subsided, she began to strain and leap against her masking tape making it obvious she was a prisoner. She did not need to be a human female to see the disgust in the sailor's faces, men used to a bar and floozy women.

Now unfortunately for Posidonus he was waving his scalpel in protest at this strange intrusion into his fantasy world, and was wondering if he was dreaming and the best way to find that out is to pinch oneself.

That is why he was shot where he was holding the scalpel. Well, his hand plopped to the floor as well and goes to show *"Don't go playing with knives?"*

Planet Rhegid

He also fell to his knees holding a cauterized stump, just as well laser weapons where the fashion and since no one in the boarding party had any sympathy for him, he was dragged to his feet and try as he might to retrieve his hand, saw it stood upon and kicked aside as if it was human **trash**, which it was as it was his!

Aelfric Europe, expert in robots would have been happy.

As for Nesta she did not even need asking for help, she was freed and covered up, so, she had her dignity back and had no need to cover her body with her hands; she was in the company of men with true grit.

Her FEAR of dying also went and she began to shake from shock.

And to Posidonus's horror, "Human girl welcome to the Rhegid Empire, we are friends of The Man," and Nesta fainted with relief and shock and next woke lying in a warm bed tucked up under a sheet, cozy but even more so, SAFE from FEAR.

And all the evidence of what Posidonus had done to the

other survivors of Vegas Hotel that had boarded this craft was recorded, all the tissue samples taken; Posidonus was going on trial as a deterrent to others for,

NOT ALL ALIENS BEHAVED
AS HUMANS OR
CYBORGS.

But he was still thrown in a cell in chains as he was recognized to be a dangerous mind, and the jet was put in a Technological Museum for kids to see on school outings.

But Posidonus had his wish; he had made it to Alien Land.

Now by the time Nesta had recovered and been taken to visit the Rhegid Emperor she was dressed fitting a human female which meant she looked like a Manga drawing, and if you have never seen a Manga drawing, everything is exaggerated and in the fashion of Buck Rogers and bodices made of tough ceramics to stop a laser.

She was a handsome girl, and all understood why she was a friend of The Man.

This she found embarrassing which meant she flushed often.

And the bodice was embedded with diamonds, so it sparkled and her arm and leg plates with rubies and emeralds and a gold skull cap given her.

Her cloak of Rhegid red wool softer than human silk hung from her shoulders.

FREE GIFTS form the Rhegids were doing their best to separate themselves from the bestiality of Posidonus who was human; she was also a friend of The Man,

so, she claimed.

And to banish FEAR weapons had been given and accepted and Nesta had enough intelligence to know if she used them, well? She was one and they millions,

she was a bright girl.

And Nesta looked for a woman, the rumored Rhegid princess who was one of The Man's ex's; ex's already and Nesta had not even been on a date with The Man, she was all human female?

Imagine: Mosaic walls depicting Rhegid life. Smell: Polish
and varnish.

Now she was escorted to the emperor by a platoon of warriors dressed in a variety of colored woolen cloaks and all carried weapons.

Now when they entered a large courtyard fresh air and animal sounds, birds, and pets she heard and clapping for the Rhegids were showing their appreciation of how good she looked, and she now felt good and walked with pride.

Now because all these well-dressed people formed a processional line at the end of which she could see a man siting, she knew she was about to meet the Rhegid Emperor, a friend of her man The Man; indeed, Nesta had confidence in her abilities and unlike Po Wei did not have to resort to devious ways to become a ruler of millions, unless the ways of a woman can be classified as DEVIOUS.

Tintagel the Clone.

And a hundred feet further on Nesta saw him.

ONLY A YOUNG BOY.

And the closer she got she noticed his eyes were lit up

with eagerness, **and where had she seen that look before?** What could he do to her, he was only a boy even not as tall as his courtiers; and they Nesta saw, apart from their red skin and lankiness and hair color that ranged right through the color palette looked no different from any human?

And their eyes, the eyes of cats.

"I am the Emperor An t-each Mall which meant The Slow Horse, for a wise horse moves slowly through space and is also quick to gallop when his warriors are needed," his voice had not broken.

"I am Nesta, personal pilot to The Man, Dictator New Saturn 12."

"As you have told us."

PAUSE as the eyes of the boy emperor roamed her; *'he is only a naughty boy,'* she told herself.

"The Man is our friend, so you are welcome here till he collects you. In the meantime, travel with me," and An t-each Mall rose on a metal disc and his court dropped to their knees as a hundred wind instruments gave the signal to do so.

As for Nesta she found the disc floated in the air and An t-each Mall took her through his garden, where she saw strange plants and animals, handfuls seemed ferocious for they were chained snarling.

"I have many wives and appreciate beauty, The Man is lucky to have you as his pilot and so close to him," the emperor went on and Nesta, *'He's only a boy whose voice hasn't broken.'* Just how young did Rhegid boys have to be to get interested in girls? And this was an absolute ruler who got what he wanted.

Then the emperor stopped and clapped his hands and a scribe naked apart from a lion clothe appeared from the foliage.

"Look into the machine he carries," and Nesta investigated what seemed a portable screen and saw Posidonus shivering in a cold cell.

"He is on the Coin Nu Ko-yn, The Dog Planet awaiting judgement and sentence will be delivered and his execution will be his game he inflicted on others; he will not escape." An t-each Mall.

And Nesta saw wild beasts' approach Posidonus ready to tear him apart; nature's real doctors and at first felt no pity for this evil man until, he began to whimper.

Posidonus had no dignity in the face of approaching sentence.

"The Man my friend will be pleased," An t-each Mall and neglected to tell Nesta The Man was nearing his Rhegid boarders coming to get Nesta.

The absolute emperor was being a naughty boy indeed.

He also did not tell Aelfric Europe had arrived at the border with a fleet of ships demanding an audience with 'these unknown aliens?'

Nor that the Master Priest had landed and was confined to quarters which meant he was being subjected to truth serums. So knew all about the virus and The Master Priest was making an antidote for he too had seen the sentence of Posidonus approaching.

And The Master Priest was not pleased doing something for free but then he had seen those claws on that were- like- creature and fangs and fur.

SHAME.

And The Slow Horse Emperor would feed the antidote to Nesta in a special dish for he was a collector of fine China ware, and now Nesta had a flaw, the virus needing fixed.

As he boasted to her, "I collect beautiful things.

I have sixty-six
wives already. I am
incredibly good in
bed."

'Listen girl he is only a boy whose voice is not cracked yet?' Nesta told herself for the hundredth time.

And all about her evidence the boy emperor collected things for the plants, animals, strange alien slaves, vases, statues, different architectural styles in the columns and roof supports were evidence.

And a group of small children burst out behind ferns, 'daddy papa,' they shouted and gathered about An t-each Mall whose disc floated down, so he could hug them; and Nesta said to herself 'So boys here are sexually active, well done Nesta, you certainly pick them?'

He was truly the ABSOLUTE dream of Aelfric Europe, and his empire was ten times the size of Augustus Sutherland's empire.

And he had read The Man and being absolute believed he was ENTITY, the law and justice that all could come to for help. But he had a problem; he fancied Nesta as wife 67 and wondered what his friend The Man would do?

Do you see Rhegid society was bound up in a warrior code of protocol, honor, and valor, he was not as absolute as he cared to be? But there were sneaky ways to get what you wanted as young boys knew extremely well?

AND HE WANTED NESTA.

And that night Nesta ate a special dish and something ridiculously small in her died, the virus, was not mourned and glad it had died for it had begun to be more human with the passing of time, and no longer wanted to eat Nesta all up and billions of other citizens in the bargain. It was a distant speck of protein on the humanoid evolutionary chain; it was more human than it knew, it was human?

It also was not into cannibalism.

CHAPTER 24

Friends

The boy emperor

Color Backdrop: Yellow, purple, red grasses of Planet Rhegid; millions of tall Red colored men.

Aelfric Europe was informed of The Man's approach so quickly he disentangled himself from Madam Butterfly Chou and hurried to switch on his private screen.

"I have him at last?" He screamed and did not think

it might be the other way round?

"Who?" Madam Chou asked.

"The Man," he replied and gave instruction for part of his fleet to close upon The Man's ship New Saturn.

Now Madam Chou decided she must save The Man and the future of space. She would destroy this vile robot Aelfric but how? She gazed at the coffee table with the lacquered top of the Mona Lisa; for Aelfric being modelled on a human liked his luxuries and with that went vice.

He liked human wine.

> Human
> women.

> Human
> food.

> And he trusted Madam Butterfly Chou and trust belonged to flesh and

blood

> Not cogs and ball bearings.

She plunged a wine glass deep into the back of his neck and twisted. It was horrid, blood splattered her and digging deeper with the glass saw wires which she grabbed just as he turned to face her.

ASTONISHMENT WAS WRITTEN ACROSS HIS FACE.

"You are a robot like me?" He gasped.

Her reply was yanking the wires
out of his neck. BANG and PUFF
of SMOKE.

Whatever she had pulled certainly did something to him because he was sneezing flames and smoke was coming out of his mouth.

For good measure she rammed what was left of the

glass into the front of his throat and slashed this way and that.

Aelfric tottered and fell backwards as arms and legs jerked uncontrollably as his tongue streaked in and out of his smoking mouth like a snake.

Somewhere in him was a tiny control box, she wanted it and taking his dagger from his belt cut him down the front; she had no idea where to look.

She stuck her hand in

BANG.

It was a very brave
thing to do. Robots
run on high voltage.

Madam Butterfly Chou flopped on top of him like a fish out of water. Now Aelfric used his auxiliary power to regain partial control and dignity in his jerking limbs, and bowel movements and so throwing Chou off stood up and saw himself in a full-length mirror.

FEAR had him, he looked a mess and being very much human saw what Posidonus would see!

HE WAS EXPOSED.

NOTHING BUT A JUNK HEAP OF ROBOT WIRES. HE COULDN'T AN- SWER

HIS GUARDS WHO WERE DEMANDING IN.

HE HAD CONVINCED THEM HE WAS NOT A ROBOT AFTER VESPA'S ANNOUCEMENT.

HE HAD DOUBLED THEIR PAY ALSO.

NOW THEY WOULD SEE HIM AS A LOUSY ROBOT AND NO ROBOT BULLIED A

HUMAN AND SURVIVED.

"He typed into a keyboard for an electrician to be sent for and one was.

At that moment he caught a movement, Madam Chou was reaching for the wine beaker, and he started to give her a kick in the mouth so she would need a dentist, but there was a puff of smoke, and his leg froze sticking out like a sore plum.

Madam Butterfly Chou knew her ancestors were still with her and did not need telling what to do.

She stuck the beaker and contents into Aelfric's exposed groin, so LED lights blinked, and discs whirred.

There followed an almighty BOOOOOOOOOOOOOOOOOOOO-OOOOOOOOOOOOOOOOOOOOOOOOOOOOOOOM.

And Aelfric was thrown against the door and Madam Chou scrambled onto a bunk.

bed and did what The Master Priest did so often, and experience in working in beds had taught her, she EXITED his ship on a tube, a lifeboat.

*

"Ships and a tube approaching," The Man was informed.

"Take the tube aboard and search it well and send a welcome to our friends The Rhegid," The Man.

There followed a twenty-one-gun salute but the boy emperor wanting not to be outdone replied with a hundred-gun salute, then The Man moved his ships to do battle with

what remained of Aelfric's Traders?

*

Smell: Overpowering stink of electrical fuses burnt out.

"We cannot get an answer," the guards complained to the electrician outside Aelfric's door.

The captains and admirals where here too, not happy as they had been given an order to surrender unconditionally from The Man.

And at last, the electrician got the door open, and all saw Aelfric sitting on the edge of his bed in a hooded robe, the room also stunk of burnt electric train engines.

"Fight, fight I order you," and Aelfric dismissed his captains and admirals who just wanted away.

And the electrician was confused, a medic was needed not him. "Come here."

The electrician approached, the door slid closed, and Aelfric grabbed him by the throat and disarmed him. Eventually the sailor looked up into his own pistol and the ELECTRICAL WOUNDS OF AELFRIC.

He understood.

He knew the truth of Vespa's radio statement. He had been serving a dam robot.

He was a dam fool.

He was going to die and begged Aelfric for his life. "Mend me as much as you can then I will let you live."

The electrician went to work; he had his chance to live by putting the red wire into the blue socket and the green wire into the black socket but did not, he had been offered life and besides the pistol was pointed at him all the time, so worked correctly.

He was just an electrician with two wives, one on New Earth and the other on New Jupiter who did not know about each other and each other's kids. He should be going home he hoped on leave, it was the Augustus's birthday soon when Aelfric usually allowed a month's leave.

He wanted home when the tree went up and the kids got their presents in their stockings and then they ate the turkey afterwards. You see he was not motivated by VEANGEANCE, and Aelfric shot him in each eye just in case a medic read the last images on the back of the retina and saw he was a robot and Vespa had not lied.

Now Aelfric dressed in gold chest armor opened the door.

"Madam Chou has shot the electrician and escaped in a tube and how is the battle going?" And wished he never asked and was not believed about Madam Chou either!

His captains and admirals had put two and two together and were not dying for a metallic man; *'pull the wool over the other eye Aelfric?'*

Robot was scrawled across a wall.

Aelfric knew his time was up, blasted human crew.

And guess what, the electrician had died for nothing!

At least he would not be around when his two wives found out about each other. "I am alone all alone," Aelfric muttered in an empty ship and surrendered to the Red colored Men that boarded, no resistance, they saw only a man speaking gibberish about being the ruler of space.

Well, Aelfric was taken to meet an ABSOLUTE RULER and did not know any FEAR as his bits and pieces were not working too well. Madam Butterfly Chou had really messed him up bad; and because he was more human than he cared to admit, was suffering shock.

*

"I am Aelfric Europe; I demand the respect due to me," Aelfric shouted at the boy Emperor An t-each Mall who was alarmed because Aelfric was twitching and pouting his lips at him. The electrician you see encased in FEAR had not repaired Aelfric well, wires should have been earthed but were sticking out and it was obvious here was a robot who had forgot its place in society?

So why Aelfric got the notion he was about to treated well from who knows? Just there was no indication of the beating that followed.

Who says what goes round does not come round?

I mean you do not rave and rant showing disrespect for one of Alien Lands most powerful boy emperors who did not like Aelfric anyway, who had smoke coming out

of his body armor and he smelt of electricity gone off, like when a socket blows and

burns the kitchen black.

And then Aelfric sensed something in the air, his robot bit did, and he sensed ION WAVES that are used to transmit matter through space.

"Legendary ion waves that humankind has searched for but failed. The ions in a body are copied by a machine and numbered then sent ahead, then the originals ions are broken down and sent and join the copy at the destination and re-assembled on the copy's blank number by number but at hyper speed.

Like numbered bricks, whole armies, food, ships, medicines, all the works, like ghosts," Tintagel the Clone.

And the Rhegid officer read the ion copy print out and knew he was in the presence of a robot. Now Aelfric collapsed, not from the beating but because ion waves interfered with his circuitry.

But they still pushed him into the ion machine with a tag on his back. "Robot trash," it said.

Rhegids did not trust robots, they had a robot revolt five years earlier so, saw robots as scum, worse, TRASH and knew how to deal with them.

WORKED THEM REALLY HARD OUT IN ALL WEATHERS SO THEY RUSTED UP AND PRESENTED NO THREAT TO NON-ROBOTS.

Aelfric had come to the right place for a rest, permanently and what goes round comes round for he was not alone in this thinking that life forms were TRASH.

So, he reassembled on the back of a grilled prison wagon pulled by eight legged beasts resembling water horses except they had tusks and a spiked spine.

"I am the ruler of New Jupiter and demand respect," Aelfric shouted up at the guards sitting, one holding the reins.

For an answer one of the guards peed on him which set the other prisoners against Aelfric, and he got another sound beating.

An t-each Mal the Slow Horse had told the guards to treat Aelfric as TRASH for he was a robot, and they were.

And Aelfric looked out of his puffed eyes and knew FEAR for he was in the presence of horrid locking alien ruffians who did not need an excuse from the guards to beat him up again.

"Posidonus," he heard that name mentioned and looked about his company. "Do you know Posidonus?" He asked.

"Yes," one of the guards, "a powerful man, friend of Emperor Augustus" but he was grinning, and Aelfric should have been warned, but he was enthusiastic to press on that he was a friend of Posidonus and be allowed out of here for he saw hope.

And the guard stopped the prison wagon and dismounted.

"Posidonus, friend of Augustus?" The guard and opened the wagon door and Aelfric shuffled his leggings towards the opening, he was getting out, he would make sure these men who beat him paid.

And as he stuck his head out and opened his mouth wide to breath in air that did not reek with sweat, the guard beat him about his head and shoved him back in with these words, "Show him what we do to the friends of Posidonus boys," and they did.

"This cannot be happening to me, I am Aelfric Europe," the robot moaned, and it was happening to him, at the end of his journey they threw him out of the wagon and showed him his new home, it was about the size of a dog kernel and full of fleas, and a plate of watery slop was ready for him to eat as it was raining.

Afterwards he joined a chain gang draining out a swampy lagoon that was full of midges, snakes, and crocodiles. And since Aelfric was a superior built robot cyborg having human flesh and nerves, he felt it all.

"Why are they treating me like this?" He would ask and the toad would crock and jump away from him. A pity he did not investigate when he had power his enemy The Man, for he would have found out The Slow Horse Emperor's mother, a woman called Veig had once been ambassador to the Man's court and there were rumors that The Man had alien women as lovers.

Why one was a snake with legs, another covered in fur and growled like a bear and The Man had children from these unions, and all had more than one head.

Strange The Slow Horse Emperor An t-each Mall only had one head, so his mother was not one of these.

CHAPTER 25

Dog Planet

Color: A giant orange Rhegid condor trails Aelfric's progress. Planet Rhegid is famed for its natural bright dyes from its grasses.

The orange condor

"The sound of a thousand 6-meter-long horns greeted Aelfric Europe as he got the welcome befitting a king," Tintagel the Clone.

And Rhegids lined his passage on both sides and threw rubbish at him as he headed towards the glass palace of

The Slow Horse Emperor.

"King of Robots," was burnt into a piece of broken chipboard screwed into his back; he was a robot, scores had plugs in their feet so you could shave from them, he was a ROBOT.

" Let us pull him to pieces," and "throw him in one of his own baths," for the Rhegids had not forgotten the robot war; so, mothers frightened naughty children with the word 'ROBOT', so all these people were preconditioned to hate Aelfric before they   saw him; *but had heard about his famous baths!*

"I should never have wanted to be ABSOLUTE," Aelfric muttered as his bare feet walked upon orange grass growing up between the stone cobbles.

He knew FEAR as this world was huge, he must have been mad to think he could be ABSOLUTE over space.

"You here?" Aelfric gasped as he saw The Man and the 5, The Slow Horse Emperor, and all the mighty warriors of the Rhegid nation.

Above an orange condor circled Aelfric and the bird was not molested for the Rhegid god Tupt is a condor that circles battlefields.

And The Man felt pity for Aelfric and Nesta saw and was pleased; she did not want to marry a brute.

"Only a robot with grand dreams eh Aelfric?" The Man asked and stood on lower steps, so his height did not dwarf the living god Tupt, the Slow Horse Emperor.

And the robot lunged at The Man.

Now Slow Horse did not flinch, he was an emperor and trusted his soldiers would deal with the robot king.

"He was a god, and goddess SLEUT the cat had not visited him out of the land of the dead to make an appointment with

him to die, so was not afraid," Tintagel the Clone.

And one a robot and the other a man with implants wrestled with each other and were not interfered with.

And Nesta felt FEAR for she was in love with The Man and worried he might be slain.

And the 5 were prevented by the Rhegid mighty from helping The Man.

And the boy emperor studied his father and his human side while the fight progressed.

"Please stop them?" It was Nesta at his feet and she had come unsummoned so why guards were about to lift her away.

Now sparks flew as The Man tore away Aelfric's scalp revealing a shiny metal skull with bone in the middle layers, part robot part human.

And the boy emperor dismissed the guards, Nesta should have been flogged for her public action, but the boy desired her and so both a Rhegid and human mind   had control of him. But it was too late to stop the fight for The Man was airborne, his silver wings flapping with Aelfric on his back strangling him.

"Nets," the emperor commanded, and beast experts approached and fired nets from shoulder held cannon and the fighters fell heavily to the steps leading to the throne entwined.

Now the 5 were not impressed with the Rhegid as they tore The Man free from the nets. And the Rhegid were not impressed with them for they had seen mutants aboard pirate ships, and wondered why The Man allowed them as his companions?

"Beast," Pyoo-ur Sister said standing hard upon Aelfric, and then the rest of the 5 beat him.

In fact, this evil man seemed to be getting beatings these days; *do not forget his ways for what goes round comes round.*

And the emperor signaled to his mighty men to stop the 5 and it took 26 of them to do so and now the Rhegid were impressed.

"Suit's hell cats," they now called them, Tintagel.

Now Nesta made too run to The Man, but Slow Horse the Emperor jumped up and held her back. This was sacrilege, what he did in private was one thing, but this was a very public display. He was the god TUPT, and she a human commoner and SILENCE prevailed as Slow Horse realized what he did; Nesta should be put to death for touching him so; *but it was the other way round was it not?*

And the orange condor above circled lower sensing dinner was afoot!

It knew there was no greater honor than to die for your emperor the god Tupt and gain immediate entry into the Heavenly banqueting Hall, and as Nesta was a girl, to serve the warriors there.

Things just never change whether on Earth or Heaven?

Yes, the silence was heavy as the Rhegids expected Nesta to fall upon the nearest sword and become a maiden in heaven, but she was not a Rhegid, she was a human with different ideas, if they wanted immediate access to their heaven well, they could commit suicide, she was going to marry The Man, was she not?

And Slow Horse had unwittingly provided himself a solution in how to possess Nesta as wife 67.

"TUPT.... the great winged war god of the Rhegid empire

who spent most of his time drinking, womanizing, and fighting with his chosen heroes against the foes of chaos," Tintagel the Clone.

And both Tintagel's knew about Princess Veig and her son and had not made such a birth public. Slow Horse An t-each Mal was TUPT was he not? Not a product of a liaison between The Man and his mother; but he had to come from somewhere and not from under a cabbage leaf?

"The Senate of Lords would kill Slow Horse if they suspected human blood was in him and had put down his pale complexion to a distant ancestor not a human gene," in time when the empire needed an arranged marriage between a human to survive such a marriage would take place, but right now the empire was strong and needed no one.

"She has been blessed by TUPT," someone shouted meaning Nesta still lived because commoners had touched Slow Horse and stopped breathing as   if they had been brought up to expect to die after touching their god so did.

But Nesta was a human girl brought up to want toenail polish and purple lipstick?

And he who shouted was Tintagel the Clone from the crowd and it was taken up in sighs and gasps and "It is true she still lives?"

Now The Man knew he had a problem with the boy emperor who was not a boy? And he looked for support amongst the Humanist Party here, they who wanted closer ties with humans, but they were silent, there were too many ordinary people here under the spell of the Purist Party led by one of Slow Horse's uncles.

And Nesta looked at The Man and asked herself if quick

divorces were available, a war worse than the Trojan Horse would break out if The Man forcibly objected for, she saw the look in the eyes of the 5.

As for the boy emperor he was looking at Nesta so missed the look of impending hostility in the 5.

"Remember your mother Slow Horse?" The Man whispered to the boy emperor who jerked upright. He knew of the rumor's and that was why Princess Veig had been sent to a nunnery on Dog Planet and he looked into the eyes of his papa.

Now we are dealing with an ABSOLUTE ruler who knew no FEAR because others did his fighting and he wanted Nesta, and that was all there was too it; his friendship with The Man was secondary and besides, it was The Man who courted his friendship was it not?

And at that moment the orange condor flew down and bit Aelfric's left arm off, so, blood and hydraulic fluid came out.

And all saw he was indeed a robot, and they took him and ionized him sending him to the penal Planet of Dog, where we know, he was put to work draining swamps.

*

And The Man and the 5 were escorted back to their
ship and what could be done to save Nesta?

And a translation machine mistook The Man saying, "poor kid, Nesta," translated it as daughter and so it was presumed Nesta was the daughter of The Man.

So, the Purists were horrified, and the Humanists overjoyed with happiness and then saw such a union would mean any children would inherit both empires to be ruled from here, New Saturn would be a gateway for Rhegid traders and settlers into human galaxies, thousands of Rhegids did get rich.

"You are my sister never mind, Suet is Tupt's half-sister and there is nothing wrong in us marrying to keep the empire in the family," Slow Horse told Nesta who could not believe what she was hearing? What was wrong with this child who pretended to be an emperor, but he was not pretending, he was absolute, and Augustus could learn a thing or

two from Slow Horse.

And then Slow Horse decided to visit his mother in the nunnery on Dog Planet, if anyone would understand why he wanted Nesta she would, and so made his first mistake, he exposed himself to little germs like the cold and smallpox for he had never left his palace that was so vast it was a zoo, library, amusement park, a city of cooks and soldiers, of officials and all in antiseptically clean air.

So not a germ could survive whereas Dog Planet is where they sent robots like Aelfric Europe.

FULL OF DISEASES.

CHAPTER 26

New Enemies

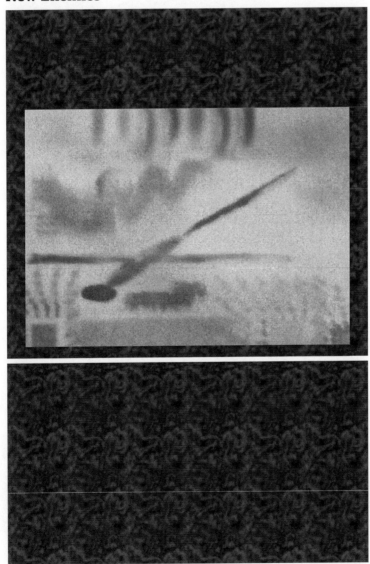

swamps

Now The Master Priest knew his worth and so when Slow Horse got sick, he was called for after Rhegid science failed to diagnose what was ailing the boy emperor. There was nothing wrong with him, yet he was not eating and was lethargic?

And The Master Priest was he not the greatest genius known saw at once the boy was pining for Nesta.

"I will find a cure for the emperor," he told the court officials and in return wanted freedom, a base and Dog Planet seemed just that, it had the likes of Aelfric and Posidonus, perfect subjects to conduct his foul deeds.

But he still felt let down by life, and all because of that abomination The Man.

Now Dog Planet is a hellish world, of swamps and were-creatures from the imagination; mutants run amuck and jungles with such thick canopies only heat seeking instruments can see the forest floor when an animal moves.

"Such a wonderful Garden of Eden," The Master Priest for he saw all these genes his to mold.

"Believe me it is Dante's garden," Posidonus whispered to the wind.

And the genius gave Slow Horse certain pills to boost his ego and drive so the emperor pranced wildly wanting Nesta in dandy cod pieces, but he was not lethargic any the more the more.

"He is only a boy?" Nesta forgetting their diverse cultures.

And The Man followed the imperial party to Dog Planet in his ship with the 5 and his crew, one ship against an empire? He could have summoned help but then WAR would have started, and billions would die. The Man was not Paris of Troy and Nesta not Helen, and both knew other ways must be found or The Man his teachings assigned to the mutterings of Augustus!

*

"Mother, why did you give me The Man as papa?" Slow Horse asked his mother in the nunnery, a Gothic structure atop a plateau that had its own clouds and circling orange condors.

"He was handsome
and kind." "Nesta is
handsome also."

"Let her go, go marry a Rhegid princess and let me home; I will do you no harm son."

But Slow Horse An t-each was ABSOLUTE and knew FEAR over the thought of losing Nesta; but it was only lust, and the FEAR would go after he had bedded then seek another to satisfy LUST.

"Do you want war with The Man?"
His mother asked.

"A puny empire."

"He is a friend and loyal friends
are hard to find."

"I am the emperor and am Tupt
incarnate."

"You are a naughty boy," his
mother.

*

And The Master Priest advised Slow Horse to come to Dog Planet to get Nesta, for he wanted to ingratiate himself with the emperor who he would use to destroy

The Man.

"Posidonus you again?" Nesta asked sickened by life. "I am alive no thanks to you."

"And so am I," it was Aelfric, but The Master Priest had not replaced his left arm, a one-armed robot was not as dangerous as one with two hands.

"Why have you come for me?" Nesta asked FEARING.

"To take you to Slow Horse," and Nesta was afraid, if these villains had the ear of the boy, then there was no salvation for her.

But she was wrong, The Man and the five had other ideas, they had landed on the penal planet as well, *secretly of course.*

Backdrop: *Orange mists drifting up from frog ponds, up to a Gothic nunnery. The many grasses are squelchy to walk on for it had just rained.*

The nunnery was something else, straight out of a Gothic Batman movie surrounded by blue leafed trees while orange condors flew overhead.

Now again these birds screeched to add atmosphere as if they knew it was required.

Also rocks below were stained white with iguana.

And the nuns used penal colonists to sweep it up and then exported it. All penal colonies had to pay for themselves and that was why the nuns were encouraged to have siblings to be sold.

"Some things never change, who would buy a wizened convict who had been collecting freshwater pond seaweed when his sixteen-year-old daughter would definitely sell?"   Tintagel the Clone.

And this is how the Rhegid Empire did expand; barren rocky outposts where slowly turned into a maze of life by Terra forming habitable plots of land to sell the overcrowded masses back on home planets; made of course by the unwilling hard labor of penal settlers.

"*There is always some skeleton in the family cupboard and this method of solving crime was one,*" Tintagel the Clone, "*but nothing is secret for always the box is opened and you wish you were never born, better to be bored and safe than play the fool?*" Advice for those wanting to be ABSOLUTE who needed spies to be ABSOLUTE and put FEAR into those they needed to be spies.

And the spies were the penal inhabitants of Dog Planet and The Man's whereabouts was known.

And in the bottom of the valley the mud brick walled adobe fort of the governor of this hell: where barren vegetation grew, and slaves and convicts toiled the rusty brown soil to get it to yield food.

Whereas the nuns lived in a cool cloudy palace, had fertile soil and the children of the nuns toiled the rural landscape and is called 'PRIVIAGE,' being the nuns of Tupt

of course.

You see the Rhegid Empire was only semi secular, these people were superstitious, and their lives regimented by saint days and how to eat and use the toilet and even what position to lie in bed with a woman? But the empire was changing; contact had been made with humans from the dictatorship. Not good models to judge humanity upon and The Man's ideas of liberty were infectious.

Now bells sounded as The Man and his party approached the nunnery and the inhabitants came to see what all the fuss was about as a flock of starlings chased flying insects above.

"Go and inform The Master Priest at once," it was the governor in his mud fort.

And word was brought the great perverted mind The Master Priest and at his feet folk fawning for potions; Dog Planet was not healthy, why the toad infested bamboo fields where full of cane flies that caused constant bowel irritations, until The Master Priest gave a potion, green it was and tasted like chocolate; genuinely nice.

"Your prey awaits you Aelfric," The Master Priest and since the one-armed robot did not move but sat staring from a sofa out the black marble veranda across those toad infested fields, the robot found his neck being jerked from a spiked collar attached to a cord for his new master to summon.

Posidonus chuckled, he did not have to FEAR his friend these days; in fact, his friend did the FEARING.

Supposed to anyway, but this was Aelfric Europe who dreamed of ABSOLUTE power.

A devious person, a work addict and schemer; someone not to be seen as washed

out.

Rising he kicked Posidonus who complained to The Master Priest.

"There, my little pet, what did the naughty robot do to you," The Master Priest, Aelfric knew was taking the Mickey out of Posidonus who was too stupid to realize.

And Posidonus chuckled as a small electric current flowed through the spiked collar, so the robot jerked and fell to his knees, affected because he was made of circuits and not all flesh and bone.

Now Aelfric sat with a hundred retainers, all badly armed with hoes and old rusty lasers. The governor had not sent any garrison men yet, waiting on the side lines to see which way the wind would blow. After all that was The Man and his renowned 5 *gruesome* mutant guards.

And Aelfric sat at the bottom of the hill leading up to the nunnery he had not attacked yet? Why, because Slow Horse the Emperor was approaching also with noise and ceremony.

And above the orange condors circled and Aelfric cursed them for they were giving his position away.

A mosquito landed on his good arm and sucked his robotic blood; it was blood, synthetically made but was blood so the female midge flew away and was able to reproduce.

A green frog croaked next to Aelfric.

A green dragon fly buzzed in front of Aelfric's face. A green eel slithered between his legs.

A green water rattler after the frog and eel also slithered near him.

It was a great pity Aelfric waved the other life away for he should have remained still, and he would not have been bitten.

And all wanted battle for Nesta was he prize.

"Who says the devil looks after his own/ After the punishments handed out to this monstrous robot and Posidonus surely divine justice exists?" Tintagel the Clone.

And Aelfric pulled the green snake head away from him and stared into the cold black eyes of the snake that had yellow slits staring at him. Both robot and reptile wanted each other as dead thingmabobs.

And Aelfric felt the venom in him closing his human made parts and he felt

FEAR: he had never experienced being bitten by a snake so did not know if he would survive but after fifteen minutes, he was still holding the snake he decided he was going to live.

"And the venom made him feel as if he was riddled with arthritis for, he ached and all his retainers could see it in his eyes, but since he had not fallen dead these penal inhabitants FEARED him for, he must be a god." Tintagel the Clone.

And the robot had an idea born out of jealousy, and he led his retainers to where Slow Horse was approaching, and it took an hour but still Aelfric held the snake, and

he threw the reptile onto the emperor and fled.

"Slay them all," General Farrell Sgian whose name means Knife Warrior shouted and his *professional* soldiers guarding the emperor slew the hundred retainers of Aelfric.

A great slaughter and all looked at the boy emperor too see if he would die, or god Tupt save him.

And the snake had bitten Aelfric and used its venom on the robot, so the boy lived.

"An anti-venom exists in the governors' fort," General Farrell mused and ordered the procession make haste there; the boy should be dead, even if the general was of the Humanist Party, which was the most venomous snake on this planet of a dog!

BUT?

"Princess Veig, what are we to do about Slow Horse?" The Man asked inside the nunnery.

"You are still very handsome."

The Man sighed.

"Does nothing ever change? And what made us dance as male or female is eternal, so nothing changes, life moves forward and diversifies in color, beauty, design, and architecture,"

Tintagel the Clone.

"Who are these?" She added looking the 5 over and felt FEAR and it subsided when The Man assured her, they were his bodyguard.

"We will see our son and use family ties to avert a bloody war," Veig and The Man hoped it would be so but that night they stayed in the nunnery.

"And in those days a nunnery was a depository of unwanted women, an unhealthy place where hormones battled for babies and the mind for marriage with Suet or Tupt

and other gods; when the women should be lying on their back doing natural functions for what is unnatural is from darkness," Tintagel the Clone.

And the 5 got more than boozy for the nunnery distilled wine and exported it to other planets making a profit.

"Give me a kiss handsome?" Pyoo-ur Sister and giggled for she was flirting with a Rhegid tradesman who did joinery at the nunnery.

And he did for she had looks even though her face was slightly scarred; it was the body what mattered.

"More wine," Zagor Blue skinned demanded form a serving girl sent here because her property owner wanted her families land to graze pigs upon.

And Hairless eyed her up; a Rhegid was still a woman and did not care if she did not ask to be here, the drink was in?

"Let's go upstairs and listen to your troubles dark one?" A girl making cash

each time Morair Nobleman had a drink, and he went upstairs for he was indeed troubled, for his lands had been confiscated because he and others had risen in revolt against property owners who forced those who farmed the land for generations into slavery.

And the girl listened, and Morair the Nobleman did what men do best under the influence of drink, make a pest of themselves till they get want they want and then

fall asleep.

And whether The Man lay with Princess Veig is for others to find the answer, but she saw his heart had been stolen by another but whom?

Tintagel, Posidonus? A joke..................

Aelfric's Char-
acter update

"Why hate me, what have I done wrong apart from too have ambition?" Aelfric wailed to the cosmic dust storm above to carry his complaint to God.

"I don't believe in a God that hates robotic men anyway," yet he still had complained to what he could not see in space.

"All I ever wanted was power so I would not have to do the bidding of others, what is wrong with that? I am a robot, a slave of humankind who wants to be a master. Master of all humanity with humans the slaves. What is wrong with wanting to reverse the situation?

Man says God made man and man made me so completing the circle God made me and that means I have a soul. I am not just a pretty face with circuits and control boxes behind it; I am Aelfric Europe once one of the most powerful men in existence and I have every intent to use Dog Planet to its fullest capabilities.

I get rid of the human trash that Augustus would crucify so what difference between us except our method of execution.

And Tintagel says those I bathed where innocent dancers and opponents, but they are human trash and I know what to do with my garbage? Recycle it............

*

"You have done what?" The Master Priest upon hearing what the robot had done, "Has it occurred to you the boy emperor is my protection against The Man?" And it had and that Aelfric knew the emperor did not protect him, in fact sent him here to rust.

We can only imagine what agonies Aelfric suffered that night for Posidonus was heard to chuckle, laugh, and clap his hands often.

And screams of a robotic man drifted across the bamboo fields.

*

But the break in Slow Horse's procession to the nunnery gave The Man and his friends time to be who they were?

And they started a civil war the 5 did?

Now when news was brought The Man what Aelfric Europe had done the 5 were sent down to the old governor's fort to see what was. And he was sent word there was **no** anti venom in the fort and so stretched forth his silver wings and took what the desperately needed serum there was from nunnery stocks and flew down the valley to save his son.

And there was much intense argument in the fort for General Farrell suspected the Governor Sgian Briste that meant Broken Knife had lied; a Purist Party flag was flying from the fort's flagpole.

Not that the governor was a member of any party, it was the only flag available as the moths and weather had made a mess of the imperial flag; and a flag was needed to show the penal settlers there was authority.

Now the 5 jumped the adobe brick walls and terrified the garrison guards who fired back killing General Farrell's men; and men with guns being fired upon will fire back.

"So, the first shots of the civil war between The Humanist and Purist parties existing in the Rhegids Empire had been fired, and if that flag had not been flying none would have shouted 'Purist scum' and those shouted in return "Humanist buggers," Tintagel the Clone.

And the battle was short lived for the governor fled with his garrison troops into the toad infested fields.

Now seeing all was well and seeing the boy emperor standing directing his troops; in fact, only repeating General Farrell's orders or none might have obeyed, and when the fighting died down and the boy seemed his usual ABSOLUTE self, The Man returned to the nunnery where Princess Veig waited for him and the infamous 5 went

with him, leaving sighs of relief behind.

*

And Slow Horse made a great show of himself on Dog Planet for he drank his way up to the nunnery in a great procession of courtiers and warriors and bands making a din; for he was Tupt and those that lived on Dog Planet were the products of his justice.

And they the penal inhabitants looked upon him with an insane hatred and their children and went back generations hated him, for they were confined to Dog Planet and had started farms and co-operatives to sell their produce and sometimes themselves when officials came from Rhegid needing salves.

"It was one sure way to get off Planet Dog!" Tintagel the Clone.

Now at the nunnery Princess Veig and The Man awaited the boy emperor. "Daddy," he muttered a whisper for The Man was imposing; and he was heard by those that carried his floater. Now they did not need to carry the floating disc as it floated by itself so were not subjected to any discomfort, but the poles sticking out of the disc were for symbolic purposes.

And those that heard the uttering of their emperor said nothing, later when they were alone did make sure what they heard became the hottest news about.

"Son, give Nesta back to The Man and I want away from here, I am not suited to this type of religious prison," his mother said and then bowed. She should have bowed first but was emphasizing the point he was a boy, and a naughty one at that.

"I do not have Nesta; The Master Priest has her and will give her to me shortly." "What him again, is there no limit to that man's ability to cling to life? And if he has Nesta she is in grave danger, so where is he exactly?" The Man annoyed and alarmed, and it did not go unnoticed on the disc bearers that The Man spoke down to their emperor.
And it did not go unnoticed on Slow Horse either.

"Leave me," he told his bearers and the crowd of courtiers beginning to crowd into the great hall of the nunnery.

The boy did not want the world to see daddy and mummy chide him, he was an emperor not just their son.

"I will drag you down from your disc and beat your bum good boy if Nesta is harmed because of your stupidity," The Man and the conversation went on like this for a while until Slow Horse threw open the nunnery hall's doors and stormed out, took four steps a time and halfway down the steps leading up to the nunnery, remembered he had forgotten his disc.

He was not going back up there, The Man had put FEAR into him, and parents always speak down to their children making them small.

So, Slow Horse the boy emperor ordered a chair brought and sitting in it demanded his bearers lift him. He did show his parents he did not need his disc; the last laugh was on him and led his procession to The Master Priests laboratory.

"It is fitting a human emperor is lifted on a chair, and not on a disc," was what Slow Horse heard and looked about furious; they knew, they all knew he was half human and not Tupt incarnate; Tupt their god would never incarnate in an alien human.

> *Why not? A human had a body and things just as a Rhegid did.*

*

"We must follow him, he will lead us to Nesta," The Man to the 5 and they followed, and the penal inhabitants left them alone and cast sour looks not at him and

his party but at Slow Horse.

They knew who The Man was and showed him the way to The Master Priest, anything that would annoy Slow Horse they would oblige for his justice had sent

them here.

And that is why Aelfric had been recruiting amongst them a sizeable mob that he was training and arming with cleavers and mining explosives. He still dreamed of being ABSOLUTE even if his subjects were the inhabitants of Planet Dog.

And one was the Governor who had been told he would remain here indefinitely for speaking up for Princess Veig, and since his little conflagration in the fort, *well?*

And scores joined the ranks of Aelfric's mob, for the soldiers here were of the lowest, deliberately sent here to abuse the penal convicts therefore enforcing punishment.

> *"Dog Planet had a reputation of being hell to live up to!"* Tin-

tagel the Clone

And The Man reaching the laboratory saw these retainers lounging about the grass picking and eating grass stalks.

"There are six of us, you leave this lot to us, and you go in and get Nesta before Slow Horse gets here, and at his speed the processional march will arrive tomorrow," Zagor Blue skin and he was not joking, Slow Horse had dissent amongst his courtiers, and he could hear the raised whispers that he was human.

*

"The Man is here master," Posidonus told The Master Priest who looked at Aelfric in an annoyed manner as if to say, "Why are you here and not out there bringing me my enemy in chains?"

And Aelfric saw the look and was annoyed, certainly positions had changed and Posidonus enjoyed Aelfric's discomfort for he was Posidonus and knew where his butter came from?

"Ah Nesta, sweet pretty Nesta," The Master Priest eyeing the girl appreciating why Slow Horse wanted her; now if he had time, he did take her first before giving her to the royal boy, but that was risky, she had such lovely limbs he did bite and feed upon. Oh, he was so hungry, and she was so tempting. She certainly beat the penals who were meat gone off!

"Come with me dearest," he said and droids prodded Nesta after him.

"Had he given in, would he blame Posidonus?" Tintagel the Clone.

Now Nesta knew FEAR for she was alone with him held by droids and knew his reputation.

He stroked her neck feeling her arteries and veins, so thick and containing scrunches food.

His fangs dropped out and he was dribbling. Nesta wiggled to free herself.

"Is this the end of Nesta?" Tintagel the Clone.

And The Man burst in, sent laser into the two droids who dropped Nesta, and The Master Priest jumped at his enemy to bite The Man's neck.

A mistake, his exist was not blocked, he should have run, Nesta was free.

And she kicked him ridiculously hard with these precise words, "Bite me, would we?"

"Well aimed, are you harmed for we must hurry so the 5 can disengage and retreat with us to Princess Veig and my ship before Slow Horse gets here," The Man.

"I am alright, Posidonus and Aelfric are here also," and Nesta kicked The Master Priest again. She did like to have killed him, but she was a good girl and pity rose in her heart so left with The Man.

And The Man was made of sterner stuff and as he was closing the door sent a laser bolt into his enemy for all the women he had drained of blood.

"Ah," The Master Priest groaned as the door shut, he was not bleeding, the laser cauterized as it went through him; so, bent down and picked up his left foot that the laser had taken from him.

"Where's the blooming droids, never here when you need them," and he pressed a button and Posidonus heard and came.

"Master," and The Master Priest gave him a look that said, "Never would I trust

you to be my medic," "NOW GET ME A DROID."

Now outside Aelfric was not having the time of his life, these 5 mutant warriors' danced rings about his retainers. If only he had an army like them? Once again, the dreamers dream, and empires are made.

And the governor hearing The Man was here at last sent Aelfric reinforcements; the garrison was on its way for the governor hurt much at being left to rot on this Planet Dog. Now this news made Aelfric bold, so he showed himself urging his retainers on.

"Let's get out of here," The Man and seeing Aelfric sent a laser bolt at him.

And the one-armed robot screaming fell backwards down a hill, rolled into a thorn bush, and was impaled there where he *feared* to move less the thorns rip his flesh; but he was safe?

*

Now Slow Horse wanted to cry, he was angry and hurt, He had a papa, and he knew The Man had never been a father to him, Never played with him, given much time to him, always fighting away. Besides Rhegid law would prohibit their emperor cuddling into a human dictator.

Then why not, he was
the emperor. He did not
want a war with his
dad. Dada.

Daddy.
Papa.

He really did have a dad and his religion had separated him from a normal childhood.

A papa to take him to the parks and play games with.

He had a mother also, but religion had tucked her away in a nunnery for silence.

Was being emperor worth it?

He was a boy for he talked to Jimmy the fantasy mouse under his bed. He wanted to be hugged by his dad and have stories told him; and for a moment he forgot about Nesta and his wives and wanted out of his robes; he was a boy who was an ABSOLUTE boy.

"He is crying, it is his human blood," he heard whispered. "The emperor is a boy," and he agreed.

"Tupt will no longer bless our planet."

"He should quietly abdicate to avoid scandal."

"I am your emperor, and you do what you are told before I send you all to live here."

And the whispers stopped, for the moment for members of the Purist Party was here and wanted the boy removed.

Also, present members of the Humanist Party who opposed the Purists because were on different sides.

*

And above a tube existed the battle wagon New Saturn, Madam Butterfly Chou was coming to visit Posidonus for a cup of tea.

One planet was just like any other to Madam Chou, cities and domes, spires and traffic, whores and bars and of course willing customers always.

"*But Madam Butterfly Chou had never been any good at geography and besides nothing existed in the human worlds about Dog Planet; woof.*" Tintagel the Clone.

CHAPTER 27

Nuclear Winter

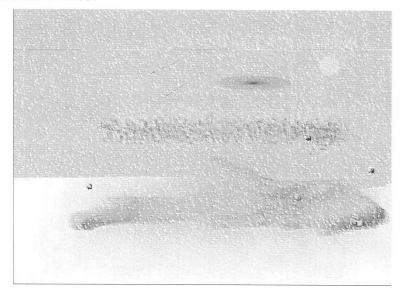

Snowed out

Since the adobe fort was out of bounds the Governor sought refuge in the laboratory with The Master Priest.

And all because he had raised what flag was available a party flag and so started a civil war?

And The Master Priest was not impressed with what he saw; he did not see the garrison troops as fit; they had suffered years of excessive use of the nunnery wine and penal inhabitants. You see The Master Priest saw everything as food but compared to the locals these men should be like softened tenderized veal.

And The Master Priest heard his stomach rumble, he had not been to a feast in a long time.

It was just bad timing, The Master Priest was packing his bags and getting the locals to transfer his crocodile suitcases to an old ship that he had been repairing. It had crashed here years ago in a cosmic storm, its survivors adding to the population as desperately needed fresh genes.

Now the governor had looted the ship and kept quite so none knew of its existence, except for The Master Priest that is.

"Master?" Posidonus called and the silence made him realize something was amiss? "Master?" He called again and saw the empty laboratory rooms, equipment missing.

"And you see why there were so many crocodile suitcases!" Tintagel the Clone.

So Posidonus breathing hard fled out of the laboratory intending to follow the packers who had left a trail of flattened vegetation through the long safari pink grass, where blue flamingos rose to the air in panic, for Posidonus grunted and sweated for he was unfit.

Now the yellow flowers of this type of blue grass produce pollen so Posidonus went into an allergic reaction, sneezing and coughing so his eyes watered much as he stumbled, fell, and felt little legs walking across his face.

Terrified he brushed the insect aside, but it was a scorpion and its sting sunk into his hand. The chances were that if he had left it alone it would have crawled off him; but this was Posidonus who did not have nerves of steel.

"A man who ate all the wrong things because science allowed him too, cream buns and definitely no vegetables!" Tintagel the Clone.

And the venom made Posidonus vomit often so dizzily he called "Master Priest where are you? It is Posidonus."

And then he saw salvation, a tube was in front of him, he could escape, go away, and have nothing to do with Aelfric or The Master Priest.

"But he had no cash these days and did not eat his vegetables?" Tintagel the Clone.

Thus, with a dream of starting afresh on a new world he fell into the tube in a sitting position and the venom inside him began to make his muscles relax, *"All the better for the scorpion to eat its prey, normally insects, birds and small mammals,"* Tintagel the Clone.

And then a snake was dropped onto his lap, and he screamed and tried to get up so stood and fell on the reptile and so it bit him.

Madam Butterfly Chou took the reptile from behind the head and directed it to bite Posidonus six times more on the face.

"Why?" He groaned.

"The dancer," VENGEANCE replied.

And because Madam Butterfly Chou was gloating and not paying attention the snakes' head turned and bit her wrist.

So startled dropped the snake back onto Posidonus as she staggered backwards terrified, she was going to die.

She could feel the pain and heat in her arm as the poison rushed through her body.

Her heart began to pound faster out of panic not venom.

She imagined her breathing was difficult and it was, she was having a panic attack so, gasping for air, she sank to her knees.

Then fell onto her back and with wide eyes stared at the racing yellow clouds in the green toxic atmosphere above and felt dizzy. All she had to do was to shut her eyes and calm down, but Madam Butterfly Chou did not like snakes, she was convinced she was dying.

"Bugger Posidonus," she shouted swallowing her tongue as she gulped air and choked and began to turn blue.

Posidonus seeing all laughed, he was not going out alone.

Backdrop: white freeze up.

"The laboratory has fallen, I believe the 5 led the charge through the gates," I owe you much but did not add papa.

And tears ran from Slow Horse's eyes as the sounds of distant canon reached him, civil war and it was all his own doing.

"I am just a boy," he cried.

"Son, I am here, my fleet will arrive in two months, and I will drive the Purists from your world," The Man for them outside the laboratory to hear.

"Will you really help me after all I have done?" And still did not say papa and The Man had not learned anything.

"We are friends, friends always help each other, and you are my son, a good kid at heart," The Man and showed he had learned nothing by using the word 'kid.'

And Slow Horse looked at the 5 and did not want them as friends. They were horrid looking mutants, worse looking than The Man.

"The governor Sgian Briste escaped," we have nothing to do here so we will chase him down," Zagor Blue Skin as Pyoo-ur Sister looked the boy emperor up and down making him nervous, he did not want her as a wife no matter how exaggerated her curves and bosom.

"Where is Nesta?" He asked.

The Man did not reply as he watched the 5 charge out of the camp to seek the governor. "Tomorrow we will return to your capital, and you can be an emperor?" The Man meaning equity not a boy playing at absolute power, and again had learned nothing for he was speaking down to a boy.

Now outside away from the emperor "How are we going to take his capital?" Tintagel the Clone asked suspiciously.

"You told me General Farrell has driven out the Purists, all that boy has to do is act regal because the masses of his people see him as Tupt incarnate," The Man replied wondering what Nesta was up too, glad he had left her aboard his ship; that boy was an adolescent teenager whose hormones could not be trusted because he was too used to being ABSOLUTE

.

Nesta's diary.

"I knew he was mine the moment he entered my room and shut the door, deliberately making sure I saw him lock the door.

I did not say anything but sat there on the edge of my bed challenging him with my eyes. I was not going to give in that easy, a girl is the boss, and the men follow; so, the silence was getting to him.

We women could be so cruel, and he looked funny in his pink pantaloons. So, I helped him out by giggling and then turned the lights down.

Nesta's diary.

Princess Veig was made Consort to Tupt which meant I

was safe because the people remembered her with affection and Slow Horse already had one civil war on his hands!

The boy emperor had managed to call The Man 'papa' because it suited his whim to have a father about and then The Man announces he after the Purists had been defeated would leave for his own world. "With a Rhegid armada and my own forces I shall force Augustus to abdicate," and that meant Slow Horse would be under his own *absolute* hormonal influences again.

Nesta's diary.

The nuclear winter was the result of a proton reactor due to neglect exploding in the north of Dog Planet. This huge reactor had been built here to send energy back to Rhegid

. *"Of course, no sound mind wanted such a dangerous monolith on Rhegid, let it be with the dogs up there,"* Tintagel the clone.

So cold unpredictable winds suddenly blew south dropping temperatures well below freezing point.

Leaving a swath of ice and frozen life that had been too slow to move away, such as Posidonus, who had been found with a snake on him and lying next to the tube, Madam Butterfly Chou, also frozen.

And The Man had taken us all to see to verify the claims that the evil Posidonus was dead at last.

"Take him to the north pole of this place and leave him there. Tell no one, it will be our secret and put a sign about his neck with these words, "An evil man, let none awake him," and then The Man lifted Nesta's chin so he could look into her eyes, and he saw all the pain there Posidonus had given her. "You must go forward with me."

"Shall I have Madam Chou taken aboard and cloned Master?" Tintagel the Clone. "Indeed do, we will bury her elsewhere, all worlds owe her a debt of gratitude. We shall make pomp and show out of it. A lesson and warning to evil men who pervert the sexes for profit. I just cannot imagine any world without Madam Chou and her girls," The Man grinning at Tintagel the Clone who grinned back, for only men could think like that.

"Such the acts of VENGEANCE, a pity she knew so much FEAR when she died," Nesta added.

Nesta Diary.

And we on small cutters from the New Saturn saw below more of what the 5 had found looking for Sgian Briste the Governor of Dog Planet; a blue rusty ship whose doors had not been closed when the cold freezing wind had descended upon it. So penal laborers were now frozen testimonials to the nuclear winter.

"They say it is The Master Priest's ship," Hairless, one of the 5... "We must go down and see if he is dead inside," Zagor Blue Skin. Then the wind blew again so all shivered.

"Wrap up well friends," The Man and I Nesta thought nothing of any danger, my man was with me.

And we landed and made our way to the ship in knee deep snow as the wind frosted our visors on our helmets.

Then we all saw him, standing at the entrance that was open to the wind, dressed for the summer.

THE MASTER
PRIEST.

In a white cotton smock, as if he were a druid reincarnated and unaffected by the freezing weather?

And behind came Governor Sgian Briste, always there is another Posidonus, existing under the woodwork like slaters; also holding a large butcher's knife. Now jumping he charged at us demonstrating threat tactics that we should leave or be killed.

But the snow was deep, and he disappeared in a drift, emerged choking and wet, and to be wet here is fatal and he flopped about like a fish trying to get back to the ship he emerged from.

"It was also obvious The Master Priest was not amused by such clownish behavior," Tintagel the clone, *"and The Man was half bionic, so his eleven fingered hand reached out and took the knife hand, clamping shut like a vice."*

"I condemn the guilty," The Man shouted and forced the knife back into Sgian Briste's body, opening a dam so fluids gushed out and froze, making an ice bridge to the governor, who quickly froze as well.

"It was an execution for the benefit of The Master Priest for his appointed time to go home was near," Tintagel the Clone.

"I condemn the guilty," The Man shouted and using his bionic legs sprang at the doorway and his victim taken by surprise fell backwards fumbling as he did so to press the button to shut the ship door.

"You see one might hear tales of The Man's agility but unless you see it you just don't believe, because you cannot do the same feats," Tintagel the Clone, *"for most of us have difficulty lifting our message bags."*

"Help me," The Master Priest and those that would help him where his penal helpers hoping to catch a lift off this Planet of DOGS.

"Kill," they came as if zombies out of a Hammer horror film.

"It was The Man who swung these unfortunates this way and that until his friends came aboard and thawed out,"

Nesta.

"He is doing remarkably well by himself, does not need us anyway," Morair Nobleman and that annoyed me Nesta, so stood beside my man and fought like a she were-cat.

With shrugs of embarrassment the 5 went to work; such a one-sided fight and I am sure mercy would have been granted if the penals had JUST asked for it, *but they did not*, The Master Priest had promised them a passage and they fought hard to escape the years of misery they had suffered.

*

A cockpit bathed in red infra-red light. Colored LEDs

And a genius had donned flying goggles and leather jacket and had no idea how to fly; droid 34A was missing but he belonged to same class as The Man, Tintagel, the 5, even Augustus and Aelfric, they were people who did not behave as ordinary people did because they were different.

Wow.

Where had they all come from? These comic book heroes and villains?

"At last, we are alone," The Man behind the Master Priest wondering which lever to pull to get the ship airborne, any lever would do for he was in a hurry to escape.

"Mercy, I beg," The Master Priest.

"Of course, and The Man drew his short sword to dispatch the evil scientist quickly, thus showing mercy.

Any lever would do? What about a throttle handle and The Master Priest pulled it all the way back so the ship boomed to life zigzagging across the snow throwing The Man onto the back of his victim?

"From such an advantageous position The Man could

smell the iron on The Master Priest's breath as the later turned to bite him," Tintagel the Clone.

"I am hungry, I will feed upon you, die dictator die," the vampire that was The Master Priest said gloating bringing his fangs down. And by gloating and boasting and wasting time he gave The Man valuable seconds to lurch backwards.

That is when the ship came to a stop in a snow drift, completely burying itself; but the action threw The Man forward and his short sword went home so that the leather flying gear of The Master Priest was pierced.

"This is my mercy to you foul beast," The Man pushing his sword home and then left the vampire to die on his chair. Now The Man opened the windows, so the freezing air blew in and left the cockpit shutting the door behind him.

Thus, The Master Priest began to freeze and as he did so realize the cockpit would be his icy tomb.

"Is he dead?" I Nesta hoping.

"Yes, it is time we returned to Planet Rhegid and prepare the downfall of Augustus," The Man seeing vast armies and armadas.

"We have many prisoners," Zagor Blue Skin.

"Give them substance and tell them they can have the fort, they can make their own government and rule themselves," The Man and dozens of penals overheard and it went about them a fast whisper. The Man was giving them not only life but freedom and their FEAR of him vanished.

Nesta's Diary

"I was not in a hurry to marry The Man, he had wars to

fight and I did not want to frighten him off. But what I was making sure was that he had an intelligent partner so read as much as I could about life. No one was going to say I was a jumped-up courtier, I was going to get the ordinary citizens to say I was kind,

and just and with Tintagel the Clone as a teacher I could not fail.

CHAPTER 28

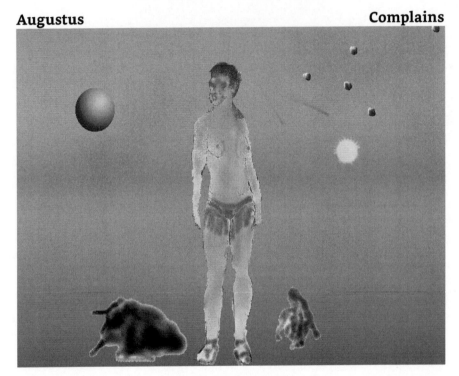

General Wilhelmina

"I am Augustus and where are my admirals? Where Po Wei and the traders? All gone, dead or run away. Now I am alone, and The Man approaches with evil intent to rid me of life.

Is there no one to help me?"

"I will help you," and Augustus turned and looked at a young woman whose stare was stern and unflinching.

"I am sure I know you," Augustus replied and the young one was hurt; she was one of the Praetorian Guard so always close to the emperor who now failed to recognize her, such her importance in his life.

"I will lead your armies against The Man and be victorious," she said now suffering mixed feelings of ridding the throne of a debauched emperor who showed no gratitude to her for years of service.

"You, you expect me to make you my general?" Augustus on the point of laughing and the young one remained calm when another might have run a sword into Augustus.

But none of the other Praetorian Guard laughed for they knew the young woman's reputation and what generals present looked the young one over and were affronted by her cheek.

"What is your name, Attila the Hun?" Augustus joked and his courtiers laughed except for his guard for they were trained to be sterner stuff.

"Sergeant Will, Wilhelmina Dodd," the woman's reply and Augustus stopped his theatrics for it dawned upon him what sex the soldier was? And twirling suddenly Augustus took off the soldier's helmet and was confronted with a handsome face, but the ginger hair was cut short, but the face was still feminine, the soldier was a boy, surely a member of a religious church castrati choir so the voice would never break; and the hymns sung so angelically, for Augustus borrowed these choirs when he walked up the processional way to his throne so all would believe he was divinely appointed.

And Augustus now with a new toy to fascinate him undid the warrior's cape so he could notice better the chest amour designed for a, girl?

"By the gods you are?" Augustus as he noted the armor mold for bosom "unless you are of the third kind," he is meaning being of one sex but in the body of another.

"I am Sergeant Will of the 1ˢᵗ Martian Cohort assigned to protect my emperor," Sergeant Will coughed out and Augustus marveled, indeed the voice was husky, but because its owner voiced it to be so; yes, Will was a Wilhelmina and to prove it Augustus undid the trooper's body armor, so it fell to Will's feet, and she flinched not.

"My I never noticed," Augustus appreciating the girl standing at attention in front of him in short kilt and white vest with a strange bird motif on it. It was the motif of the cohort, but Augustus never noticed such details of the people he asked to die for him, well that is what they were paid to do was it not?

"And how will you save my throne from the beast that approaches?"

"Train your men like praetorians and replace your incompetent generals with real generals," Will looking at a spot above her emperor's head.

Now Augustus knew what she meant, his privates were soft and generals those who had bought appointment and he saw greatness in her and was reminded of Boudicca the warrior queen and of Amazon female archers who cut off a bosom so the bow string would not be interfered with as they let loose an arrow at a Greek mercenary hoplite.

"Pick up your armor General Wilhelmina," Augustus on a whim for he was thinking bad thoughts and generals present began to draw their weapons to kill the upstart soldier, but the praetorian guard present were quicker for they trained hard as soldiers.

"Armies of such?" Augustus dreamily inspecting the guard and he liked what he saw and wondered why he never noticed any of the handsome men and women that made them up?

"Augustus was absolute, and power had ruined him, did not those Emperors of Rome brought up at court make bad rulers and those emperors taken from the ranks make just rulers?" Tintagel the Clone.

*

Character update. From the diary of Wilhelmina, General of the Empire. "I was born a girl and wanted to travel space I think to get away from the debauchery about me, but even as a flight attendant on a liner I was expected to have no morals.

What could I do so men did not give me a wink and expect me to jump into bed with them?

I would become a soldier, not one of Augustus's regulars who barrack antics were mimics of their emperor, but a real soldier.

I joined the Praetorian Guard and earned respect for my capabilities not because I was handsome and female, but because I led men into battle and brought them home alive. I will train an army for the empire it has not seen the likes of till The Man appeared. Like me they will take an oath of loyalty to the emperor who I hope changes and acts for once in his life like an emperor.

Call me 'witch' but I am not. I admit in my diary that I hear voices from unseen faces but respect the unseen power that has made me. It is this naivety that is my weakness for like my fellow citizens I see body functions as natural but there are limits, and what I see about me shames me and has made me withdraw from the joys of living."

CHAPTER 29

Nesta Sits upright?

General Wilhelmina stepping
out of Light Hole

From Nesta's diary.

"He has done what?" The Man surprised, "Surely this is not his idea, he is incapable of such thoughts," when it was reported a girl had been appointed a general to raise an army to defeat him.

And I looked at her hologram that arose out of Tintagel the Clones notepad and saw at once a girl in armor, with minimum padding for comfort and was alarmed for here was one who was a real solder like The Man.

"I am told what regiments she trains half desert, and she is happy master," Tintagel.

And I saw at once why she this new general was happy with what she had left, people who wanted to be soldiers and who followed Wilhelmina not Augustus.

"We shall see what their mantle is made of, where are they stationed, better to eat the hardboiled egg before to many eggs appear," The Man and he was not amused for he saw the threat such a general was too him, why she could be one of his deserters and did ask Tintagel to search the military lists for one.

But none was found.

"Is that wise master, if her men defeat you the moral boost to this new general will be unstoppable, let us keep nibbling away at the empire weakening it and by weakening the empire we weaken this new army of Augustus of supplies," Tintagel his opinion.

I liked The Man's idea, it was woman's jealousy speaking, a woman knows instinctively when a threat to her position has appeared and wants to deal with it before the opposition gets out of hand.

I studied the hologram carefully; the girl was handsome, only a man would see her as a boy.

"Augustus is not worthy of such loyalty," The Man was saying, "where has this girl come from," and immediately knew FEAR for that is what was said about The Man.

"Surely this woman has morals and courage and lots of wisdom and can gaze at the stars," I advised and there was silence. What I had said frightened them all, "why else will men fight for her and not Augustus?"

"She is crazy, deluded, her oath is to a man not worthy of her allegiance," Tintagel, "why it is said he ordered her to have him, and she still swears loyalty. It is said she obeyed because her liege commanded and cried for her heart was elsewhere."

"She took an oath and once you start breaking oaths you become spineless, is that what Augustus wants, to break her, is he frightened of her too, or is he such a fool he doesn't know what his actions will do? Tintagel you must get her onto our side," The Man.

*

"It was said Augustus took his new general the day he appointed her to her lofty rank for he thought it a game and by his action showed his old generals he favored them but was allowing the girl lee way to see what she could produce.

I do not think Augustus believed anyone could save him from HE WHO CONDEMNS THE GUILTY, but the girl was comforting for her firmness gave him hope and where there is hope no FEAR.

For The Man's sake I hope Augustus's immoral action for it was so, drives his new general away but for my sake not into the arms of my man The Man.

This new general had set an example to all her troops. Obey your emperor for he is the emperor. Augustus does not deserve such loyalty.

And a horrid wish also born from jealousy came into the right side of my head, "It would be cool if she was burned a witch," and shut the thought off for it was so cruel and hideous.

But in my heart, I knew this new general was not a spark in the pan. In fact, looking at her hologram that I had badgered Tintagel for I can see the girl is a girl, built much along my own build. Not as stunning but then I am full of The

Master Priest's genes. The girl looked rustic as if fresh from a farm, used to getting up early to milk the cows and collect the eggs. Just the type of girl a hungry looting soldier hopes to find searching for fresh bread.

And that was why she obeyed her emperor, she was naïve.

CHAPTER 30

Resurrection

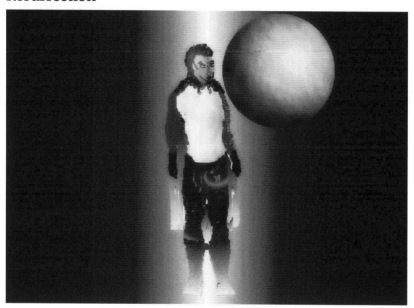

Master Priest

Nesta's diary

"Master it is reported and confirmed the bodies of The Master Priest, Posidonus and Aelfric have vanished," Tintagel the Clone reported to my man and knew immediately who was behind such deeds.

"She will use them as third elements," I said, and The Man looked at me knowing I was right.

"Order an attack on General Will's base, Planet Sirus, I knew I should have done this at the beginning, let us hope she is not too strong now?" The Man.

"I accept responsibility," Tintagel.

"For what; one must decide but to dither is to become ill, so I weighed the facts and decided wrongly.

*

Wilhelmina's diary.

"I wondered why The Man did not attack earlier and glad he did not for waiting my emperor's enemy gave me time to prepare.

It also stopped Augustus listening to his male generals that I am a joke for even Augustus sees the attack means The Man has taken me seriously.

I feel no pressure as I feel close to the unseen so have unseen helpers, I call them angels so feel no fear and wish Augustus never did what he did to me, for it reaffirms in the eyes of his generals, I am a woman and to be used as one.

Men left my legion after the news broke, but those that stayed respected me more when they heard I cried for it was an order.

"We serve Will not the emperor," I heard the whispers and hoped my liege Augustus did not hear.

And my men defended themselves against The Man's attack. It was a great moral boost, and my men love me, and recruits are going up for news travels fast."

I have met Posidonus the Clone and know of the evil he is

capable of so have secretly established him on New Saturn 12 to work his FEAR. I do not exactly like what he will do, cause FEAR amongst The Man's citizens, FEAR to walk alone home at night, FEAR when you open the knock at your door, it might be Posidonus not the meter reader.

And Aelfric I have given a complete overhaul and wonder if it is the same robot for, cyborgs have souls for they can think and reason and have light in them, energy.

The Master Priest I cloned as well and have set him to work developing a warp engine, for ships to travel at warp speed cutting down travel time so the emperor's ships may raid and disappear before The Man's battle wagons arrive.

*

Nesta's diary.

All The Man talks about is this Wilhelmina and I FEAR jealousy will cloud my opinions and so give the wrong advice to the dictator. But the more this imperial general hurts my man the more he talks of her, and I FEAR he will become obsessed,

and then what will happen to me?

*

Wilhelmina's diary.

My emperor visited my front-line base and made sure the press put his picture on the billboards with a telescope viewing The Man's lines so my victories will be seen as his.

He is my emperor and is my duty to serve him.

That is why I lay with him again and feel disgust for my emperor. He no longer is fit to command my loyalty. I had never read The Man and when my emperor returned to his throne, I obtained a copy and began to read.

What I read amazed me, but was it all true? Did liberty exist in the dictatorship? I had heard The Man was worse than my emperor, a looter, rapist, murderer, and child killer. But my emperor had hurt me twice and I wished he did leave me alone.

*

"Posidonus well you have no FRIEND to protect you now, do we?" Aelfric Europe meaning, he was not a friend and grinned for the pair of them were in a rented property in New Saturn, smuggled in.

"Aelfric, I am different, whatever the other Posidonus did to annoy you went with him to the clone vats, come let us be friends," and Posidonus offered his hand, but Aelfric looked past him at the table where a man lay dissected barely alive. Unlike the clone in front of him, Aelfric had a hard drive that remembered everything about the original Posidonus and could see no difference between him and the clone.

So, Aelfric took the offered hand and using his new bionic strength squeezed tightly till Posidonus fell to his knees whimpering.

"Nothing changes, does it?" Aelfric and let go and wondered off to a hologram fax machine where he spent the next few hours organizing a smuggling network into New Saturn 12, smuggling coke sticks and what he was buying from Flesh Markets.

He only stopped when he heard the man on the table give a big gasp and knew he was dead. It was time for a break, humans were all the same, trash, nothing changed, who said leopards change their spots; Aelfric still dreamed of being Absolute and thought General Wilhelmina foolish to repair his circuits and establish him here? He knew he was too work as a third element, but he dreamed of expanding his smuggling network across chartered space into Alien Land, especially the Rhegid Empire where a boy ruled, revenge was not the sole property of Madam Chou!

"What would life be without a droid?" Posidonus wondered as a droid disposed of the body in its body and exited the room.

Aelfric looked at Posidonus, what did he do to deserve being housed with him?

*

"Please," the girl begged of The Master Priest, "please," and as he advanced towards her, she was forced back onto a work bench, where experiments were conducted and behind her a black board with scribbles and equations on velocity and warp speed.

The Master Priest had hold of her from the local internet pimp market; she was a Goth so should be ecstatic as she had met a real vampire.

But she was not, she could see the demon in front of her disrobing as he advanced, at first, she got worked up smoking a coke stick, it made things easier until The Master Priest allowed his fangs to drop out.

Long and sharp hollow needles and when he took her wrist and kissed it, she was cool, until he bit and drank. It hurt and she was used to the Gothic vampire scene and a bit of blood drinking, but there was something different here, he was really sucking up her blood nonstop; he was getting carried away.

That is when she pulled her wrist away, the bites were deep, and she wanted to bandage them to stop the red spread. But The Master Priest had tasted and wanted more, and she saw in his eyes a look of anticipation, of dominance, and the girl knew this was no game and edged backwards, "Please."

And he pushed her back, so she lay on the bench, and he filled his special gut. "Life is good," he said, "nothing changes."

*

"My new general pleases me much," Augustus mused as he headed home in a fast ship. She was so incredibly loyal, incorruptible, naïve, childish but could win battles.

In a way he knew she was fighting on the wrong side and when victory was his, he would dispose of her, her ethics where as dangerous as The Man's. Her soldiers he knew where loyal to her not him; they could go as well.

Twice he had forced her to lie down for he was her emperor and enjoyed abusing his position; it was a reward of the job. It assessed her loyalty to the limits; it also helped to break down those morals she had. A little vice in her would bring her round to the true imperial way of thinking:

HEDONISM.

*.

"I look out the window sighing for her," Slow Horse as he looked up at the stars wanting Nesta, the toy in the window he had been denied. Would Santa bring her to him?

"I hear General Wilhelmina is a woman, these humans are crazy letting females do a man's job," and he looked at her hologram. She was rustic but appealing and, in his mind, imagined her in his menagerie along with Nesta. "I must get her here; I am an emperor and can get what I want?"

Things never change; he was still a naughty boy.

CHAPTER 31

They Meet

Posidonus the assassin was behind General Wilhelmina

"He has done what?" Augustus shouted when he heard a massive Rhegid armada had invaded his space, planets, galaxies, and dimensions.

Shouting he frog marched himself to his war cabinet where generals had quickly assembled; none wanted the emperor's wrath, he was remembering the
CRUCI-
FIER.

"Where is Wilhelmina?" He shouted staring at a huge table that was a screen for pressing a button layer of space below the planets he saw now appeared.

The screen was alive, ships were moving, and comets calculated years in advance blazed ahead of naval engagements.

It was the ultimate in war gaming and Augustus could see a large concentration of ships in the far right.

"Where is Wilhelmina?" He asked again.

Where indeed, she was about to fight an invasion herself and could not be in two places at once, except her invasion was The Man's doing.

Now Augustus had fought his traditional enemy The Man for a hundred years and more and in his mind would continue to do so for another hundred years, but these aliens, now that was an unknown factor; it was said they ate humans: never mind his own soldiers ate babies of the vanquished.

"Order Wilhelmina to defend the empire against this Rhegid tick," but did Augustus really know what he was doing?

And when Wilhelmina got the order, she could not believe, in front The Man, to the north Rhegids, so did what The Man would do, she fought him hoping even in defeat to slow him down and get time to go north and stop the alien invasion.

Augustus did not deserve such a loyal general.

"She has done what? No one disobeys me, not even Wilhelmina," and he thought of crucifying, there was always generals on the make, she was replaceable, a great pity for he had enjoyed her farmyard roughness.

But things did not go as planned, for Aelfric Europe had other ideas for, he represented more than anyone the darkness astronomers see that moves across galaxies swallowing whole universes, civilizations, milky ways, empires for darkness is always hungry.

*

"Posidonus, you look marvelous in body armor, who would know it was you?" Aelfric cheekily.

"I am against this," Posidonus moaned.

"I have arranged a meeting with her, but it will be you she meets, and you will tell her I am waiting for her secretly so none suspects I am in her employ, she should come, tell her I have important news about The Rhegids, for her alone," the robot aspirer told Posidonus who was not a happy man.

"What if I refuse, Wilhelmina has been good to me, without her I could not work as a doctor again," he moaned, and Aelfric lost his humor.

"Stupid man, you are not a doctor, a maniac yes and if you do not do what I order I will give you a bath, understand?" And so, saying stuck his bionic fingers up Posidonus's nose and lifted the later off his feet, so they wiggled like trotters for indeed Posidonus was making grunting sounds.

Then he withdrew so Posidonus collapsed in FEAR.

"Understand?" And Posidonus understood as his nose bled and Aelfric wiped his stained fingers on Posidonus's hair.

Now feeling better Aelfric sat again dreaming and scheming for he was an absolute dreamer was he not?

And time passed so Aelfric watched Posidonus do what

he was told.

Wilhelmina's diary.

"But none had foreseen the ferocity of The Man's attacks, so his troops over ran the imperial front lines, and I Wilhelmina a true general went to the front line to stop the chaos.

I saw him, knew at once who he was for, he was silhouetted against the moon like a demon with silver wings come to wreak havoc on the empire, and then heard his screeching war cry.

I needed time for my troops to regroup and rally, there was only one way to save my men and had a solder accompany me waving a white flag advanced towards him.

Either I knew him from his writings, or all his writings were lies, and he did kill me as I walked."

The war went silent, a bird, a scarlet crow made its dry sounds but there was no more killing.

I saw him too advancing towards me, I saw her also, knew she was Nesta and that must be Tintagel the Clone.

I saw the 5 also and a little FEAR crept into me. I had brought no escort, relying on the book 'The Man' for protection, this was not my emperor Augustus who did not know what honor meant.

Then he stuck his white flag into the churned-up mud, and I did likewise. "Brave woman," was all he said but I felt Nesta's eyes on me.

I also felt the 5 look me up and down and search the immediate area for a trap but found none so searched me and The Man did not stop them.

I understood, I might be a suicidal wired to go off.

"You are too good for the empire, come and fight with us?" Tintagel suggested and I was tempted a little after my ill treatment at the hands of Augustus, but I had sworn an oath.

"Now I know who I fight, a face to a name, a real man or are you all bionic?" I asked.

He laughed and I saw Nesta was furious, jealously had risen in her heart, I did play upon it, make my adversaries' life hell.

"I am all me, no replacements," and looked Nesta up and down and Tintagel put his hand on her shoulder, he was onto me.

"I like what I see, again I say come and fight with me not against me?"

"I unlike you am loyal to my emperor," and I opened my legs so stood displaying myself as a breeze blew my cotton kilt between my thighs. I knew he was looking, so

was Nesta, The Man would pay later for looking! A victory I had won a victory.

"You are not married?" I turned the screw deeper into Nesta, "Have you never found a woman equal too you?"

It was too much for Nesta who moved forward a foot, but her intention to slap me was obvious, so why Tintagel held her back.

Now I had ordered a table to follow me from behind and servants carrying food, all planned, I needed time for my men to rally.

"Nesta we must be friends, sit next to me and eat?" I asked but she did not sit until The Man sat for, he was curious as to what was going on, and the soldiers on either side seeing came out of their fox holes and walked towards us; then one kicked a football and a game started.

"Sending Aelfric to work against us was smart, but their actions debase your morals," Tintagel advised her.

"All is fair in war and love," I replied and felt the heat glowing from Nesta; she was indeed beautiful and could see why The Man kept her close.

Now because I was engrossed in trapping The Man, I did not realize one who had come close was Posidonus.

*

Posidonus

"I had to wait till the little friendly lunch was over and both sides went back to their lines where they were supposed to be, who ever heard of the enemy stopping a war to sit down and eat together and play games? It was crazy, against all the rules of war, they should be at work killing.

But on the way back Wilhelmina I knew would get in a hover scout car and I made sure I was in the back as a guard, my face disguised; never mind what Aelfric told me to say, Wilhelmina I hoped would continue to be good to me.

It was an easy thing to do, I had lots of practice so waited till behind the lines. I shot the driver and held the pistol at my general's head.

"I know you from somewhere," she said just before I sprayed a gas into her face,

and she fell asleep.

We were off to meet Aelfric and a naughty boy emperor.

But what I could not reason was why Aelfric was endangering his smuggling network by biting the emperor's hand? Surely retaliation would come, and I did not want to be frozen again, even a clone can feel the remembered pain of the ice creeping through the original's innards, of no longer shivering, of the body packing in, turning into a solid block of ice.

It was The Man I wanted revenge on, not Wilhelmina,

but what a toy to play doctor on?

"But you will not for she is needed elsewhere to expand my empire," Aelfric butted into my thoughts, and he had droids carry Wilhelmina into a ship. There I saw in his eyes he wanted to play also, but if I could not play then he was not.

"The Rhegid will know you have touched her, and he will be your enemy and not friend?" I Posidonus in a subdued tone.

It worked for the look Aelfric gave me, so sour, full of dislike, he did not need reminding, *but he did, did he not?*

So, course was set for the Rhegid fleet, and I knew that galaxy was far away, time to play for politics change as does the breeze changes direction.

And saw Aelfric was thinking the same, Augustus could buy her back and if not,

The Man would.

Life was picking up for the likes of us.

*

Nesta's diary.

"When I heard I was overjoyed something had happened to the bitch, but when Tintagel suggested Aelfric and Posidonus might be involved my heart melted its jealousy and I became concerned.

"How could the emperor get rid of his only hope against you?" I asked The Man. "Because he is absolute and sees Wilhelmina a threat, the troops are loyal to her

not him, history is full of generals becoming dictators," and The Man smiled at me and when he did that, he always disarmed me.

Tintagel smiled also, equilibrium was restored to the

household, and I was not foolish enough to make The Man's life a living hell for flirting with Wilhelmina, I was not his wife, he had a court full of beautiful women and knew he was attracted to Wilhelmina's rusticity; they were both generals.

Me I was just a pilot, a jumped-up street urchin, an assassin sent to kill The Man originally, but with Tintagel we were a team and there was not room for a fourth member, especially Wilhelmina who let the breeze blow her kilt between her thighs, I saw his eyes have a good look. Men ogle and believe no one notices!

I know what Wilhelmina was doing, The Man was too man to notice for he was not thinking with his brain any the more the more *was he?*

It takes a female to know a female.

"And that is why you work for me, what you have said is enlightening, together we shall watch The Man," Tintagel the Clone and I was relieved another had believed me.

"But we don't have to worry about her, others have taken care of her?" He added.

Yes, others had, but why?

None thought it was the boy emperor playing his absolute naughty game again for the Rhegid fleet was already engaged with the imperialists. Perhaps if it had just appeared I might have put two and two together.

"She was a good soldier," The Man saying her epitaph.

CHAPTER 32

Highest Bidder

"I am delighted to meet you," Slow Horse the boy emperor said very polity.

But Wilhelmina was no fool, this was a secret meeting, obviously this boy was afraid of someone but whom? It was the creeps behind her, Posidonus and Aelfric who were not taking the slightest efforts to conceal themselves?

So, who was the boy afraid of?

"Come up here with me," Slow Horse and she knew it was a command as he held out his hand down to her, so with a shrug she took the hand and mounted his disc.

"Kneel," Wilhelmina directed this towards the creeps who startled looked at the emperor.

"Kneel," the emperor said, Wilhelmina knew now what the boy wanted of her, and asked the same question Nesta had, *"He is only a boy?"*

Aelfric shrugged and knelled, he knew what was going on, the emperor's new toy would be discarded soon, and he would not need to kneel again until another toy was required.

Quickly Aelfric tugged the evil Posidonus down, too much was at stake.

"I met The Man the other day," and Wilhelmina did not

know what prompted her to say this, but the effect was immediate, the boy seemed to shrink, so this was whom he was afraid?

Was The Man that powerful even this alien trembled at his name, why? And Wilhelmina remembered 'The Man' the book and saddened her emperor was not like The Man and in her heart knew he would never be.

Suddenly she straightened, a hand was under her kilt, it was the boy; 'He is only a boy' she told herself.

But unlike Nesta did not have a bionic general to rescue her.

"We are rich," Aelfric muttered and Posidonus knew he meant 'I am rich.' "I am poor," and Aelfric knew Posidonus meant there goes my paymaster. "Better do everything I tell you to at double time had not we?" Aelfric and

Posidonus groaned hating himself for handing Wilhelmina over to this boy emperor who would get to play instead of him.

"You are sick," Aelfric further down the audience hall and slapped the back of his servant's head so Posidonus stumbled.

Together the two evil men watched Wilhelmina disappear with Slow Horse and together they exited the Rhegid ship, one an extraordinarily rich robot man and the other wondering why he was still poor.

"Be lucky you still breathe," Aelfric answered for the ears Posidonus.

*

Nesta's diary

"What ails your son?" I asked The Man fearing he was not my man any the more

the more.

"Takes after me," The Man providing a poor joke and Nesta was silent. "He is certainly incorrigible," Tintagel meaning the exact opposite. "Aelfric has offered Wilhelmina to the highest bidder?" The Man.

"If anyone can save her it would be the likes of him?" I really feeling sorry for my opponent in love for I had been with Slow Horse remember, "One thing he certainly isn't is a boy, might look like one, squeak like one, think like one yes, but those Rhegids are like rabbits and rats," I added and watched my man for a reaction.

"Sweetheart, I will bid for her because she will make one of my finest generals," my man The Man and I cursed longevity for it meant an individual could seek many partners; parting in death no longer existed; never did, we all meet again in the ion fields were a soul can be reassembled in the Earth physical plane, so what the hell, if he wanted the farm girl for a while, let him, I did be here when he came back with Tintagel, servants of the dictator. See I was not that stupid not to realize I could not put a ball and chain about a soul like The Man. For one he had lived longer than me and was a dictator, absolute.

"Sweetheart, listen, Augustus will abandon her; already he has appointed some useless cousin of Po Wei General in Chief. Soon I will be standing on the marbled Appian way into Augusta the emperor's capital, You and Tintagel will ride in my chariot as we go up that cedar lined avenue and put an end to corruption," The Man.

"An admirable dream master," Tintagel.

'Yes, an admirable dream and he could dream on about

Wilhelmina,' and felt bad, she needed help, but she was our enemy; but The Man respected worthy opponents and had made it clear he wanted her on his side, and I had not caught The Man thinking about Wilhelmina but had seen the look in her eyes.

There was more to uncharted space than the Rhegids as Tintagel has pointed out to me heaps, room to send Wilhelmina too if The Man wanted her as a general and then why not leave her with Slow Horse, what was all this concern about an enemy general for anyway?

"What happens if she refuses to give up this stupid oath to Augustus" I asked defensively.

"Sweetie, she will, she is so full of vanity, valor and honor she would have to commit suicide to escape taking an oath to me," The Man replied.

'Now that sounded well, maybe I could bribe Aelfric to do the job? Wicked, try a stronger word, JEALOUSY.

And after the oath she did be his willing servant, how sickening,' I thought.

*

"So that is where she ended up?" Augustus mused.

"We can get her back master?" Aelfric thought and since thoughts were alive the proton reassembler descrambled his and Augustus read them; it was the new message sender, fast and you could see who you were thinking about also; it as all the FAB.

Now the emperor was not as much a fool as the robot thought!

"It seems this cyborg has learned nothing from The Man, so I will teach him what my name means," and he scanned his court and a little man, not ugly or deformed, but a courtier, no higher than a foot, a third of a meter is whom the emperor's eyes settled upon.

"You, you will deal with this problem," and there were no protests, just obey, thousands of empty crucifixes on the roads into the capital Augusta.

And the little person was called Mcer of Old Pluto.

'Christ he would pick me, what have I done for this job, I was only sent here to court by my mother to be rid of me, to advance and pay my own bills. Well, my bills have never been high, I hang glide, sometimes drink, like a girl when I am in the mood, and hate this assignment. Just pronounce my name as Mcer, OK and who knows maybe The Man will ask me to join him?'

And Mcer picked up his emperor's thoughts thus:

"Your mother advanced you into the ESP classes for she told me you where gifted and I know you are reading my thoughts now, so listen, use your gifts against my enemies and that is why I choose you. Are you big like The Man, cunning as Aelfric, evil like Posidonus, who knows, you work for me now?" Augustus.

"Do your job and be advanced at court and know fame, wine women and song and fortunes," and Augustus then imagined he was pulling down a shutter in front of his mind, so shutting Mcer's mind out, and went to seek the little man's mother who was

gifted in other ways for the empire was corrupt.

*

From the memory banks of Posidonus.

'I investigated my piggy bank that I kept hidden from that monster Aelfric for I had extracted much from the citizens of New Saturn 12 where Wilhelmina had sent me.

Yes eureka, I had a billion silver imperial dollars.

So secretively thought up a name for me. Pony, Star Gazer, Bafular, oh bugger no name seemed suitable so just sent my bid for Wilhelmina as ANOYMOUS.

Was I coming to rescue my paymaster? Certainly not, I was very indignant that the boy should get to play with my toy first.

So, you know how long I have spent cringing and crawling at Wilhelmina's feet to draw her into my way of thinking to tell me her ills? Then I can be her doctor, yes?

*

More Wilhelmina

"They say Aelfric dreams, dam them both, Posidonus is crazy, never do I dream of his evil ways, he is filth, damned to hell. Are the men nuts, obviously so, a smile from me means I want to play doctors; can no one smile for the smile is mistaken for an invitation? He can go to hell; he is there any way so can go to a deeper hell." Wilhelmina when she heard Posidonus's thoughts played back from the proton assembler.

"But what listening to Posidonus has meant to me is that I believe more strongly in The Man with the hope the dictator sees the likes of Posidonus as ill and not for the bath? The Man is too much like Augustus and his crucifixes!

Ill enough to be sent away out of society for even a thousand years till they can be part of society.

The Man's ways are good enough for the beginning of a new age, but once things settle down and all the drug barons and child molesters are bathed, then when there is time and stability you must cure them instead of playing God.

A trooper once said to me he saw the enemy in his sights so shot him in the ankle, then the leg when he tried to get up and again in the other leg because if he stood, he did be shot by another.

"Why did I not kill him, he was made in the image of God," the soldier replied.

I have never forgotten his reply and that is why I carry the generals cross on me back with responsibility and my oaths are strong.

But The Man is The Man and Augustus, Augustus and I am just Wilhelmina a prisoner.

Bugger Posidonus to hell, I am the victim not him.'

*

"Do you believe these messages from Posidonus, one giving the terms for Aelfric to deliver Wilhelmina to The Man and the other want terms what would The Man give for Aelfric?" Tintagel amused.

"When thief's fall out?" Nesta.

"We will bid for both, the imperial forces are reverting to their old types, easy to bash?" The Man grinning.

Nesta saw him as a boy and wished he did never grow up and lose his aura of innocence that was his secret appeal to women.

"Cannot you just ask Slow Horse to hand her over before Augustus gets her back?"

"Might pay him to keep her you mean until Augustus is no more," was The Man's reply and that suited Nesta.

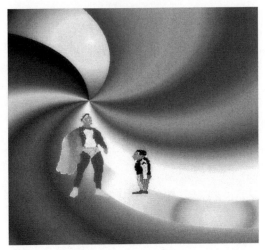

Mcer was tiny compared to Augustus

CHAPTER 33

Papa Here

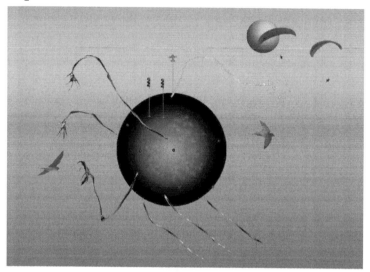

A droid buzzed about fly like so got swatted good.

From Nesta's diary

"I was about to meet Slow Horse again and it produced FEAR in me because he had come so close to keeping me as one of his wives. I was not a mare in his stables but an individual human being with feelings and aspirations of my own; a destiny laid out before I was born to follow.

And there he was on an emerald throne that floated on an exceptionally large disc supported as usual by pole bearers that were symbolic only.

He seemed longer and skinnier and there was no sign of Wilhelmina and what a poor actor he was; he had the easiest part to look stern like a regal emperor which he

was anyway!

"Son," The Man and waved and strode from the disembarkation pad towards him.

I followed with Tintagel and I against the latter's advice, "Don't wear such flimsy apparel, you know what he is like?"

"And that is why I AM wearing the latest summer body armor to emphasis I am not his too touch, to produce strong desires in him for me and away from Wilhelmina. My apparel shows I am papa's not a naughty boy's.

"Who am I, to fathom the ways of a woman?" Tintagel answered.

And I knew Slow Horse noticed me and behind him on a smaller throne Princess Veig who I hoped was holding the reins to her son tightly.

And after small chat "Where is she, you cannot go around space kidnapping girls you fancy? It just I not what emperors do, gives us all a bad name son, so what do you want for her, and do not give her back to Augustus," The Man.

"What's he done this time?" Princess Veig asked alarmed, horrified.

Of course, Slow Horse denied it and wondered how we knew for few knew and for effect said, "That's what happens when you play with rogues," The Man rubbing it in about the company he was keeping these days.

Yes, that made him go very pale as if he had caught something nasty and part of me hoped he had then remembered

Wilhelmina and felt ashamed.

"Bring her out lad?" The Man again and we all looked hopefully at Slow Horse.

But time never stops for anyone especially where the wicked are involved? "She is not here?" Slow Horse postulated when told by an aid. All could see he was genuinely perplexed but was not believed till all the players received a message

from the auctioneer.

"I already paid them to give me her?" Slow Horse vivid and by not controlling his anger gave away his involvement in Wilhelmina's original abduction.

"I think we better talk," his papa and Slow Horse:

"This is my galaxy, here I am emperor, get off Rhegid," for the boy feared daddy for The Man was the dictator.

And just as guards appeared his mother slapped the back of his head, so he tottered forward; the guards stopped, they did not know what to make of things.

"Arrest her," Slow Horse shouted.

But the Famous 5 suddenly stood between the guards and Princess Veig.

"I am Empress Consort, it is you who shall be arrested, guards confine my son to his apartments," his mother truly angry slapping her sons head.

"He is our emperor?" One of the guards protested ready to fight

"Well son, either go to your rooms or everyone on

Rhegid will know what you have been up to, and this time I will not help you out," The Man.

Then the guards attacked and the 5 fought well.

"Stop," Slow Horse shouted not wanting his people to know he had obtained another human woman for a wife; he remembered the civil war and Nesta. "Mother

do not ever humiliate me in public again or I will?" But she cut him off with a hard slap to his face.

"You humiliate yourself by the lust between your legs," and his mother kept slapping him.

The guards did not move, they were bloody and torn and faced the Famous 5.

Nesta's diary.

"I did not feel sorry for the boy emperor and wondered how we had managed to pull off humiliating such an absolute ruler and still lived? It was his mother's intervention that carried the day in our favor. I do not think The Man would have assaulted the boy although his physical strength and body build was threatening; it was the Empress Consort who now ruled the Rhegid Empire.

And surprisingly Slow Horse was quite happy to retire to his sixty odd wives and zoo and collect beautiful things, also oddities.

He knew he was not ready to be an emperor even if he was still called Emperor An teach Mall, the Slow Horse.

He had brought disgrace upon himself for he was the incarnation of Tupt. And powerful courtiers of all parties were glad he had gone into retirement, till he was older of course, and hoped when he reappeared, he was an adult?

Two months later

"What do you mean Augustus has put in the lowest bid?" Mcer annoyed.

"It is true, look for yourself," Aelfric replied and, in the shadow, Posidonus hoped his high bid would win; but the damage done to Mcer was unrepairable. His intention of biding his time till he overpowered Aelfric crumbled. Why was Augustus abandoning Wilhelmina his greatest asset?

"Because she is more popular than he is!" Aelfric responded as if able to read thoughts.

Mcer winced.

Posidonus went off and took a white rabbit from a cage and went to a world where the creature became Wilhelmina and he disappeared. Rabbits do not scream so none bothered to check what he was doing.

"How can you put something up for auction that you don't own?" Mcer asked. "But I do own her, do you think I will give her to a BOY?" Aelfric asked, "Wilhelmina is a woman."

And after pressing a button Wilhelmina was escorted in by armed droids. Mcer stood and bowed in respect to the general.

And Aelfric saw the glint of light in Wilhelmina's eyes and knew not to trust Mcer, not that he did?

"What do you bid for her Mcer? Bid for her for yourself, your emperor has abandoned her," Aelfric and looked at a screen, "Anonymous has won, she will be

sent to Anonymous; your fate is sealed dear," and Aelfric had the droid leave Wilhelmina with him and escort Mcer away.

He did not want to leave Wilhelmina and was in shock that Augustus was not worthy to be anyone's emperor.

"My dear," and Aelfric undid the clasp of her cape, so it dropped to the carpet.

At that moment Posidonus entered holding a pair of rabbit ears and seeing Wilhelmina dropped them.

"Get out get out," Aelfric screamed and started to beat the evil man.

At once Wilhelmina seeing the droid shift to protect its master grabbed the laser arm and pushed the droid into Aelfric.

He screamed as the droid fired.

Posidonus also as laser light passed through Aelfric into him. Unfortunately, Posidonus was all tissue, so the damage was colossal.

Aelfric turned and Wilhelmina pushed again so the droid made Aelfric tumble

over a prostrate Posidonus, so fell droid also.

Wilhelmina ran to escape.

In the corridor she met Mcer attracted by the screaming. "Come with me," and he took her hand and started to run. She followed no options otherwise.

"Where has she gone, I will tear this place to shreds to find the human," Aelfric shouted behind.

"In here," and Mcer pushed Wilhelmina into a tube and got in himself and exited. Where has this situation happened before?

Was it Nesta and Posidonus?

Was Wilhelmina to be subjected to a man at close quarters? Was the character of Mcer good or bad?

Was Mcer aroused at being squished against a woman?

Was he like other men, what were his hands doing?

"I am not sure where we are going?" He said trying to look at the viewing screen.

In fact, they went into the street landing atop a hover fruit wagon coming in from an agricultural dome full of watermelons now squashed.

The screaming driver demanding recompense drew a crowd; it also drew Aelfric?

But this was New Saturn 12, The Man's world and Aelfric had presumed all the players in the game where still on Planet Rhegid? Foolish robot, silly robot, moronic robot, The Man was here.

"Kill him," Aelfric ordered his droids for he had like Po Wei had gotten used to absolute power.

The first droid opened and Mcer pulled Wilhelmina down under the floating lorry.

A scream as the lorry driver was hit in the abdomen.

No one knew his name, he was an extra, a no body, but he had a woman who lived with him and two kids.

A police officer in the crowd fired at the droid; the droid exploded covering Aelfric in sparks.

"Kill him," Aelfric meaning the police officer and the droids turned their attention on him.

"Come with me," Mcer said but he said it to empty space.

Wilhelmina was leaping through the air kicking Aelfric in the side of the head, so the robot king spiraled away into a gutter.

Do not be too disgusted, this is New Saturn 12 where gutters are slow moving so lilies will flourish and frogs and newts and eels and carp will flourish and the scent of the lilies and water roses nice.

Mcer shut his eyes to use his ESP powers and built it up in his third eye in the middle of his forehead.

*

"I think we are needed," The Man being notified Aelfric was in his capital and the famous 5 grinned for they were bored of practicing in the gym and wanted real action.

"Coming dear?" Tintagel asked Nesta.

"Of course," she was not going to miss this?

*

Now Aelfric Europe ran back to his hideout leaving his droids to battle it out with Wilhelmina.

But Wilhelmina had other ideas, she was after him.

Mcer pushed the remaining droids together and made them float into the air and ran after the general; by doing so he broke his concentration, so the droids fell noisily to the ground.

Above a large hover transport was approaching; in it The Man and his friends.

Below the city watch were gathering to subdue the droids and find from the crowd where had those responsible for this outrage fled?

"That way," they knew by the time The Man arrived.

"I won I won," Posidonus gloated holding his cauterized belly wound unaware of the turmoil heading into his life.

And he went to fill a bath for he was terribly upset Aelfric had not told him and was not going to give him his prize.

"Who does he think he is, I know how to deal with the likes of him, he is only a robot," and soon Aelfric's private washroom was filled with the strong smell of acid.

"I will make my Wilhelmina happy as I have made others smile on the table, I will give her pleasure as she pleases me," Posidonus was ill and a lost soul.

"What was that?" He queried hearing the commotion of Aelfric entering and Wilhelmina kicking the door open he was trying to close.

He had tremendous strength and could not understand why he could not close it?

Behind Wilhelmina stood Mcer with closed eyes sending his mind at the door.

Behind Mcer the 5 were approaching.

Behind them The Man.

Behind him Nesta and Tintagel.

Behind them a cohort of his dictatorial guard.

Behind them police.

Behind them the crowd were it was safe.

Because of Mcer the door flew open into Aelfric who shouted an oath as his human nose burst and he fell back.

Straight away Wilhelmina kicked him in the hilly and each time he stood up was kicked repeatedly.

But she like Mcer before her was to find she could inflict a fatal blow to A BIONIC ROBOT.

And she was sweating now, New Saturn was a hot planet even if Aelfric liked air conditioning, he was a robot and could survive without 95% of his human flesh; he was a cyborg, was he not?

And Wilhelmina kicked one last time with all her strength and the robot king burst through a door into a corridor that sloped down to his private quarters where Posidonus should not be?

And because he fell down a slope he was away from her savage kicks and doggy fashion panted to cool his circuits under his bruised living flesh.

And by the time Wilhelmina reached him he reached out and grabbed her leg up ending her, shaking her in a rage that she had the arrogance to try and destroy him, Aelfric Europe.

But Mcer was at the top of the slope, and he shut his eyes. "Argh," Aelfric grunted feeling thought energy slam into him. But he still held Wilhelmina.

But he did not know the FAMOUS 5 had rushed past Mcer.

But Mcer distracted opened his eyes and saw the shadow of The Man fall upon him.

But The Man wanted Aelfric and could see Mcer was attacking his enemy so therefore must be friend?

Free of ESP energy Aelfric still holding Wilhelmina fled further down the slope.

The slope could be activated like an escalator, but Aelfric was in too much of a hurry to remember that.

But Posidonus was not, he was about to come up from the bottom and activated the slope.

The sudden jerk threw everyone off their feet.

It gave Wilhelmina a chance to stick her fingers in Aelfric's eyes, she was a soldier, she was trained to kill, and he was her enemy who was going to kill her.

It gave Posidonus on the now moving slope time to see what all the noise was about.

It gave Nesta and Tintagel time to stand next to Mcer.

It gave time for the following dictatorial cohort to enter also.

It gave the police time to try and tape off the door into Aelfric's secret hideout. It gave the crowd time to push past the police tape.

It gave time for the reporters to work their cameras. It gave Mcer time to know when the goose was up.

It gave time for The Man to slide down to Aelfric.

It gave time for droids to arrive who were programmed to protect this dwelling.

Wilhelmina screeched, in front of her where eyes should have been camera lenses.

"Bitch," Aelfric hissed and reached his other hand to gorge out her throat. Bad move, The Man taking that hand twisting it.

Wilhelmina screeched again as Aelfric refusing to let go flopped her upright savagely.

"I am off," Posidonus behind trying to run down the moving escalator. "Allow us," it was the famous 5.

Aelfric fled not wanting too really, believing alone he could defeat The Man, bionic against bionic.

"Out of the way fool," Aelfric pushing

into Posidonus.

"My prize," a reply.

Aelfric stopped, in the heat of battle he was amused, Posidonus was Anonymous. "Defend your prize, want her, fight them for her," Aelfric and hurried away.

"Argh," Posidonus gasped as Zagor Blue Skin pulled his hair knot and swung him and let go so he flew after Aelfric.

But the robot was fast and Posidonus landed heavily on the moving escalator that was taking him back to the FAMOUS 5 for more harsh treatment?

Poor Posidonus he was full of FEAR?

"Well, let us get a move on, I take it you need to see Aelfric?" Tintagel asked Posidonus.

"No, but it is better if I do, more accurate." Mcer replied and began to move down the escalator. Now ever try to go against an escalator.

Tintagel switched it off, that was the sensible thing to do. The sudden stop gave Aelfric his freedom as e zoomed off ast the top.

The sudden stop made all fall.

It allowed Aelfric to escape because he was no longer on the escalator.

It allowed the droids time to counterattack.

"Oh, bloody hell," Nesta seeing the droids appearing out of walls.

"Oh, bloody hell," the dictatorial guard and fired at the droids.

"Oh Crap," the spectators at the door.

"Oh Crap," the reporters also at the door.

"Oh I want my prize," Posidonus and stood up and ran after Aelfric before the robot shut down this part of his house and filled it with nerve gas?

Could he do that?

Would he not kill himself?

Never mind, his robot side did survive but The Man would be dead, or would he?

CHAPTER 34

Bath Time?

Ionization pulled you apart down to your ions.

Aelfric banged on a red fire button, but it was not a fire button, which was too fool people, it was what Posidonus feared worst?

"Bloody hell all die, scumbags, I am Aelfric, Aelfric do

you hear."

"I hear you," The Man replied, and Aelfric hearing lost his composure.

"Die please die, oh please die," Aelfric mumbled and now because he was no longer running and heart pounding could feel his human pain, "God almighty," he shouted in agony and began to stumble away seeking a tube to exit.

Tubes existed like the pores in an insect allowing the bug to breathe, in this case to escape.

But what about The Man?

There was an explosion, explosion?

*

Now the new supreme commander of Augustus,
Po Lee had ordered the invasion
of New Saturn 12.

"My enemy The Man was not there when this decision was taken, he was on Planet Rhegid, so I was told?"

"Why must I come too, I will be in danger Po Lee?" Augustus had asked. "You will not be in the battle but merely observing from a safe distance. Your presence will inspire your men to be brave, and may I suggest you double all pay for combatants and the promise of New Saturn 12 will not be under military law for a week," Po Lee replied bowing.

"But that will mean the solders will rob me of every-thing valuable, they will loot the city clean," Augustus annoyed.

"But you want to inspire them to fight do you not my emperor, what will be gained, The Man's home base, just a psychological blow and what will be lost, we are losing anyway," Po Lee was brave to remind Augustus of this fact.

SILENCE.

"Fail and I will crucify you, understand Po Lee?"

"I understand," and Po Lee planned to live, he was not going to be executed for the likes of Augustus; already a fast schooner was loaded with bounty and would accompany the fleet as his personal comforter. Yes, the ship would give the appearance of being full of Madam Butterfly Chou's girls but was his escape route into uncharted Alien Land.

*

And there was an explosion as an imperial missile hit the house of Aelfric by chance, one in a thousand probabilities and the corridor was ripped open and fresh air came in and nerve gas went out into the street.

There was also another small explosion muffled by the bigger, for The Man had used plastic explosive to blow the door open.

"Bugger him, he's gone," The Man viewing an empty room.

"He will lead us to him?" It was Zagor Blue skin, and he was holding Posidonus up by his hair knot again. It was obvious the evil Posidonus was suffering discomfort.

And he pointed to a wing of the house, and they went throwing caution to the wind, the FAMOUS 5 where here and had Posidonus stuck out in front full of FEAR.

"There he is?" Hairless one of the FAMOUS 5, for on a ledge five floors above

was the robot still holding Wilhelmina upside down. Seeing

his enemies and fearing he might not be able to escape in his tube he was trying to get in, he held Wilhelmina out over the ledge.

He got his way, all stopped.

But The Man was now absent, his planet was under attack, he had to defend it, the FAMOUS 5 here was more than capable of rescuing her.

And he left Tintagel and Nesta to make sure humanity and not mutant urges came first where Wilhelmina was concerned. But what about Nesta's jealous urges?

Now would the FAMOUS 5 have stopped if Tintagel had not restrained them?

And none knew at the time The Man had left but now Tintagel was informed, and he knew Wilhelmina must not fall into the hands of imperial troops as that would be a disastrous blow. Her presence would raise the enemy's moral, and she would lead them

to victory.

*

An hour later:

An absence of talk can happen in an hour especially when attacking The Man for Po Lee rained destruction upon New Saturn 12, but not as much as he would have liked, for

for having broken the code for the defense energy shield meant to excite the atoms in a missiles head so it would explode, he thought the planet exposed to conquest.

But it was not, his ships had been painted in ion paint so they would merge into the ions of anti-gravity and gravity lines that made up space, so his ships were undetected.

But he was fighting The Man.

Ion reassembles machines existed here, so large for Tintagel had invested wisely and when the machines were activated dozens of Po Lee's ships were never seen again.

To where they were sent no one knows, and it is a secret whether The Man, he who used supermarket plastic bags with this message, 'Send more,' reassembled them at the other end?

Only you can guess, he was a dictator.

"What is happening?" Augustus asked, the ship he was in breaking up. "I don't know," Po Lee thinking of his schooner.

In fact, the ship was being pulled apart by electromagnetism that Maxwell eons ago in Edinburgh had discovered. You see, lot can happen in an hour; this was New Saturn 12 not Hope, where children once lived?

And Augustus fled his ship and entered a lifeboat, as The Master Priest had used long ago but it too was breaking up.

"Every man for himself," someone shouted, and he was no longer an emperor, but someone in the way as all fought to get in a tube, a lifeboat.

"I am your emperor; Po Lee tell them."

But Po Lee was gone; he was heading for a schooner anchored just outside the fleet.

"What the?" Augustus as he was pushed into a tube as parts of a sailor hit him, not from an enemy weapon, but from the melee in front of him as all fought to get into a tube.

And as Augustus lay heavily down the tube automatically closed and exited into space.

He had never really been this close to the stars, and he was terrified. He was alone; my he could reach up and pluck a star. All about him was silence and he felt he was buried alive in a coffin and FEARING death, because he was The Crucifier he began to scream to be let out.

Silly man, let out into what?

And he had no idea how to operate a tube which automatically headed to the nearest inhabited world; New Saturn 12.

Well, what goes round comes round!

But it had not come round to Aelfric who found as he moved away from the ledge those below advanced.

But he knew he needed an exit tube fast.

But he knew if he let go of Wilhelmina those FAMOUS 5 mutants did be upon him in seconds for, they were better bionics than him.

But he knew The Man would be back, the sounds of battle seemed to be fading.

But he knew an idiot had attacked New Saturn 12 and been ionized. But he knew Wilhelmina must come with him in the exit tube.

But how?

He moved away from the ledge.

He heard them coming up
the stairwell. He knew he
had too hurry.

He thought he heard "My prize, give me my prize," 'bloody idiot Posidonus' he thought and hurried away.

He gave vermin a bad name like the black rat in the ventilation shaft above hating him for he had brought disturbance to its life, for it wanted out to roam the kitchen for scraps and big fat tasty juicy roaches that spread disease because they could eat through concrete and get to your essentials.

*

And outside exit tubes began to land on New Saturn 12, hitting the city domes and slid down it into uninhabited land where the air was full of green polluted gases.

And dozens went through the holes where missiles had hit the domes and landed on the streets amongst spectators now that the attack was over.

And the spectators opened the exit tubes and hauled the survivors out and did not give them hot coffee and warm bread and a cozy blanket to wrap themselves in for shock.

Instead, they shouted, "Imperialist scum?" and tore them apart literally, yes, scores took each appendage such as a foot or hand and pulled while others hit with fists, bricks and wooden laundry poles and tore exposed soft bits.

The killed had brought war, FEAR and death and The Man was busy elsewhere, since victory was assured, he handed mopping up operations to his generals for he had business elsewhere did he not?

CHAPTER 35

Master Priest and other loose ends.

There are new beginnings out there.

And The Master Priest developed the wrap engine, so the ships of Po Lee had travelled across space so fast went unseen.

"Augustus is lost?" The Master Priest upon hearing the fate of his emperor and knew it was time to fill his crocodile leather suitcases and seek employment elsewhere?

And he took down a portrait of Wilhelmina, "You were good to me in my old age,"

and packed it away. He must hurry as he knew the engines did fall into The Man's hands and that monster did be here on Augusta very soon.

Then there was the sound of chimes as his doorbell went.

"I wonder who that could be; I haven't booked a taxi yet?"
*

And The Man being told it was stale mate between the
FAMOUS 5 and Aelfric crawled up the exit tube towards his
prey. It was an extremely dangerous thing to do, if the tube
came out, he would be impaled by its nose.

"Hello," he said emerging from the exit and squeezing
out between it and the tube. Aelfric did not need to turn
to know who it was.

He dropped Wilhelmina.

"Murdering scum?" Zagor Blue skinned shouted.

And since Aelfric did not have a hostage now used his
bionic legs to spring him to a roof beam above where he
sought escape.

And The Man seeing he could do it knew he could also.

"Must you follow me," Aelfric and lounged a foot
out towards The Man. The foot was grasped and
twisted.

There was a
snap. Aelfric
screamed.

The Man pulled with all his strength and the foot came
away.

The Man jerked this way and that snapping
wires and freeing ball bearings, so they rained
on those below.

The Man threw his trophy away and it fell into the
shadows.

The Man lunged for the other foot that was
doing its best to kick. The Man felt it in his

face but was not put off.

The Man took the other foot.

Aelfric screamed begging for mercy and as the foot came away dripping human blood and hydraulic fluids. Aelfric grabbed ceiling wires and tried pushing off into space. And found his body weight too much and the wires began to rip free from the ceiling as Aelfric descended fast.

And in the shadows, one picked up his thrown away feet.

And tucked them under his arms.

And followed Aelfric's decent wanting to get to the robot before anyone else. And this one was hidden by the shadows, so we do not know who it was.

And The Man seeing the wires had failed the robot would fail him too, descended as quickly as he could fire ladders and when he was near the ground jumped for his ankles might not take his weight from a higher jump and break.

And he saw Wilhelmina standing there unharmed.

"Mcer shut his eyes and brought her to him as she fell catching her and landed her gently," he must be a god?" Morair the Nobleman amazed.

"No ESP and Aelfric is getting away," Mcer replied embarrassed, he never got used to the applause and wonderment. So, then Aelfric went into the shadows because the last wire ripped from the ceiling landed him there into waiting arms.

"Get me out of here," Aelfric demanded.

"You are heavy, and I am doing my best," Posidonus replied slipping them both into a hidden wall chamber and freedom.

Now outside, "Where did the buggers go?" Zagor Blue Skin.

And Pyoo-ur the Sister opened fire with a laser machine gun and made thousands of holes in the wall, doors, ceiling, and floor where might be secret compartments.

And Posidonus because he was using his body to support Aelfric was unharmed but not Aelfric who was a shield. So was hit so much human blood and cyborg fluid ran from him making him dizzy, weakening him.

"We are almost there," Posidonus quipped, and Aelfric began to worry the evil runt would try and operate on him. He was having nothing to do with it and pushed Posidonus away. A good thing for the Posidonus as a chunk of plaster blew bizarre and hit Aelfric on the back of the head, covering him in bricks and mortar.

"Let's go in, they must be in there somewhere," The Man.

"I think I know where they are going," it was Mcer's voice and Posidonus knew he had to hurry.

And those under stress get adrenalin rush so he carried the robot to another locked doorway and entered, then threw the robot heavily down and summoned a remaining droid to carry Aelfric to his destination and when reached: "Make sure I am

not disturbed," Posidonus told the droid who went to guard the main door to this compartment. And Mcer knew of its existence because he had picked up Aelfric's thoughts who wanted him here to save him from Posidonus.

Was he afraid of his servant, well the air was heavy with a funny strong smell? "All is ready, already prepared for me, thought you did get rid of me would you

and you cheated me out of my prize," and threw Aelfric's two feet into the special
bath.

Aelfric was not sure where he was, but his brain was telling him that was his bath.

Unfortunately, hydraulic fluid squirted into Posidonus's eyes blinding him momentarily.

That was all Aelfric needed, seconds and there was a big splash as he pushed Posidonus in.

"AR," Aelfric hissed as acid splashed onto him burning him. Behind him an explosion and the door were kicked in.

Standing there Zagor Blue Skin ahead to make sure no bobby traps would kill The Man. In front of him a nightmare, Posidonus had managed to stand up in the bath in an attempt to get out. He was no longer recognizable; what goes round comes round. "And The Man behind Zagor shot out his eleven fingered bionic hand and arm and hit Aelfric in the chest, so as is balancing on the remains of his leg fell easily backwards into the bath toppling what might be Posidonus.

"No," Aelfric screamed as his circuit melted and he could not get up as Posidonus was now on top of him; so together both melted away amidst stinks.

"Out of primeval chaos came matter from the actions of light that is word and inventive mind and back to chaos our bodies go," The Man so saying words over the acidy grave of two evil beings.

*

Backdrop: The Man did use the new wrap engines and he did not fight every planet on the way to Augusta, the imperial capital but by passed them all. He went straight for the heart of the corrupt empire and took it. With no emperor all fragmented with this Count proclaiming himself King of Pluto and that Duke ruler of the Milky Way, and that Tribune promoted himself to an Earl and ruler of the Moons of New Uranus and aliens seeing the borders of the empire unguarded invaded and took human chartered space for their own.

The Dark Ages had arrived and in the far-flung corners of the empire learning was pushed aside and replaced by FEAR, FAITH and PAGANISM and inflation and barter system replaced the central banking system and the steady imperial dollar Po Wei had built up over a long lifetime.

But now fast ships had brought The Man to Augusta, so war ravaged the Appian Way and all where disgusted when they saw the crucifixions.

So, none felt sorry for what had happened to the Emperor Augustus when he had been torn to pieces by the mob.

"This is the house I rented for him," Wilhelmina assured them all outside a house with a walled garden.

"I wonder who that could be; I haven't booked a taxi yet?" remember who said this, the Master Priest that vampire.

Then the door was knocked off its hinges onto The Master Priest.

Opening his eyes, he looked up into The Man's face and trembled and there behind him his monstrous mutant bodyguard and what was she doing here. He had been betrayed as soon as he could he did remove her picture where he had packed it away.

And then the FAMOUS 5 pulled the door off him and yanked him to his feet.

"How do we get rid of him making sure he doesn't come

back?" The Man asked. "Give him a bath," it was Nesta, and all looked at her amazed at her cruel and wicked statement, but it was the truth.

"Proclaim me your regent here dictator and my troops will swear allegiance to you," Wilhelmina said.

Now all had come to know Wilhelmina as an honest woman, even Nesta who being a woman did not want the likes of this saint near The Man. He was a man after all and so liked the idea of leaving Wilhelmina here in Augusta since she had no emperor to swear loyalty too, she would swear to The Man.

But the problem was with all the mopping up it was not safe to venture out into the streets with The Master Priest.

"Then we must kill him here, burn him till nothing is left, sweep up his ashes and bathe them," The Man and The Master Priest had a funny turn listening to his fate.

You just did not describe one's execution in front of one, did you?

What where the times coming too?

And Zagor Blue Skin picked up The Master Priest so Pyoo-ur the Sister could slit his throat, then he and Red would upturn him so did bleed like a chicken and be dead?

And as the knife was drawn across the evil vampire's throat he arched back and kicked out, so Pyoo-ur the Sister tumbled backwards and then he somersaulted, so he dislocated his shoulders, never mind he was The Master Priest and they popped back, and he was free running for his life.

That is when he found the power of thought was like a fist hammering into his back so he spins across the floor.

And "What ghost is here to kill me?" When he saw the

knife with no human aid float towards him.

He did not know about Mcer and ESP.

And slithering he got to where he wanted, an exit tube and pressing the button flopped in and just as the tube sealed, the knife went in with him.

It had belonged to the mutant warrior Pyoo-ur the Sister so was designed to look wicked and was at least a foot long; more an ugly looking dagger.

Then the tube existed just as those representing VENGEANCE reached it. It shot far and none saw it land if it did?

"We must search for him, he is an evil spore," Wilhelmina. "I have no way of telling if the knife stuck him?" Mcer.

"We will know if he lives when women appear drained of blood," Red, one of the FAMOUS 5.

"We will stay and help Wilhelmina hunt him down," Zagor Blue Skin.

"Follow him wherever he appears," The Man adding "as evil spores multiply and will be with us till the end of time?" An epitaph for evil.

THE END

BOOKS BY THIS AUTHOR

The Man

A mammoth story of a good dictator and his romances,
his friends,
his enemies,
his wars.
The Man believes in 'Rulers are here to serve the people, not the
other way round.'
There is a vampire in the tale,
and is an arguement for early Christian dogma of reincarna-
tion, predestination.
A mirror of our present society, so come meet the vampire
Master Priest.
Meet the 5 mutant bodyguards.
Meet Tintagel the Clone.
Travel distant universes and be amazed at the color.
We are not alone.

Ants 169 Illustrations Science Fiction

82652 words 169 illustrations. 262 pages
Mammoth adventure with Luke of The Ants, a rival to Tarzan,
whereas Tarzan was brought up on ape milk, Luke is raised on
Black Ant milk.
Amazing strength and he battles Insect Nobles for the domin-
ant species on Planet World.
Humanoid Insects from chromosome splicing.
Human genes into insects to make them taller, handsome, at-

tractive but cruel masters of Planet World.

A good hero needs a side kick, Luke has Utna, a giant Black Ant he rides, saves shoe leather. Come row a galley with Luke.

Look at the crimson moons, fill with him 'spring fever'.

Planet World, Ant Rider Book One, Illustrated

Is Book One of Ants 169, 47619 words, 219 pages.

Ants 169 is so large needed halved.

Book One has Luke finding out his aims and becomes a hero by fighting for human rights.

Full, of adventure, example, Luke ends up a galley rower and saves the ship from pirates.

And like a dog, Utna pines for Luke wondering seashores seeking Luke, his friend, and like a dog, loves his master.

This book is about love, the power of it, it sings across space as Light. Come and be lit then.

Phoenix, Ant Rider Book Two, Illustrated.

Is concluding part of Ants 169

48439, 187 pages.

Luke concludes his epic struggle against the humanoid Insect Nobles, become this way by gene mixing.

The Insect Queen, Nina and he race to the star ship Phoenix, a human ship that crashed on Planet World in the Time of Myths.

What secrets does it hold?

Is the Insect God Enil a human? One way to find out, come join Luke and be his friend.

Ghost Wife, A Comedy Of Errors

74256 words, 159 pages.

Oh, Morag dear, you died so do what ghosts do, Rest In Peace.

"not on your Nelly, I am very much alive, and stop ogling the medium Con, dear." Lots of madcap ridiculous fun. Information on the After Life, pity our world leaders would not stop and listen, might be no more wars.

Is comic mayhem, fanciful rubbish to tickle. The ghosts here will not haunt but make you laugh, so do not worry about holding bibles, these ghosts are clowns.

Ghost Romance

54980 words, 218 words.
A nonstop ghostly ridiculous adventure from Borneo to New York Zoo, with Calamity the orangutan in tow. So, load up on bananas and figs as the ape eats non-stop.
"Ook," is her only word spoken.
Do not worry about the extras feeding the crocodiles, they come under a dime a dozen and are not in any union, and better, made of indigestible rubber.
Not to worry animal lovers, a vet is on standby by for the sweet crocodiles, sea water variety so bigger, nastier, fierce and wanting you as food.
This book speaks heaps for food out there, a mixture of local, Indian, Chinese, Portuguese, Dutch, British, you name it, it found a way onto the menu.
Come eat more than a banana and drink condensed tea milk to sweeten you up.

Mungo, Books One And Two.

97334 words 450 pages
A mammoth adventure for Mungo, the boy raised by lions on New Uranus, humanoid, all creatures here are about humanoid thanks to genetic engineering.
Of his first love, Sasha, daughter of Red Hide, King of Lions, to his war with Carman, Queen of Lizard Folk.

These lizard folk like humans at a barbecue, as the burgers, steaks, and sausages.

No wonder Mungo wars against them.

And no one wins in a war as a human star ship arrives and enslaves the lot.

Advanced humans see other humans as undesirables.

Run through the red grass, climb giant rhododendron flowers, smell the clean air of the mountains, and only found here with Mungo the lion rider.

Mungo, Book One.

50632 words, 201 pages.

Mungo travels his world to the floating city of Huverra.

Meet his friends and enemies.

Meet more mazarrats as they provide a parallel story.

Mazarrats a cross between a mongoose and a baboon is said.

Not true, they are cute singers looking for a home.

Mazarrats, you want to take home with you.

They run a story themselves between the lines.

Discover the technological wonders these lizard folks have.

Printed in Great Britain
by Amazon